The Golden Thread

# The Golden Thread

A Novel about St. Ignatius Loyola

*by Louis de Wohl*

IGNATIUS PRESS      SAN FRANCISCO

Original edition published by
J. B. Lippincott, Philadelphia and New York

Cover design by Riz Boncan Marsella
Cover art by Christopher J. Pelicano

This edition published with permission of
Mrs. Ruth Magdalene de Wohl
Executrix of the Estate of Louis de Wohl
and with permission of Curtis Brown, Ltd.

Published in 2001 Ignatius Press, San Francisco
ISBN 0-89870-813-3
Library of Congress Control number 2001093604
Printed in the United States of America ∞

BOOK ONE

# CHAPTER ONE

"We are liberated", said Doña Mercedes triumphantly. "God has heard the prayers of Navarre. This is the greatest day of my life. Ana, go and open all the windows. I want to see our victorious troops."

Old Ana opened the nearest window in long-suffering obedience. There was no need to open another as Doña Mercedes was sure to forget about it all in the next minute.

"Victorious troops", she croaked contemptuously. "There hasn't been a battle, not even a skirmish. And if that cater-wauling is supposed to be singing . . ."

"It's sweeter than the choir on Easter Sunday to me", cried her mistress, approaching the window, a billowing black cloud of silk with a stout woman in her forties as the storm center. "Here they come, our liberators. What a day! Juanita, Juani-taaa! Where is the wretched girl now . . .?"

"Here, Doña Mercedes", said a girl of sixteen, entering. Her finely chiselled face seemed to give the lie to her simple clothes. "I did not hear you ring."

"I didn't ring. I called—shouted—screamed. Look—look at the fine boys. They ought to ring the church bells. If they do it for every poor sinner dying, they can do it for Navarre coming into her own again."

"French boys", sniffed Ana. "What's so fine about them? And Silvio says the citadel has not surrendered."

"Ana! I've always suspected where your sympathies are. If you hadn't served in this house for thirty years . . ."

"Thirty-two", said Ana. "And the good Lord will take them off my time in purgatory."

"Listen to the ungrateful woman! You are a secret Spaniard, Ana, admit it."

The old retainer drew herself up. "I'm neither a secret Spaniard nor a Frenchie, I'll have you know, Doña Mercedes. I'm a Navarrese."

"Well, what do you think I am, you fool? All good Navarrese should rejoice today."

The girl Juanita gazed at the two women. Ana's like a very ripe old olive, she thought, and Doña Mercedes is like one of those huge, fat night moths that squashed their heads against our windows last spring. La! I shall have to confess this. Lack of charity, calling Aunt a squashed night moth. But it will make Padre Gómez giggle again, as he did last time, when I told him that I had called old Silvio a coppernosed mule. Is it a sin to make a priest giggle?

Doña Mercedes was talking at the top of her voice now, because she heard some of the words that the troops were singing so lustily, and it was not exactly the kind of song Juanita should listen to. In fact, it was not the kind of song anybody should listen to, or sing, and she had been very wrong to compare it with the choir on Easter Sunday. She prevented Ana from listening to it, too, by giving her a lecture about the political situation, which was clearly one of supreme significance and importance. The commander of the liberating troops was French, true enough, and so were many of his troops, but he had come to give the ancient dynasty of the d'Albrets back to Navarre, and that meant that it would cease to be a wretched province of Spain.

"We shall be free, independent, our own masters. Our dear city of Pamplona will be a capital again. I daresay it means nothing to you, Ana, but I can't tell you what I felt when the Cuéllars from Madrid were here a few months ago, and everything and everybody here were called the most shameful names. 'You here in the outer provinces.' I could have thrown my soup into Concepción Cuéllar's stupid face. Outer provinces indeed! How I wish she were here now! Santísima madre, I'm crying, I believe. Fetch me a handkerchief, Juanita. Oh, it's a great day, a great day. What a pity my poor José didn't live to see it. No, not one of the good ones, Juanita, it's such a pity for the nice lace, a simple one, I want to blow my nose."

"Do you think that Don Francisco will be with the army, Doña Mercedes?" asked Juanita when she returned.

The patriotic lady blew her nose resolutely.

"Don Francisco? Nonsense, he's only fourteen, a mere boy. His brothers will be, of course, Juan and Miguel. They will avenge the death of their father, who had to die in exile because he was faithful to his king."

"Don Francisco is past fifteen, Doña Mercedes."

The stout lady gave her a quick appraising look.

"And since when are we interested in whether a boy is fourteen or fifteen, Señorita? Are you shaking your curls at Don Francisco Xavier, by any chance? It won't do you any good, little one. The Xaviers are of ancient lineage, not just gutter nobility, as so many whose patent is scarcely dry. They own two castles that were standing before Charlemagne's day. You'd do better looking for a nice young man of your own rank, or he will have a sad surprise when he meets your family. I don't know what young girls are coming to nowadays."

"I haven't any curls to shake, Aunt", said Juanita, ruffling her long black hair, a matter of sheer despair to her, because it was not curly at all and yet somehow managed to look untidy. It had always been like that. Mother used to say that the only way she could possibly look tidy was to cut it all off and put a nun's coif on her bald pate.

"You certainly haven't. You look like a gypsy, and if you aren't careful about the way you behave they may take you for a Morisca next."

Now at home, in Barcelona, Juanita had played with all the children of the neighborhood, whether they were Moriscos, gypsies, Jews, or "Old Christians". Seaports are usually less affected by racial prejudices than inland towns. Aunt Mercedes' words therefore did not hurt her as much as they would have hurt another girl. But Juanita knew that she was supposed to be hurt, and she sniffed dutifully and tossed her head in the best style.

Doña Mercedes noticed it with some satisfaction. The girl was not bad, really, considering María's ill-starred marriage to that man Pérez. "That man Pérez" was the only way Doña Mercedes spoke of her brother-in-law. To say that she disapproved of her sister's marriage to a man without rank and of doubtful ancestry, to a man who wrote poetry instead of acquiring honors or at least riches, was a gross understatement. She had fumed and thundered against it and flatly refused to be present at the wedding. And true enough, the absurd versemaker had died two years ago, leaving María nothing but a bundle of papers with his verses, and Juanita. But the girl was not bad. Curly hair was not necessarily a sign of pure blood anyway, and that little widow's peak of hers would look well under a veil of really fine lace, the kind they made in Valencia. The eyes were lovely. It was that little slant that did it; the saints knew where she had it from—or perhaps the saints were the last people who would know. The best thing the girl had was her figure, of course, or rather the figure she would have one day, for now it was still a little gawky, hips too narrow—they either were too thin or too fat before they ripened. Later on it was the same thing again. Alas, a woman had to rely on a few fleeting years in this life.

However, she was going to see to it that little Juanita did not miss her opportunity when the time came, and part of that was to nip in the bud all attachments that could lead only to disappointment and heartbreak. Don Francisco! She might as well wish to marry a grandee. It was the wisest thing poor María had ever done in her life to send the child away from Barcelona, where everybody knew about her impossible father, to stay with a lady of means, in a well-ordered household. She had written that to María, and she could only hope that her sister was as grateful as she ought to be. One could not be sure about anything with María. She had always been a little erratic in her ways, and that man Pérez was bound to have brought out the worst rather than the best in her. He had left his mark on Juanita, too. She was much too impulsive, she could be wayward, and she had a most unbecoming habit of making remarks about her betters, remarks which no doubt she thought were humorous and even witty, but which did not come well from the lips of a well-brought-up young girl. Old Ana, of course, spoiled her wherever she could.

Was she really in love with Don Francisco? She could not have seen him more than two or three times, and that only for a few moments. It was sheer nonsense, and anyway this was not the time to bother over the dreams of a little girl, even if she was one's niece.

"Ana, I want the best silver on the table today, and fresh flowers, and a pitcher of the Xeres wine my poor husband was so fond of."

"Yes, Doña Mercedes."

Juanita helped to lay the table. Surely all the three brothers Xavier were with the liberators. She remembered how they had spoken of the coming days of freedom the last time she had seen them, when Doña Mercedes had taken her to the mayor's reception. Everybody had been very quiet and deferential as long as the Spanish commander had been present, a glittering *caballero* all in black velvet and gold lace. But as soon as he left, everything changed. It seemed as if everyone began to breathe freely. Information had gone from mouth to mouth that the great day was very near, and Juan Xavier said crisply, "We Xaviers are ready."

They all drank to that, even the ladies. Nobody seemed to worry very much about the Spanish commander. Miguel even made some allusion to the fact that it might be possible to deal with him in a friendly fashion. "Herrera is not such a difficult man to approach", he said, with a twinkle in his eyes. "At least there is some hope that he will not be too obstreperous—if he finds himself up against sufficient superiority in numbers." Little Francisco said, "One thing is certain, I will not be left out of this." And big Juan patted him on the back.

It must be rather wonderful to be a man, thought Juanita. Men could do things. Even little Francisco.

Fancy Aunt Mercedes thinking that she was—what was it?—shaking her curls at Don Francisco. If ever I do fall in love, I shall certainly see to it that she doesn't know, whether he is a grandee or a cobbler—or even a Morisco. Father had always said that it did not matter what a man was, but what kind of a man he was and whether I really loved him. He did not count ancestors and old castles and things. Of course, Aunt Mercedes would say that was because he had no ancestors and no castles—except in the air. But what nonsense that was. Everybody had ancestors. And Father was invited to the homes of grandees and of simple people and liked them all and was liked by all of them, but that was because he was a poet. He admitted that. "Poets are like sparrows", he said. "They pick their food everywhere. Poets, you see, and sparrows, are no respecters of persons, and that they have in common with God. It's always a good thing to have something in common with God." It was the sort of thing that made Padre González in Barcelona scold Father sometimes, and then they had a heated discussion, and it always ended with Padre González laughing till he was purplish in the face and slapping Father on the shoulder and saying that Father would have to spend a long time in purgatory, no doubt, but that it was perhaps a good thing not only for him but also for the other poor souls there, because they would have something to laugh about at least. And once Father replied that he thought all the souls in purgatory were laughing anyway, and Padre González looked at him with horror, but Father looked back at him very firmly and said, "I feel quite sure of that, Padre. Wouldn't you laugh, too, if you knew that now you could be quite certain of going to heaven? You aren't certain now—or are you?"

Padre González admitted quickly that he was not and crossed himself, and after a while he said that perhaps Father's theory was not so bad after all and maybe at least some of the poor souls in purgatory were laughing, and what a pity it was that Father had not become a theologian.

Mother had told her never to speak of Father in the house of Aunt Mercedes, and she had obeyed her—so far. But it made her think of him all the more, and of what he would have said about this house, where everything was so tidy and nothing ever seemed to be thrown away.

Aunt Mercedes seemed to be everywhere at once, and nothing escaped her. Old Silvio complained that she always knew exactly how much wine was left in a barrel or a pitcher.

"Ana," Aunt Mercedes commanded, "before you go back to the kitchen, take a goblet and drink with us to the health of our gracious king." She even went so far as to fill the old servant's goblet with the precious Xeres wine. "To King Henry," she announced, "and may all his enemies be scattered."

They all drank.

As if in answer to the toast, singing started again in the street. But this time even Dona Mercedes' patriotism could not find it edifying. It sounded more like howling than singing, and suddenly there was a scream—the shrill, piercing scream of a woman, followed by a salvo of raucous laughter.

"French boys", said old Ana. "I knew they were no good."

Doña Mercedes had paled a little. She put down her goblet, rose, and walked to the window. What she saw made her recoil. "Ana! Tell Silvio to lock the door quickly. Don't go to the window, Juanita; stay where you are. No, run to the back door and see that it is closed, too."

"But surely, Aunt Mercedes ..."

"Obey at once", snapped her aunt, and Juanita left with no more protest than a little shrug.

A fairly long, winding corridor led to the back door, and its walls were thick. She did not hear the angry knocks at the front door, the low grumble of Silvio's voice, the excited cackle of old Ana.

Silvio had reached the door just a moment too late.

CHAPTER TWO

THE DOOR WAS OPEN—as any door would be when Sergeant Jean Garroux knocked at it with his armored shoulder—and it took more than the combined effort of the two old retainers to close it again. For now Garroux had his foot in it.

The huge, bull-necked man gave it an almost contemptuous shove, and it flew back, knocking Silvio over and pinning Ana against the wall.

"Enter, scum", snapped Sergeant Garroux.

The four men behind him stepped forward, a little unsteadily. They were Gascon infantry, hastily banded together by the noble bishop of Couserans, Charles de Gramont, so hastily that there had been no time to supply them with uniforms. Malicious tongues had it that the noble bishop had made his levies in the very last minute to save the cost of their equipment, but others, better informed, insisted that according to law they had to pay for their own equipment and that the good bishop had left it so late in order to spare them a financial burden they could not possibly carry, Gascons being notoriously poor.

A decent campaign always paid for itself anyhow, and up to a couple of hours ago the Gascons, as indeed most of the army, had been in excellent spirits. By then, however, it had become obvious that Pamplona would surrender without even a gesture of resistance. The mayor had paid his visit to the commander-in-chief, bowing and scraping and sweating profusely, and delivered the keys, and news had come that the Spanish garrison in the citadel was about to surrender without a single shot.

No campaign—no loot.

The annoyance of the army was considerable, especially as the Spanish garrison was much too small to constitute a real danger. The only thing left to them was to spend their own money in the inns and brothels, and that was not much.

They were not the only ones who were annoyed. The inn, shop, and brothel keepers shared their feelings fully. They had expected a roaring trade and now found that these devils of liberators either did not come in at all or, when they did, took what they wanted without payment.

Some of the merchants suggested that the rich people of the town did not seem to know what they owed to their liberators and that it would be a good idea to remind them, especially as the liberators were keen on spending money in the town, which thus would not lose any of its wealth.

The idea was taken up with alacrity, not only by the Gascons of his lordship of Couserans but also by the regular infantry under the command of Lord Elgobarraque, mayor of Bayonne. Like every really good idea, it spread with lightning speed. The inns and *posadas* were emptied; the troops searched and found suitable objectives, and soon women and girls began to scream in many houses on the more elegant streets of Pamplona.

Doña Mercedes Olverón y Fuentes did not scream.

Rushing to the front door, she found old Silvio groaning on the floor, with blood trickling from a wound on his forehead; old Ana still pinned behind the open door; and a number of large, sweaty, and obviously drunken men in tattered clothes staring at her in a very disconcerting way.

"How dare you force your way in here in such a fashion?" she snapped. "Behaving as if this were not the capital of the king. You ought to be ashamed of yourselves."

Sergeant Jean Garroux gave a slow grin, exposing strong if yellow and irregular teeth. "Bernac, I think you like them that way. She's too fat for me."

"She isn't bad", said Bernac. "Got nice earrings, too." He stepped forward.

"Don't you dare", shouted Doña Mercedes. "I shall speak to your captain about this. It's disgraceful."

"I wouldn't bother about that, lady", said Sergeant Jean Garroux. "He doesn't like them fat either. Excuse me . . ."

He ambled past her, giving her a not too gentle push that sent her straight into Bernac's arms, and now she screamed, but the scream was drowned in the thunderous laughter of the men. Bernac's short, dirty fingers hooked into the top of her bodice and tugged.

Squealing like a sow, thought Garroux on his way deeper into the house. There could be no man here, except for the old dodderer at the door, or he would have shown up by now. Where would she keep her jewel box? In the bedroom, of course; they always did. Silver dishes, eh? Nice. But jewels were better. Worth more and didn't bulge.

Suddenly he stopped.

Before him, straight, alert, and slim, stood a very young girl with wide, frightened eyes.

"Pretty", said Garroux. "Prettiest little jewel box I could hope to find. Let's take the jewel out."

The girl recoiled too quickly for his outstretched hands. "Who are you?" she asked in a trembling voice. "What are they doing to Aunt Mercedes? Why—?"

This time he caught her before she could recoil again. "They haven't taught you much yet, have they, little cat? All right, I'll teach you. Here's the first thing. A pretty girl doesn't use her mouth to talk with, but . . . No use wriggling; you can't get away. Just leave it to Jean Garroux, will you? Couldn't find a better teacher in the whole damned army. Ouch—aie—you—you—wait, I'll teach you how to scratch. . . ."

But Juanita did not wait. When Garroux let her go for one short moment to protect his eyes against her fingernails, she twisted her body away and fled down the corridor toward the back door.

17

It was like a bad dream in which some horrible monster stalked after her along an endless corridor. She could hear the heavy tread behind her, and she could hear his laughter, chuckling and coarse, as if he were quite sure that she could not escape him.

The door—she had only just bolted it. With flying fingers she pushed the bolt aside, tore the door open, and rushed out into the street. The sun beat at her eyes with blinding light, and she staggered and would have fallen if something—somebody—had not caught her in time.

"A little lady in a great hurry", said a deep voice that seemed to come from far above.

The blindness left her, and she looked up into a lean, weatherbeaten face with amused blue eyes. Had she been less excited she would have seen also that there were a few laughter wrinkles at the corners of those eyes and a fairly long scar over the left one, right up to the brim of his hat. She would have seen that he was in his mid-twenties, wore a brown leather camisole, and carried a two-hander, an over-long sword with a blade as broad as a hand, as well as a heavy pike from which half a dozen things dangled, including an iron helmet and a bundle wrapped in leather.

She saw that it was not an evil face, and before she could say anything she felt herself torn away from the man and heard a hateful, coarse voice bellow, "There are lots of girls in this town. Do your own hunting, you Swiss mule. This one's mine."

Then she was lifted bodily and carried back into the house, and all she could do was to stretch out a helpless arm and cry out, "Help, for the Blessed Virgin's sake, help!"

A moment later the door closed behind her.

The young man with the scar hesitated.

The little lady did not seem to like the idea of what was in store for her. But she had that in common with a great many other young ladies in Pamplona—and a whole army of young ladies all over Christendom. A dozen little wars and a few middle-sized ones were going on just now.

The little lady had screamed for help in the name of the Blessed Virgin. But they all remembered the Blessed Virgin when things went wrong, and usually only then.

The little lady was pretty, but not prettier than a good many others.

Why should he get himself into trouble over her?

No reason for it at all. None.

He had arrived at the back door. It was closed, a fact that somehow irritated a man already in a sullen mood. The girl was a confounded nuisance.

"Long" Ulric von der Flue, double soldier in the Free Corps of his Lordship Charles de Gramont, bishop of Couserans, walked along the twisting corridor and right into pandemonium.

A couple of Gascon soldiers were busy bagging valuables. An old man was shrieking for mercy, and a third Gascon soldier clubbed him over the head. He fell on what seemed to be the body of a very old woman in servant's dress. And the big fellow who had caught the girl had just got her down and was staring at him over his shoulder.

"A sergeant, too", said Ulric von der Flue bitterly. "You ought to know better."

Garroux's fleshy face was suffused with blood. He rose to six feet of towering rage. The girl's head fell back with a bump. Ulric gave her a fleeting glance. Knocked herself out, probably, he thought.

Garroux's porcine eyes remained fixed on him as the Gascon, surprisingly quick for a man of his weight, slid over to a heavy armchair and seized the sword he had left leaning against it.

19

Ulric grinned at him. He made no movement to interfere.

"I told you to keep out of this", said Garroux hoarsely.

"So you did. And you're a sergeant. Not my sergeant, though, thank God. He doesn't call me names, and he has no need to force women, because he doesn't look like a scurvy ox."

Garroux broke into a stream of abuse that would have shocked the most foul-mouthed fishwife. Then he called out, "Cahors! Bernac! Varel! Beauxregard!"

Ulric shook his head. "If you want to know how to swear, you ought to go to Hungary", he said. "They picked up some beauties from the Turks. Is that the whole army under your command? You and four men?"

"My, if it isn't Long Uli." Varel grinned, his mouth full of grapes. "What's he want of you, Sergeant?" He finished off the grapes and wiped his hand on the seat of his trousers. "Not up to trouble, is he, Sergeant?"

"He's dead", said Garroux. "But he doesn't know it yet."

Uli frowned.

"Listen", he said. "You know as well as I do that this is no way to behave. The old man over there is dead, and maybe the old woman is too. This isn't enemy territory. If the provost hears about it . . ."

"The provost", interrupted Garroux, "is a very busy man today. I didn't intend to bother him. But now that you have nosed your way into other people's affairs, I shall have to. D'ye think I have called in my men because I need help against you? I'd deal with three of your kind, single-handed. What I need is witnesses. Four good, true, reliable soldiers to give witness about who disturbed the peace. Eh, Bernac? Eh, Beauxregard? Varel? Cahors? Give me that sword of yours, Swiss mule. You have no more use for it. You're under arrest."

Uli nodded. They would make him the scapegoat for what they had done. They would finish off the girl, too, so that she could not give evidence against them. It was just the kind of plan to be expected from Garroux, who was known as a completely unscrupulous man, but whose extraordinary fighting value had saved him more than once from the provost's rope. What a nuisance that girl was.

The scar over his left eye had darkened and seemed to pulsate, but his tone was almost gentle as he said, "If you want Little Hans here, you must come and get him."

He dropped the pike, helmet, bundle, and all and drew Little Hans from its sheath. With one swift movement he measured the height and width of the room. The two-hander was over five feet long, one foot and three inches less than its owner.

"*And* resisting arrest", said Garroux. "Get him."

But the movement of the four men was stopped by a swishing circling stroke of the two-hander, and Cahors cried out as his sword fell out of a hand suddenly short of two fingers.

"One", said Uli. It was Cahors' right hand, so he was not likely to throw the knife in his belt with the left, not with the pain doubling him up as it did. "Who's next?"

"You are", bellowed Garroux. He picked up a heavy chair and threw it at the Swiss, drew with incredible speed, and rushed forward.

Uli sidestepped the chair, and it crashed against the wall, but bumped him fairly heavily on the rebound, upsetting the stroke of the two-hander. The terrible blade bit deep into the wood of a table, and Uli had to let the handle go. He eluded Garroux's wild stroke with a jump straight at Beauxregard's body that sent the soldier sprawling and made Uli land at Bernac's feet. He seized the feet and pulled with all his might. Bernac fell with a crash, and Garroux, rushing in again, had to swerve to avoid a collision.

It was Uli's good fortune that he was wearing no armor; the plates were carefully assembled in the tight little leather bundle that adorned his pike, and they weighed a great deal. What is more, they impeded movement in the kind of scrap he was in. His body, left to its own devices, and acting purely on instinct, coiled up and seemed to shoot itself over to the table, where the two-hander was still in the process of sinking, dragged down by the weight of the handle. Uli grasped it with greedy hands, tugged at it, got it free, and drew a flashing circle with it around himself, as if trying to erect a magical barrier between him and his enemies.

He did, too, although the geometrical figure never got further than a semicircle. For then it was stopped by something extremely heavy and hard, and the collision was so violent that Uli almost lost Little Hans for the second time.

Sergeant Garroux had also performed a semicircle in the irresistible dance to which Little Hans had invited him and then had fallen with a crash, with half a dozen pieces of what had been a perfectly good shoulder-plate ringing metallically around him and gradually coming to rest.

"Two", said Uli, panting. "Who's next?"

But there would be no next. He knew that. Despite the red mist flickering before his eyes, he thought he could see all four scurrying away.

The first thing he did then was to give a very careful inspection to Little Hans. No dent. He passed his thumb all along either side of the blade. No need even to resharpen it. He lifted the two-hander and peered along the blade. He knocked against it with a bent finger and listened to its voice. He nodded with satisfaction. Little Hans was all right.

Long Uli was all right, too, except for a few bruises.

Apart from that, nothing seemed to be right.

He walked over to the bodies of the two old people.

They were dead, as he had thought they were.

He walked back to the girl. She was still unconscious. He pushed a cushion under her head.

At least that's one for whom I have not come too late, he thought. Then he began to explore the other rooms.

In the next one he found somebody lying on the bed—a short, stout woman, with a face horribly distorted by pain and fear. Her eyes were dead eyes. There was blood all over the bed, and the room was a shambles.

There seemed to have been a fight, and after that one of Garroux's men, or all of them, had searched the room for something, the dead woman's jewels, most likely. All the cupboards were open and their contents scattered.

In eight years as a soldier Uli had seen too many dead women and devastated houses to be much shaken. He went on with his search. It was quite a large house.

## CHAPTER THREE

JUANITA CAME TO. Everything was quiet. Very quiet.

She had had a nightmare. She had had a nightmare because she had forgotten to say her prayers. Mother always said . . .

She was not in her bed. She was lying on the floor. Her arms hurt, as if someone had . . .

Memory came back with a rush of batwings, and she sat up, groaning. That man—that awful man. But he had been driven away. The other one, with the large sword, he had driven him away.

Where was he? Where was Aunt Mercedes?

There was a low, slithering noise, as if something were being dragged along the floor. She turned her head. Her eyes widened. She wanted to scream, but no sound would come.

The nightmare was not over. The man was still there. He was crouching on the floor, on all fours, like an animal. There was blood on his arm, on his face, but he was moving, moving. Was he moving toward her?

She wanted to get up, to get up and run. She could not move. She was made of lead, as one is in a nightmare, when the monster comes, ready to devour.

And then the monster looked up and saw her.

His eyes were bloodshot; his lips slobbered. It was the devil. Holy Mother of God, it was the devil, and he came, crawling, inch by inch, toward her. And she could not move.

Nearer and nearer he came. She could see the little purple veins on his cheeks and his nose, the stiff little hairs growing from his ears. And all the time he stared at her from his small, bloodshot, red-lidded eyes, and now he stretched out an arm ...

But not toward her, toward the table. He was gripping the table; he pulled himself up, up. There he stood, terribly high; the whole room was blocked by his enormous body.

He did not look at her any more; perhaps he never had looked at her. He had wanted to pull himself up; he had needed the table to pull himself up. And now he was walking; with a strange sort of stagger, he walked past her and disappeared in the corridor. A moment later she heard the door slam.

He had gone. Gone. Gone.

And suddenly life came back into deadened limbs, and she jumped up and ran.

"Aunt Mercedes—Aunt Mercedes . . ."

In the door to her aunt's bedroom she stopped.

The nightmare was still not over.

But this time she screamed.

It brought Uli running back.

"Hi!" he shouted. "Come away from there."

She did not move.

He went up to her, put his hand on her shoulder.

"Come away from there, little lady. It's no sight for you."

Still she did not move. Then he saw that her eyes were blank, quite without expression in a face of snow.

But at least she did not resist when he led her away, gently. She did not push his arm off; she did not run away and hide as some did, when this sort of thing had happened to them.

"Sit down for a moment."

She obeyed mechanically, always with the same blank expression. He went over to where the table was laid. The silver had disappeared, of course, and they had drunk most of the wine, but there was still a little left. He cleaned the rim of a goblet with the tablecloth, filled it, and brought it to the girl. She was sitting just as he had left her.

"Here. Drink this. Drink, I say."

But he had to hold the goblet to her lips; she would not or could not take it.

"Come now, little lady", he said. "I know it's bad. But it's all over now. This will do you good. Just one sip. Good. Now another one."

But she could not take another one. If she would only cry.

"Who was the poor lady? Your mother?—Come on—say it—who was she?"

"Aunt. Aunt Mercedes."

Better an aunt than a mother.

He began to think of Garroux and his men. They would probably come back as soon as they had got reinforcements. Garroux at least would see to that. Uli had to get out. He had to get the girl out, too.

"Do you know the neighbors? Now come on, pull yourself together. You aren't safe here. Do you know the neighbors? What is their name?"

"P-padilla."

"Right. That's where we are going. Want to take some of your things with you? You'll have to be quick about it; those men may come back."

That sunk in. She rose on unsteady legs.

"Lean on my arm. Where do we go? To your room?"

She shook her head.

"All right, then. You can always come back for your things when the troops are gone."

He picked up his pike with all its paraphernalia and led the girl out by the front door. He looked about cautiously. The street was empty. A few small reddish-brown spots on the cobblestones made him smile grimly. Garroux would not find it difficult to make his way back here. He had left a trail behind him, like a slug.

They had to knock many times before the Padillas answered, and even then the door was opened only when they had seen the girl and recognized her.

Cautious people. Good. They took the girl in, when he explained that things were not so good in her aunt's house. He did not give them time to ask too many questions. As for the girl—well, they would see soon enough that this was not the time to question her. She had taken no part in the conversation, but when he turned to go, she stretched out her arms and said something. He could not hear what it was. He grinned at her, nodded, and walked away.

And that was that as far as she was concerned. She would recover. They did, when they were that young, and after all, he had been in time.

He grinned to himself now. In time for her. But now something had to be done—and done in time—for Long Uli. What Garroux and his men had done was the usual thing, when a town had been taken by force. But Pamplona had not been taken by force. Pamplona had been liberated. A man could still have his fun in a town he had liberated, but that fun had certain limitations. You didn't enter into a decent house, murder three people, including two women, and make up for it by trying to get the surviving young female with child. Garroux and his men were not the only ones who had behaved badly; Monseigneur of Couserans had not been too choosy about the kind of soldiers he got together for this campaign, and the Bayonnese fellows were worse.

But if the general heard of it (and he was bound to, unless these Pamplonese were the worst cowards under the sun and did not even dare complain), then this sort of thing could not be left unpunished.

The thing to do was to inform one's own sergeant. Sergeant Philippart was not exactly the sort of man who would have been accepted by the papal guard or by the emperor's bodyguards, but when he was not drunk, he could be quite sensible. Unfortunately that was not often.

The trouble was, Uli had been with them two months, and there had been no opportunity to show them what he was made of. Otherwise, he could have gone to the captain himself, de Brissac. No captain likes to lose a good man just because of a little misunderstanding with a sergeant. But as it was, de Brissac knew Sergeant Garroux as a good soldier, and he knew very little about Long Uli. Worse still, they were all Gascons. He was the only Swiss.

Bah. Maybe Garroux had found a good *posada* by now, had got himself royally drunk, and was in no mood to go after a disagreeable Swiss soldier who had hacked him in the arm.

Even so, he was not the man to forget this kind of thing, especially as it had happened in front of some of his men. Sooner or later he would want to pay his debt.

Uli stopped suddenly.

A troop of about a dozen soldiers was turning the corner. They were marching abreast, and the man in the middle looked very much like Garroux—it was Garroux. And the two men at his side wore the scarlet coats at whose sight the worst fight in an inn or *posada* stopped as if by magic. . . . They were the provost's helpers.

They had sighted him now, and Garroux pointed, and they began to run.

Uli stood motionless. There was another fellow among them whom he knew, the one who was missing two fingers.

He smiled cynically. And it did not surprise him when he heard Garroux bellow, "That's the man. We caught him red handed. He has murdered three people in the house over there, and he attacked us when we were going to arrest him."

"Hand over your arms", snapped one of the provost's helpers.

Uli nodded good-naturedly. "Catch, then", he said and threw his pike over to him. The man caught it with both hands, but its weight was such that he doubled up under it.

"There you are", said Uli. "I knew you'd give me a courteous salute sooner or later. Here, you, take Little Hans, and mind you, treat him well. He's a faithful one."

"I don't think you'll need that toothpick any more", said the second provost's helper. "Here, Garroux, hold it a while. I've got to tie his hands."

Uli shook his head sadly. "You shouldn't have done that", he said. "Give a decent steel like that into such hands. Very wrong. Where are we going?"

"Where the trees are high enough", said the man in the scarlet coat.

But this at least was not true. No tree grew on the Plaza Mayor—unless the contraption they had built right in the middle of it all could be called some kind of a tree. It consisted of two large vertical beams, rammed into the soil at a distance of about ten paces and topped by a horizontal beam. Thus it looked like the most primitive type of triumphal arch. Perhaps in some way it could be called a tree after all—a fruit tree. For from it hung about a dozen fruit. They were human, or had been; one was still twitching a little.

The tree of death, thought Uli, and then he wondered what made him think of that and whether he would be the next fruit to be added to the tree.

Hundreds of people were cramming the Plaza Mayor, citizens as well as soldiers, and the noise sounded from afar like the humming of bees.

Behind the plaza rose the steep, gray walls of the citadel. Uli gave it a keen glance. There were pikes visible behind the walls. He could see two guns. And the citadel was still flying its flag, the Spanish flag. It had not yet surrendered. What was the commander-in-chief doing, letting his soldiers mix with the populace, when the citadel had not surrendered? But there were not many soldiers on the plaza, not more than a hundred or so. And over there, covered by the colonnades, armor and arms were glittering, and the mouths of all the streets south and west of the plaza were packed with soldiers.

The men in the citadel seemed to be as slow about their surrender as the townsmen had been quick. Perhaps it was foolish to have this—this tree erected here, where it could be seen from the citadel. It made the defenders think of what might happen to their own necks.

The thought made Uli laugh, and the grim provost's helper at his side asked him what he had to laugh about. Uli told him.

"You're an ignorant fellow", said the man in the scarlet coat. "All those who hang here are soldiers who have disgraced our army, as you have. His excellency the supreme commander wishes to show the men in the citadel that he will tolerate no lack of discipline."

Uli stopped abruptly, and so strong was the drag of his body that he made the two provost's helpers stop with him.

"Just a minute", he said angrily.

Everybody halted now and looked at the prisoner.

"What's the matter, fellow?"

"Only this", said Uli. "I've been accused of something, and you have arrested me. Well and good. But there's been no trial so far, and as long as I haven't been convicted and sentenced, you have no right to talk of me having disgraced the army."

"What impudence!" roared Garroux. "I'll show you what a disgrace you are." He hit the Swiss in the face before the man in the scarlet coat next to him could stop him.

"Stop that", the man ordered. "No interference with the prisoner."

"It's all right", said Uli. "No one has taught him what disgrace is, or he wouldn't hit a man who has his hands tied. Maybe he'll learn something before he is much older."

"Quit arguing, you", said the scarlet coat. "You can do that later, with the provost marshal—if he lets you. Come on now."

When they reached the plaza itself, they turned right and entered the colonnades.

The provost marshal was sitting at a table that somebody had borrowed from a nearby shop. He was a round-faced little man with cherubic cheeks and cold, watery eyes.

"Who are you?" he asked in a bored voice.

"Ulric von der Flue, double soldier, company of Captain de Brissac—and a very silly ass."

The provost marshal blinked. "Maybe this is one man who knows what he is", he said. "What's the accusation?"

"Murder, entering a peaceful house, with the intent to steal, insubordination, armed attack against a superior", said Garroux quickly.

The provost marshal looked at Uli. "Anything to say?"

"Yes", said Uli. "Sergeant Garroux is going too far in his confession. He has done all he said, but he did not to my knowledge attack a superior. I'm only a double soldier, as I said before."

The provost marshal shook his head. "Anything to say?" he asked in a sharper tone.

There was a commotion on the plaza. It looked as if the invisible hand of a giant were stirring it with an invisible spoon. Crowds of people ran in circles and then were sucked into the streets far away on the left. Drums sounded on the other side, and one single, long-drawn trumpet call.

Uli began to tell his story.

"Lies!" shouted Garroux after the second sentence. "It is he who entered the house, and we found him there. I have four witnesses for that."

"I still want to hear his story", said the provost marshal coldly.

Uli went on, but he saw that the provost marshal did not listen very closely. His watery eyes shifted again and again to the plaza. Several detachments of soldiers in orderly lines began to take up their position there, and a group of straining, sweating men brought up a gun.

"Something seems to have gone wrong", said the provost marshal thoughtfully.

". . . so they got out", concluded Uli, "and decided to make me pay for what they did. That's why I said I am a silly ass. If I weren't, I would have let Sergeant Garroux take care of the girl the way he wanted to, and someone else would have discovered that three people had been murdered in that house. The worst of it is: I'd do it again."

The provost marshal gave him a blank stare. "Witnesses", he said. "Sergeant Garroux says he can produce four witnesses. What about you?"

A detachment of heavily armored infantry passed by. One of the officers shouted at the provost marshal, "Get your men out of the way. Commander will be here any moment. We're storming the citadel."

"I've got only one witness", said Uli. "The girl. But at least she is not under suspicion of murder."

"Maybe not", said the provost marshal. "But she isn't here. And we have no more time to lose. I'm afraid you must hang."

They were rolling up another gun, a short, wide-mouthed thing like the head of a giant toad, and the noise was overwhelming. Uli could not hear what the provost marshal said, but he gathered what it was when one of the helpers beckoned the thin little priest to approach the prisoner.

The long scar on Uli's forehead began to pucker.

"My company's moving up, sir", he shouted. "Let me march with them. You can always hang me after the attack, if you think you have to."

But the provost marshal was in a hurry now. He waved his hand to the priest, to get on with his job.

Uli looked about desperately for Captain de Brissac or Sergeant Philippart, but his company was too far away for him to distinguish any particular face or figure. They were taking their position next to a detachment carrying long ladders.

The sharp, sad features of the little priest came into his vision and the provost's helpers stepped back mechanically.

The little priest had that day looked into the eyes of many men about to die. They had dragged him to the plaza as soon as he had said Mass, and he had had no time to have breakfast. He knew he would probably have no time to eat anything all day, for there would soon be many more men dying, though in battle, instead of on the scaffold. He had thought how terrible it was that so many crimes could be committed between the time a priest said his Mass and that of his first meal, between the meal of the soul and the meal of the body, but it was a fleeting thought, forgotten when he met the next pair of condemned eyes, flickering and desperate, and far more hungry for life on earth than for life in heaven. He felt too light, too flimsily inadequate for the great stream of God's compassion to flow through him. His mouth was dry, and his voice cracked; it could not penetrate the infernal din going on all around him.

Even so the tall, lean man with the scar over his eye seemed to have understood what he had said, but he shook his head; he had no wish to confess his sins. Straining his thin neck, the little priest caught some of the words the prisoner said: "... no need ... innocent ..."

The priest sighed. It was difficult to believe that a man could lie when his death was imminent and inevitable. He lifted his crucifix. "You are not the first to die innocent of the crime you are accused of. He did, too, didn't he?"

That also the prisoner seemed to understand; he nodded, and there was the shadow of a smile around his mouth. The little priest gave him his blessing, and the prisoner went down on one knee, as soldiers did. It looked like an act of courtesy rather than of faith, and the little priest sighed again, because he had seen so many men and women whose only relation to God was an outward courtesy, to say nothing of those who lacked even that.

As soon as the prisoner rose, the two provost's helpers seized his arms and began to lead him to the primitive triumphal arch in the middle of the plaza.

They were followed first by the priest, then by the provost marshal, and finally by a throng of others, including Sergeant Garroux and his men, who nudged each other, grinning.

But their procession was slow.


## CHAPTER FOUR


THE ATTACK AGAINST THE CITADEL had started. Two thousand men of the Bayonnese infantry had advanced against the main gate and had met fierce resistance. Skilfully placed arquebusiers had thinned their ranks before they could place the first ladder, and when they pressed on regardless of their losses, streams of boiling water emptied the few ladders they could get into position.

General André de Foix rode up with his staff, including Monseigneur de Gramont, bishop of Couserans, and Lord Elgobarraque, mayor of Bayonne. Never a paragon of patience, the general was pretty near exasperation. For seven hours his envoys had been parleying with the commander of the Spanish garrison, and then, when Herrera seemed quite ready to accept all his conditions, a stupid incident had brought everything to naught again.

Some Spanish subaltern—the envoys had not even been able to report his name—had jumped up, enthusiastic and pale, and made a fiery little speech about Spaniards not being the kind of people who surrendered, even when there was no wall between them and the enemy, and surely his commander could not even consider such a thing for one moment.

Herrera had been considering it for seven long hours, but the subaltern's speech seemed to have infected most of the other Spaniards present, and Herrera, who had weakened to the envoys, now weakened before his own subalterns and became the proud, unyielding commander again.

It was quite ridiculous.

And now de Foulard reported that the attacking column at the north side of the citadel had not made any headway either and had lost almost sixty men in the first attempt. The guns were being brought into position there now, but they were few in numbers, the treasury having been mean as usual, and these walls were infernally solid.

They were solid even here at the south, as if the man who built them had expected that an enemy might hold the town of Pamplona before attacking its stronghold.

The commander gave a nod to Captain Labrosse.

"Tell them to make us a hole in that molehill with their guns, if they can. If it doesn't help, it will at least chase some of the defenders off the walls, when I attack from here."

Labrosse turned his horse away, but found it difficult to reach the corner of the plaza, where the artillerists were busy with their three guns.

"What's holding him up?" asked Monseigneur de Gramont. "Why, I believe ..."

"Mordieux", swore the commander. "They're hanging a man in the middle of my battle!"

"So they are, so they are", said Monseigneur de Gramont nervously. "Shall I tell them to stop?"

André de Foix hesitated. Then the humor of the situation made him laugh. "No, my Lord Bishop, let them go ahead. We must not disappoint the poor devil."

The bishop, in helmet and armor, crossed himself and murmured a short prayer.

The slow procession of the provost marshal reached the foot of the tree with the human fruit. The wooden contraption they had to mount had been pushed aside, and they spent a few laborious minutes getting it into position again. It was an improvised, makeshift thing, with but eight steps leading up to the small platform, instead of the traditional thirteen, but it had done for the eleven men whose twenty-two legs were dangling so close over the heads of the workers that they had to push them out of the way again and again.

"I would be glad to help you, sirs", said Uli politely. "But unfortunately my hands are tied."

A faint titter went through the crowd, whose attention was divided between the hanging ceremony and the sector of the citadel that could be seen from the plaza.

Only two hundred yards away cursing officers tried to re-form the badly battered remnants of the first assault, and the little priest who did not share in the work of getting the wooden contraption into position looked anxiously toward the spot slightly nearer the walls, where many more men, scalded, shot, bleeding, were now waiting for the last solace of religion.

Just then Captain Labrosse reached the artillerists on the plaza and delivered his commander's order.

The master gunner, a sergeant by rank, was old François Pitoux, who like most gunners had started out as a blacksmith. He nodded. "I'll try." He began to spout orders right and left, and his men busied themselves with their powder bags, waddings, and long matches. Behind each gun was a small pyramid of cannon balls.

"Wait till I get back", said Captain Labrosse, frowning. "My horse is nervous."

Under the gibbet the provost marshal wiped his brow.

"Now then", he said. "Get him up there, and be quick about it. We're holding up the army."

The helpers pushed the prisoner up the stairs, and the provost marshal himself followed with the rope.

The little priest brought up the rear, praying.

The five of them filled the small platform to capacity.

Uli closed his eyes, as they threw the rope round his neck. It was a stupid way to leave life, but probably as good as any other. Burns hurt more, or so they said. Life. Kaspar Jost could sleep safely now, with Margaret. That is, if he knew. But he probably never would know. We never know when we're safe and when we're not. Are we ever? Well, he would soon know everything—or nothing.

Probably nothing. Could a soul talk when it met God? If there was a God and if there was a soul to meet him. But there probably was. Nothing could come from nothing, as Father Pulvermacher had said back there in Sachseln. And there was a soul, because if there was not, what difference would there be between him and one of the eleven bodies hanging all around him now? A man is not the same as his own corpse.

The trouble was, God did not bother. That he knew. If God would take a little trouble, his world would not be what it was, and Uli would not hang for something Sergeant Garroux had done.

If I meet him, thought Uli, with a shrug, I must ask him why he doesn't do something about it—except for that one short attempt a long while ago. Now this was going to hurt a little. . . .

"Ready?" asked the provost marshal.

"Ready", said the helpers.

"Up the rope."

There was no "drop" that mercifully broke a prisoner's neck. They just had to string him up, and at the sound of the word "Up" they did.

A man may resign himself to die, but his body does not.

Like every one of the others who now were fruit on the tree of death, Uli began to dance jerkily in the air.

There was a tremendous, thunderous crash.

When the swirling red mist vanished, Uli found himself sitting on the platform.

The rope must have broken, was his first thought.

He was angry, and he felt a little sick. Anger and nausea battled each other, and anger won. He said hoarsely, "If there's anything I hate it's a hangman who doesn't know his job. Test a rope before you use it on a man's neck."

He was so angry that he got up, despite his hands being tied behind his back. All he wanted to do was to give the provost marshal a piece of the mind that strangely enough had remained stuck in his body.

But the provost marshal was not looking at him. Nor was anybody else. They were all staring at the guns, hidden by an enormous cloud of dirty brown smoke.

When the smoke eddied away, they saw that the number one gun had exploded. There was nothing left of it except a few twisted pieces of metal. The rest had torn the four gunners to pieces and wounded at least a dozen soldiers, including Master-Gunner Pitoux.

They don't know their job either, thought Uli grimly. No one seems to, these days.

Only now he began to realize that the scarlet coats had been so frightened by the sudden explosion of the gun that they had let go the rope.

Out there they made ready to shoot the next gun. The soldiers around it recoiled as far as they could.

"A plague on you", shouted Uli. "That's no way to do it."

The provost marshal turned to him, but this time Uli had meant the artillerists.

"Wrong elevation", roared Uli. His voice was still hoarse, but it had regained its strength. "Wrong elevation, you doddering fools."

"We'll give *you* the right elevation this time anyway", said the provost marshal, seizing the rope again.

Then the second cannon went off with a crash.

"Duck, all of you!" yelled Uli and did so himself.

The cannon ball hit the wall of the citadel, bounced off, and came back, singing monotonously, to land in the middle of the plaza, no more than fifteen feet from the gibbet. It killed three men of the Bayonne infantry and created a general panic.

"Idiots!" roared Uli. "Godforsaken idiots. Wait, I'll show you."

He jumped off the platform and made his way across to the unfortunate gunners.

"Stop the prisoner!" shouted the provost marshal. "After him, men." He fairly danced on the small platform.

The men in the scarlet coats obeyed. At least they tried to. But the unfortunate shot of the second cannon had caused a milling movement on the plaza—there was one detachment of Bayonnese infantry that had to be restrained with much effort from attacking the hapless gunners—and anyway the scarlet coats were not popular, and there were those who had observed what happened on the platform when the first shot was fired.

"Look at the hangman's mates! What are you up to now? Want to become gunners, maybe?"

"They're still alive. A cannon likes to hit the wrong men, I always say."

"Botched your job, too, haven't you? You ought to practice a bit on yourselves first."

Their faces almost as red as their coats, the men pushed on sullenly, but their progress was very slow.

They were still far behind, when Uli reached the gunners and bore down on them like a thunderstorm.

"Out of the way, you silly mongrels. Who taught you gunnery? No one ever told you that this kind of ball bounces if you give it the wrong elevation? What were you trying to hit anyway?"

"Who the devil are you?" asked the plaintive voice of Master Gunner Pitoux. He was sitting on the cobblestones, and a leech was binding up his left arm.

Uli saw his insignia and gave him a perfunctory salute. "It's all right, Master Gunner, I learned under Frundsberg. Cut me loose, you there. I'm going to work."

He began to give orders right and left. As it did not even occur to him that the gunners might not obey, it did not occur to them either. None of them knew more about the new art than six weeks of training could give them, and Pitoux started drinking too early in the morning.

The gun was one of those new-fangled, short-nosed jobs the Swiss called *Kammerbuechse*. It shot a ball the size of a human head. Uli knew the type from last year's campaign in the Milanese region, and he loved guns as one loves a good horse or a faithful dog. It was a shame to see a noble gun ill treated by fools.

"A man must know his job," he said, rubbing his wrists, "whether it's sword work or guns or—hanging. Guns are delicate things. You've got to talk to them, so they don't get nervous."

That produced the first grin among the gunners.

"Brush work first", said Uli. "A gun is like a woman. Doesn't feel good when she isn't primped properly."

In went the heavy stick with the brush at the end.

"See all that dirt? Causes deflection. Brush it again. And once more. Now then . . ."

At the other end of the plaza the commander was looking sharply at the rampart of the citadel. Up there they were fully alive to the coming assault now. The number of pikes had doubled, and he could even see a faint cloud of steam; they had got their hot liquids into position, too, water, oil, pitch, and whatever else they had. The guns were a complete failure. Should he wait for more calamities like the last two?

Apparently Herrera now really meant to resist. Was that he, sword in hand, over there on the right, next to the group of arquebusiers?

It would cost five hundred men to storm that confounded wall. It might cost more. A siege? If they could get all that water together for boiling, they were bound to have water enough for drinking. Frontal attacks were not good generalship, but what else was there to do?

He was not the only one to have spied the Spanish commander on the rampart.

Uli was talking to his gun, now fully and carefully loaded. "See that cocky fellow up there, Señorita? The one with the plumes on his helmet, I mean. That would be just the kind of bridegroom you would like, wouldn't you now? You wouldn't bounce off him, would you? Go and kiss him, my beautiful girl—up with your mouth a little—that's it—"

A man must have the feel of gun, he had heard old Frundsberg say. If he hasn't, he'll never make a gunner.

Uli gave a last sharp look to the rampart; bent down, holding his breath; and ripped the cord. The gun thundered, and all around him became dark-brown, evil-smelling smoke.

But through the smoke came the roar of a thousand voices like an echo, and Uli paled. It could not be—he could not have missed, and the ball could not have bounced. He had to stand and wait for endless seconds till the smoke lifted sufficiently. Then he grinned.

A piece of the rampart was gone, and with it the fellow with the plumed helmet and a goodly number of the arquebusiers.

The gunners around him danced and slapped his shoulder. Old Pitoux from his corner crowed lustily.

"Ah—beautiful—beautiful shot!"

Uli turned round to them, grinning. Then he saw that two of the men who danced were wearing scarlet coats. The two provost's helpers had arrived just in time to see the gun being fired.

"Lovely", roared one of them. "A real piece of good work." He touched Uli's shoulder. "Now come back with us, soldier. And I promise you, we're going to make a beautiful job of you, too, this time."

"Thanks", said Uli. "Better wait till we get that citadel down, though. Come on, boys, primp my little lady here—in you go with the brush."

His eyes scanned the rampart again.

"Hi, look", shouted somebody. "They're storming now."

It was true.

When André de Foix saw the officer with the plumed helmet fall—and a handful of men around him—he also saw the crowded line of pikes waver behind the rampart. This was the moment to be used, and he ordered the Gascons of Monseigneur de Gramont to advance at the double.

"Lucky shot", he remarked to the bishop. "A fistful of gold to the fellow who trained that gun. Make a note of it, somebody. Labrosse! All the ladders we've got to the rampart. Speed is what matters now. Mustn't let them breathe. By Our Lady, my Lord Bishop, I think your gunner got Herrera—or that young cockerel who made Herrera change his mind, and that would be even better. There! The first ladders are going up. . . ."

There was some resistance, but it did not seem very fierce. Boiling liquid emptied two ladders, but three others came up, and then another five, and the climbers went up like cats.

"Your Excellency!" screamed Labrosse. "Look at the flag—the Spanish flag!"

"Mordieux", said André de Foix. "They're striking the colors. The rampart is empty. It's all over. What a lucky shot. Where is that gunner? Excellent. Excellent. Ride over, Labrosse! see to it that there is no mischief. You know how I want it. And, Labrosse! If by any chance that officer is still alive—the one with the plumed helmet—I want to see him. Treat him as if he were my brother. Brave man. Off with you. Faith, but your provost marshal is a cool customer, my Lord de Gramont. There he is—still hanging somebody."

They really had succeeded in getting Uli back to the gibbet, but there was a good deal of commotion going on all around it, with some men shouting that the law was the law for everybody and others protesting inarticulately.

"But that's the same fellow again", said the bishop of Couserans. "They must have interrupted his execution during the bombardment."

43

"Your Excellency! Your Excellency!"

André de Foix raised his eyebrows as two gunners brought up old Pitoux with his arm in a sling.

"'What is it, Pitoux? Did you train that gun that fired the lucky shot?"

The old man swallowed hard. "No, Your Excellency. I wish I had. It's the fellow over there, the one they are hanging, and it's a shame to do that, Your Excellency. He's too good a gunner to be wasted on a gibbet and—"

"Stop it!" shouted André de Foix. But the provost marshal either did not hear him, or else he did not know that the order was for him. He went quietly on with his work, and once more the rope was fastened round Uli's neck.

Angrily the commander spurred his horse and rode up. "Stop it, I say", he repeated sharply. "Have you no eyes or ears?"

The provost marshal doffed his cap. "This man is a condemned criminal, Your Excellency. . . ."

"I don't care if he is Satan himself. Listen, you: Did you fire that shot?"

"Yes, Your Excellency", said Uli, and the blood began to flow back into his face.

"But I thought I saw you being hanged", interposed Monseigneur de Gramont, shaking his head.

"I was, my Lord Bishop", admitted Uli. "They have just started hanging me for the second time."

The commander was amused. "How did it happen?" he asked.

Sergeant Garroux nudged Bernac beside him. "Time to go", he whispered, and, with Varel and Beauxregard, they began to slink off, slowly and cautiously.

Uli said, "First I was falsely accused. Then I was condemned to be hanged. Then they dropped me when the first shot was fired. Then I saw that they took the wrong elevation with the second gun, and that was more than I could stand, and I went over and fired the gun myself."

André de Foix threw his head back and laughed like a schoolboy. "I don't know about your being innocent", he said, wiping his eyes. "But even if you were guilty, you were only condemned to be hanged once, not twice. Provost Marshal, the man is free. What's your name? Right. Come and see me tomorrow morning at the mayor's house. One more thing: Will you admit that that shot of yours was just luck?"

Uli looked him full into the face. "I served under Frundsberg as a gunner, Your Excellency, before I had the honor to serve under you."

"A good answer." The commander nodded. "Perhaps it was not just a lucky shot—but assuredly you are a very lucky man." He gave him a friendly nod and turned his horse away.

Uli smiled. It was a strangely bitter, cynical smile. He looked at the provost marshal. "Don't be so sad, friend", he said. "You will have enough work tomorrow—on others." He rubbed his neck. The rope had left a broad red weal all around it. "Thanks for the choker you gave me, anyway. And give me back my pike, my bundle, and my two-hander. Something tells me I shall need them."

CHAPTER FIVE

JUST OFF THE PLAZA Uli stopped suddenly. His "trial" had made him miss the general alarm that must have been given when the citadel broke off negotiations, and in the mean-

45

time his company had been in action. He would have to report to Sergeant Philippart and explain what happened. Or at least some of it.

He turned round and saw a shadow disappearing behind the colonnades.

Garroux, or one of his men. They were watching him.

Well, it was understandable. They had thought to have got rid of him for good, and here he was, not only very much alive, but in favor with the commander-in-chief himself. They could not very well try anything here, with witnesses abounding, but later, when the sun had gone down . . .

Tonight the whole of the glorious army was going to get drunk—and that might give them an opportunity. What a nuisance that girl was. Because of her he would have to be on his guard all the time, at least till they had got out of this town.

The girl. They might go after her, too. He and the girl were the only witnesses alive.

Then he laughed. Garroux and his confederates were in exactly the same position as he was. They, too, had missed the general alarm and had to rejoin their company.

And here it came, the company, with Captain de Brissac at the head on his bay horse. Natural enough; the citadel had surrendered, and the commander would not need all those troops to disarm and guard the garrison.

Uli went up and saluted.

Captain de Brissac performed an act of which most of his men would not have thought him capable: he smiled. His sallow cheeks seemed to obey the unaccustomed movement with some difficulty.

"I heard about it", he said. "Want to hear more. Have this."

It was a golden ducat, and Uli put it into his pocket.

"Thank you, Captain."

"Fall in. Report to me later."

Uli obeyed. Out of the corner of his eye he watched but could not see either Garroux or his men emerge from behind the colonnades. Perhaps he had been mistaken after all.

Sergeant Philippart said nothing. Only when they had almost reached their quarters, he growled, "Now speak the truth, my boy. Don't lie to an old man. Your father was a Gascon, wasn't he?"

"No, Sergeant. He was Swiss. Does Ulric von der Flue sound like a Gascon name?"

"It doesn't. It sounds awful. But your mother, she was a Gascon, eh?"

"She was Swiss, too, Sergeant. All my people were."

"She ought to have been Gascon", said Sergeant Philippart darkly. "Why did they want to hang you?"

"Sure you want to know?" asked Uli lightly. He had to report to de Brissac, and he had a premonition how that interview was going to go.

"You can keep it to yourself, if you don't want to talk about it", grumbled the sergeant.

A few minutes later de Brissac dismissed the men and retired to his own quarters, in the *posada* The Royal House of d'Albret. Until this morning it had been The Infanta of Castile. When the liberators marched into the town, the innkeeper had hastily summoned a painter and told him how he wished to rename it. When they had agreed on the price and the painter ascended a ladder, he was promptly stopped by his client. "Don't paint it over, *estúpido*. Loosen the nails and take the board down. Then paint on the back, and nail it on again that way."

The painter gave him a quizzical look. "I see", he said. "You don't seem to think it will last. Where's your patriotism?"

"I'm as good a patriot as anybody", said the *posadero* proudly. "And I shall pray to the saints that I won't have to turn the board again. But if I have to, I don't want to pay you twice. Now do what I told you."

Uli had taken quarters at a much more modest inn. The Christopher Columbus owed its name to the sudden enthusiasm of its owner for the great discoverer, and he even went so far as to tell special guests that Christopher Columbus had spent the night here once, when he had set out from Spain to France, to find someone to finance his plan of reaching the Indies from the other side of the world. It was not true, but it was a good story, especially when told with many details about what the great man wore and what he had said. And in the first years after the great discovery the name had exercised a kind of magical attraction. But this was a generation ago, and the interest in the faraway continent had dwindled. Too many young men had gone there with high hopes and come back—if they had come back at all—fever ridden, penniless, or, worse still, with the spots and ulcers of the new disease that completely baffled the best physicians and was almost as contagious as the plague. America had gone out of fashion, and so had the Christopher Columbus.

But Uli found the old *posadero* a friendly soul, his room relatively clean, and the food edible, though of course too heavily spiced, as always in this country.

He was ravenously hungry and thus ate two portions of the roast mutton drenched in garlic sauce and covered with pepper and capers, followed by a hunk of goat's cheese, and then rinsed his protesting palate and tongue with a coarse young wine of an unusually clear red.

He stretched himself like a large cat. That strange little man, Saint Francis of Assisi, used to call his body "Brother Ass" and treat it with little mercy—far less than he had for a

48

real donkey. With me it's the other way round, Uli thought. My body is grateful and even happy to be alive. Brother Ass feels warm and contented and ready for anything. But the rest of me . . .

He fingered the choker that the combined efforts of the provost marshal and his helpers had laid around his neck.

In a few moments he would have lost consciousness. A few more, and he would have been dead.

And then?

He shrugged his shoulders. The bitter, cynical smile appeared again. He called for the *posadero*, paid him, shouldered his pike and Little Hans, and walked over to The Infanta of Castile.

Captain de Brissac received him cordially enough.

"It was a good shot, my boy. Saved us a great deal of trouble, I daresay. The commander himself spoke to you, didn't he?"

"Yes, Captain. I am to report to him tomorrow morning at the mayor's house."

De Brissac frowned and murmured something about a great honor. "Why did they want to hang you?" he asked abruptly.

"I was condemned for something others had done, Captain", said Uli quietly.

De Brissac began to drum with his fingers on the table before him. "Others", he repeated. "Men of my company?"

"Yes, Captain. And if you please . . ."

"Just a moment", interrupted de Brissac quickly. "I can't prevent you from making an accusation, if you must. But I have lost three good men to that damned gibbet already, and I don't want to be thinned out any more, if I can help it. This war has only started. If you mention names, I'll have to call in the provost marshal and start proceedings."

"I understand, Captain", said Uli, with some bitterness.

"No names, then?"

"No names, Captain."

"Good. Very good. Of course, the commander may ask you about it himself. . . ."

"I don't think he will, Captain."

De Brissac sniffed. "You never know with him. What if he does?"

"If he does", said Uli calmly, "I think I can still avoid mentioning names."

De Brissac's hawk face softened perceptibly. "We seem to have made a good acquisition in you. You served in the papal guard, didn't you?"

"I did, sir."

"Why did you leave it? Or rather, why did you have to leave?"

"Because I didn't keep my mouth shut, sir."

"How is that?"

Uli hesitated. "I was very young at the time . . ."

"You are not exactly old now." There was a flicker of amusement on de Brissac's face. "Come now, what was it?"

The Swiss raised his chin. "I thought a man who is to be addressed as Holy Father must be a holy man, sir. But it seemed to me that His Holiness Pope Leo the Tenth was not very holy, and not much of a Leo either. He was more like— like a house cat. A soft, furry cat."

De Brissac's moustache twitched. "I begin to understand why you—left. That's no way to speak of the Pope, even if . . . never mind. You know better now, don't you?"

"Yes, sir. I know how to keep my mouth shut."

De Brissac nodded. "I shall probably lose you", he said. "You were too good at that gun of yours not to be transferred to those disgusting things. A reason more for me to keep the rest of my men together. You understand?"

"I understand, sir."

"Very well."

Uli saluted and left. It was the old story. When murderers were needed, they were not punished. He knew only too well what would have happened if he had accused Garroux and his friends despite de Brissac's warning. It was five men's oath against his—and Garroux was in de Brissac's good graces. The captain had been a little worried about what he was going to say to the commander-in-chief tomorrow, but even if he did accuse the five scoundrels then, the end of the issue was very much in doubt . . . despite the fact that he himself was now in favor with that exalted personage. They had hanged a dozen men in the marketplace, true. But that was when the citadel had not yet fallen. It would have been extremely disagreeable to attack it with a downright hostile population in the rear. They had had to make a show of justice.

Now that the citadel had fallen they would sing a very different song. He had been wrong in what he said to the provost marshal. There would be no more hangings.

There was only one thing Garroux and his men had to worry about: that there might be another witness against them.

Out in the street he saw batches of Spanish prisoners passing by, disarmed and escorted by small detachments of Bayonnese infantry. There were no officers among them. They would be taken care of by men of their own rank, as was the custom.

It was getting dark now. There was something to be said for being able to see the sun rise again tomorrow morning. There was something to be said for life—despite Pope Leo the Tenth, despite injustice, gibbets, and murderers. Despite Margaret . . .

But they must not get the girl. There was nothing about her that interested him in the least. A pretty creature like

51

many others. Very young, too young to see the sights she had had to see today. Too young to be murdered by Garroux to prevent her from being a threat to his safety.

He had no great grudge against Garroux personally. They had a proverb at home, "Never expect more from a boar than a boar can give." There were many Garrouxs in the world who murdered in cold blood and hit the face of a man who had his hands tied behind his back. No use killing one of them. Kill them all—or let them go.

But they must not get the girl.

Perhaps it was just that he did not want his little effort in her house to go for nothing. Probably it was just that.

He grinned with satisfaction when trumpeters blew in the streets and a stentorian voice proclaimed a curfew for all officers and men for nine o'clock tonight.

So they wanted to make sure of their prisoners first, before they let the boys loose again on the town. Very good. At least tonight Garroux and his friends would not be on the prowl. The girl was safe for the time being.

Suddenly he felt very tired. He walked home to the Christopher Columbus and went straight up to his room and to bed.

It was the kind of bed one found in a *posada*, a palliasse of straw and an old sheet to cover it. Even Captain de Brissac would not fare better.

She was too young to be murdered. And she had invoked the Holy Virgin. There was something about the Holy Virgin that always moved him a little. A Mother for all those who had no mother. I suppose I should pray tonight, he thought. Saved from the gibbet, and he does not pray, the fellow. But it was not God who saved me. It was my own will. And what I learned under old Frundsberg. Wrong elevation, they had. Silly fools. A gun must be treated like a woman. Only better.

I saved myself. I did it. God did not have to bother. I did it all myself.

The poor little priest with his sad eyes would not like that. He looked like a good man. Some of them were.

It *was* a good shot.

Well, God—I can't ask you that question yet. But one day . . .

Then he slept.

## CHAPTER SIX

"A GOOD BEGINNING, eh, my Lord Bishop?" asked André de Foix. He was in excellent humor, although he had found the mayor's bed quite detestable and his quarters utterly inadequate for a man of rank. These things were difficult to avoid in war. He stretched himself, yawning delicately.

His lordship of Couserans smiled. "You should have taken quarters in the viceroy's palace after all", he said.

"Impossible. You have no idea of the state it is in. It has been most thoroughly looted by our loyal but rapacious populace. Unfit for a dog. I shall have to hang some of the citizens for a change. I am sorry for poor old Najera. He is not a rich man, I'm told, which speaks for his honesty. Such a rare virtue."

"I wonder where the duke of Najera is now", said the bishop, frowning a little.

"Yes, it's a pity we did not get him, isn't it? Wise old fox. Got out in time. Herrera tells me he sent one of those heroic messages: to defend the citadel or die. Easy thing to do, to send a message like that, when one is safe oneself. I rather like Herrera, you know. Witty. Do you know what he said? 'I did what I was ordered to do. It is fortunate that the duke gave me an alternative. I preferred to defend the citadel rather than die.' Now he is sitting in one of my orderly's rooms, writing a long explanatory letter to the emperor. The heroic defense of Pamplona. Ventre-Saint-Gris! We have overrated those Spaniards."

"I still wish I knew where the duke is", said the monseigneur of Couserans. "He is not a coward, you know. And he is not a traitor either. Herrera is not Spain. And if that young officer had not been shot yesterday . . ."

"Ah, yes. He was the soul of the resistance. That reminds me . . ."

The commander rang a silver bell, and an orderly entered. "Who is outside, Marin?"

"The mayor . . ."

"He can wait. Who else?"

"The prior of the Convent of Saint Dominic . . ."

"I'll see him in a minute. And?"

"A Swiss soldier who insists that his excellency wishes him to report."

"That's the man. Send him in." The orderly left. "You must never disappoint a man who has done you a service", de Foix went on. "Or he won't do you another one. Almost nineteen hundred prisoners, my Lord Bishop. I got the complete lists this morning. I think by tomorrow King Henry can safely enter his loyal capital. By then the palace will be in somewhat better shape. And set your mind at rest about the duke of Najera, I beg of you. I think I know where he is."

"No longer in Navarre, I presume", said the bishop.

54

"Quite right. He has gone to Logroño. A better fortress and a stronger garrison than Pamplona."

"It is logical", the bishop nodded. "And it is dangerous. He will use Logroño as the assembly point for an army."

"If your sermons are as sound as your strategy, I must congratulate your diocese. Najera is in trouble. He has written letter after letter to the emperor without receiving a reply. Partly because we intercepted them, partly because Charles is far too busy with the affairs of the empire to bother about this little war—thanks be to the saints. By now Najera knows that he is on his own. So he will use Logroño as his assembly point, and he will try to improvise an army. Therefore we must anticipate him."

"You want to attack him in Logroño?" asked the bishop incredulously. "That means invading Castile, the very heart of Spain. Charles *must* react to that."

"Shall I wait till Najera has got an army large enough to throw us out of Navarre again? I must crush him before he is prepared. In two weeks we shall be back here. In three at the most. I have no intention of conquering Spain proper. But I must beat Najera in time."

Only then they saw that they were no longer alone.

The orderly was back, shifting nervously from one leg to the other, and with him a tall, lean soldier with a pike like a young mast and a two-hander that Goliath might have found adequate.

Impossible to say how much or how little the two had heard—still more impossible to ask them.

Uli was acutely aware of the fact that his entrance had embarrassed the two commanders. He had been a soldier far too long not to know that it was dangerous to know too much, and he tried to look as innocently stupid as possible.

De Foix smiled thinly. "My Lord Bishop," he said, "it is only fitting that I should reward this good man in your presence. I believe he belongs to one of your units, although he certainly doesn't look like a Gascon to me. Where do you hail from, my man?"

"Switzerland, Your Excellency."

"I should have guessed it. You people have been a headache to generals ever since Julius Caesar. You had the honor to belong to the papal guard at one time, I believe ..."

"Yes, Your Excellency." So Captain de Bnissac had thought fit to send a report about him to the commander-in-chief.

"... but you do not seem to be too lucky with your employers", went on de Foix, still smiling. "Apparently the Holy Father was unable to please you, and somebody must have been a little displeased with you yesterday—yes, yes, I know you feel you have been wrongly accused, but let's not go into that now. You are wasted in the infantry, obviously. How would you like to be a sergeant in command of three guns?"

"Thank you, Your Excellency."

"Very well then. Report to Pitoux in due course. Here, take this ..." He threw a little leather bag at Uli, who caught it deftly. It was heavy for its size. "Twenty-five ducats", went on de Foix. "The ransom for the officer you laid out with that shot of yours. Incidentally, you ought to pay your respects to him; it's the least you can do when you smash a man's legs with a cannon ball. My leeches are trying to put him together again. Holà ..." A sudden idea gleamed for an instant in de Foix's eyes, and his smile widened a little. "I will do one more thing for you", he said, rising. "The officer you shot is a Basque nobleman, Don Iñigo de Loyola y Licona. A brave man. I want him to reach the castle of his fathers safely as soon as he can travel. The leeches say he is fit for travel as soon as they have finished with him. You will lead the transport of the wounded man. It is an honor, Sergeant. I should give the task to an officer, really. But as you were the cause of his wound, it seems poetic justice that you should be in charge. Orderly, get somebody to escort the sergeant to the prisoner's room, and see to it that he gets the necessary traveling expenses. Six men and a *carreta* or a litter, whatever the leeches prefer. And send in the good prior of the Dominican Convent."

Uli murmured a few words of thanks and was ushered out. Twenty-five ducats was nice. And a sergeant's wages were five times that of an ordinary soldier. Old Pitoux would not be much of an obstacle, and gunnery was more interesting than most other things in the army. So far so good.

As for the commander's idea about putting him in charge of the transport of that wounded officer . . .

Uli grinned. It was obvious enough. He had heard too much, and however stupid he appeared to be, the commander was not going to take any chances. Some of his troops might get frightened if they knew that their next task would be to invade Castile proper, and there was also the danger of enemy agents hearing about it, if the matter became known too early. It was better to send the man who knew too much on an errand where he could do no harm, a nice ceremonial task, escorting a wounded officer back to where he lived—even if that meant lacking a first-class gunner at the impending siege of Logroño.

The orderly led him across the courtyard to a small white building where the captured officers had their quarters and introduced him to the officer in command of the guard, a sour-looking oldish man—with an enormous mustache—of the name of Breveux. Then he left.

"So you are going to rid me of one of the Spanish cockerels", Breveux grunted. "Wish you'd take 'em all. That Loyola fellow! The way the commander pampers him, one would think he's a natural son of the emperor. Three physicians

57

around him; he must have this; he must have that. What's so wonderful about him?"

They were walking along a narrow corridor.

"He's in there", said Breveux and pointed with his head to a door at the end. "Take him and good riddance."

"I shall need a *carreta* or a litter", said Uli. "It's up to the medical men to tell me which."

Breveux nodded. "Both legs in bad shape. That's one who won't give more trouble to the world. Hey, aren't you the fellow who fired that cannon shot? Thought you were. Should have fixed that cannon a few inches higher. Then he'd be gone."

There was no need to explain to the irascible old man that a cannon elevated "a few inches higher" would have sent the shot right over the citadel into the blue.

Uli entered.

Breveux had not exaggerated. No less than three physicians were attending the patient, or rather they seemed to be conversing with him. He was fully conscious. They had propped him up with cushions, and a thick rug covered his body from the waist down.

Uli looked at him with some curiosity. When that man fell, the defenders had given up. There must be something to him.

He saw a beautifully proportioned head. Only the forehead was too high, or was it because his hair receded a little? Why, the man was no more than thirty. Dark eyes, slanting a bit upward, with rather heavy lids, a strong, well-modeled nose, and mouth closed so tightly that it looked as if it were used only once a year. The man was in pain, of course, and almost as pale as the white camisole he wore. He must have lost a great deal of blood.

One of the physicians walked up to Uli. "You have come to enquire about the patient?" he asked.

Uli nodded. "The commander-in-chief has put me in charge of the prisoner's transport", he said. "As soon as he can be moved, I am to take him home."

"Oh, he can be moved", said the physician hastily. "My learned colleagues and I have done everything possible for him, and he will no doubt recover more quickly in his native surroundings—if he receives the necessary medical attention, which I assume will be available, although the physicians in this country . . ." He shrugged his shoulders.

Uli looked at him with ill-concealed distaste. He had all the healthy hatred of the experienced soldier for the "leeches"—most of them utterly callous, inefficient men who hid their ignorance behind a wall of Latin gibberish. "The enemy in the rear", they were called.

Perhaps they wanted to get rid of their patient because they thought he was going to die on their hands and feared to incur the anger of the commander, who had taken such a strong personal interest in his welfare.

However, Uli had to accept their word.

"Would you advise a *carreta* or a litter?" he asked curtly.

The physician thought it over. "A litter, I should say", he answered, pursing his thick lips. "The roads are bad here, and the transport should be made as smooth as possible."

That at least was sound advice, and Uli nodded and left to see Breveux about it.

"A litter, eh? And six men to carry him in style, as if he were an infanta of Spain, God blast them all. What next? Ah, well, he shall have it. There are many of them in the mayor's house."

Breveux stomped off, just as the orderly returned with a leather bag, containing the money for traveling expenses.

The commander is well served, thought Uli as he returned to the prisoner's room. He stopped in the door.

The Spaniard was sitting upright in his bed, and he was speaking to the leeches. "You have been most helpful and obliging. Give me the pleasure to accept my shield, my dagger, and my corselet as a token of my respect for your art and your courtesy."

Those were valuable gifts, and the physicians bowed and praised his generosity, as well they might. But what struck Uli most was the young Spaniard's manner. It was not haughty, not arrogant, but the way he paid them compliments was that of a ruler conveying favors to good servants. His very courtesy seemed to draw an unsurmountable barrier between him and the three doctors, and they reacted instinctively by bowing and scraping and wishing him speedy recovery as if they had been in his pay all their lives.

Uli remembered what, many years ago, the great captain of the Swiss Guard, Kaspar von Silenen, had said, not to him, who was not much more than a boy at the time, but to some high papal official: "The Spaniards have ninety-nine different shades of courtesy, just as the Moslems have ninety-nine names for their Allah. But it takes another Spaniard to discover exactly which shade is being used toward him. I would never know the difference, except for one thing I am quite certain about: that at least ninety of the ninety-nine shades of courtesy are most pestilential rudeness with sugar on top. So we call them false. But they aren't. It's just their way of speaking, and they expect you to understand and think you're a hopeless barbarian if you don't."

It was a pity that no one could tell him exactly which shade of courtesy this Spaniard was using, but the leeches at least saw only the sugar on top and lapped it up.

Uli wiped his mouth with the back of his hand. With a man like that it was better to stick to formal ways. He cleared his throat, and when one of the leeches turned toward him, he said, "My name is Ulric von der Flue, sergeant of artillery. Will you please introduce me to the noble captain?"

The physician was a little surprised, but he did as he was told, and for the first time the young Spaniard looked at Uli. He gave him a short nod.

"Artillery", he said. "Did your battery fire at the citadel?"

"Yes, sir", said Uli quietly.

"Did you fire a gun yourself?"

"Yes, sir." This was getting rather close.

"Which of the three guns was yours?"

Uli gulped. "The third, sir."

The Spaniard did not bat an eyelid. He said politely, "I congratulate you on a very fine shot, Sergeant."

"Thank you, sir", said Uli. There was more respect in his tone than there had been when he was talking to his commander-in-chief, but he was not aware of that. He would have liked to add a few words expressing his regret about the pain he had caused the Spaniard, but he could not formulate his thought adroitly enough. Instead he said, "Your transport will be ready in a few minutes, sir. We shall be waiting for you outside."

"Very good", said the Spaniard. Again he nodded, and Uli felt that he was dismissed.

He saluted, turned, and left.

As he walked back along the corridor, he thought, if these leeches have done a good job, that man will cause a barrelful of trouble to some people.

Outside he found the litter. Breveux had picked six strong-looking men for it, and Uli introduced himself once again, but this time with less formality. "I'm Sergeant von der Flue, in charge of this transport. We'll start in a few minutes."

The men maintained a sullen silence. Probably they had been looking forward to a few days and maybe weeks of idle life in a conquered town and did not enjoy the idea of having to carry a heavy litter for days on end.

Uli's eyes narrowed. It might take several days before de Foix commanded the march on Logroño, if he stuck to his idea. And in the meantime Garroux and his men would have a free hand. This very evening they might set out to eliminate the one witness who could endanger them.

For a moment he thought of looking for them and telling them himself, but he dismissed the idea. They would hardly believe him, and it might even put the idea into their heads. Garroux was a suspicious devil.

Leaning on his pike, he began to think hard.

Then some of Breveux's men came out with a stretcher, and the six soldiers showed some relief: the man they had to carry was of slight build.

"Careful now", said Uli. "Right. Yes, sir?" The wounded officer had beckoned him to his side.

"Do you know the way?" he asked calmly.

"No, but you do, sir", said Uli.

"Take the pass from Val de Ollo toward Gone. Then cross the heights of Lizarraga. From there to Urbasa, Olazgutia, Ozaeta. Then round the port of San Juan. Then across the sierra of Elguea to Oñate and Azpeitia. The castle is there. Can you repeat?"

Uli could and did.

"Thank you", said the officer politely and leaned back.

Cool, thought Uli. He grinned. Neat way to ascertain the mental caliber of the escort leader. He certainly knew a thing or two, that Spaniard. Well, there was no need to pretend stupidity with him.

"Four men forward", he ordered. "Up the litter. Follow me."

He knew the way to the pass at Val de Ollo. The army had come that way.

62

Suddenly he knew what he was going to do.

When he came to the corner of the Calle Valladolid, he let the litter catch up with him.

"Wait here for about a quarter of an hour", he said to the nearest soldier. "I shall probably be back by then. If not, go on, along this street and the next one till you leave the town, and wait for me at the last group of houses."

Then he turned left and walked away.

The house where it all started was only a few hundred yards away.

He did not bother to ring, but went straight up to the neighbor's house. What had the girl said their name was? Padilla—or something like it. As he approached, he saw a man, standing in a doorway nearby. In a few long strides he reached him and seized him by the arm.

It was the man Garroux had called Bernac.

"What are you doing here?" Uli asked in an ominous tone. "Where is Garroux? Speak up, man, or I'll break every bone in your body."

"I—I—I only wanted to—I mean no harm—"

"Where is Garroux?"

"He is not here—he—he ordered me—he wanted—"

"Out with it. What did he order you to do?"

"F-find out whether—"

"—whether there would be a witness against him—and you and your comrades. Go back and tell him there will be no need for any witness between him and me. And if I find him or any of you scum near this house again, I'll finish the work I started yesterday. Now turn around."

When Bernac obeyed meekly, Uli gave him a resounding kick in the rear that made him fly a dozen steps and then fall flat on his face.

"Get up and run", yelled Uli.

Bernac did. He did not even look back.

Would that cure them? It might, and it might not. It would appear very suspicious to Garroux that Bernac had an encounter with the "Swiss mule" practically in front of the house where the girl was. Or he might think that he had come to cash in on yesterday's victory.

He snorted. One thing was sure: they had not forgotten the girl.

Bernac was out of sight now.

Uli walked across the street and knocked at the house of the Padillas. Perhaps Bernac had lied. Perhaps Garroux had found out where the girl was hiding and was now in the house.

## CHAPTER SEVEN

THE ELDERLY MAN who finally opened the door was trembling. "Thank God it is you", he said. "Thank God it is you."

"Why? Is anything wrong? Has anybody tried to get in?"

"No one has tried to get in, no, Señor soldier, but the poor girl—we don't know what to do. . . ."

"What's the matter with her?" asked Uli gruffly.

"We have tried everything we could," the old man assured him, "but there was nothing that helped."

Uli took a deep breath. "She—she isn't dead, is she?"

Old Padilla shook his head sadly. "Perhaps it would be better for her if she were. I am afraid she has lost her reason."

There was a pause. Uli had seen many women who had lost their reason when they had seen things a woman was not supposed to see—the kind of things that war brought into people's lives. He remembered a young woman in Hungary, sitting on the doorstep of her own half-burned house and making sweet, cooing noises to her baby in her arms. No one would have known that she was mad, if it had not been for the fact that the baby had no head. He had tried to talk to her, but she only drew the headless little torso closer to her breast and stared at him with unseeing eyes. Madness always liked to walk with an army. Hunger and pestilence came later.

Sometimes such women regained their reason, and sometimes they did not.

"Where is she?" he asked hoarsely.

"We have given her Alonso's room . . ."

"Alonso?"

"Our son. He is in Salamanca now, for his studies. Perhaps you can help her, Señor soldier. She won't speak to any of us, however hard we tried. She won't eat. And she has cut off her hair. . . ."

"Cut off her hair?"

"Yes. And put on an old suit of Alonso's. We were terribly frightened when we found that she had taken my wife's scissors. We thought she was going to do harm to herself, but all she did was to cut her hair off."

Uli shook his head again. "She sounds mad enough", he murmured.

"We have been thinking maybe we should call in a priest—or a physician."

"A priest, not a physician", said Señora Padilla, joining them. She was a haggard-looking woman in her early fifties, with a prim mouth. "The girl is possessed, that's what she is, possessed by some demon. I made her such a lovely dish of eggs this morning, and she did not even look at it. And she talks to herself all the time. Possessed."

"A physician might be better", insisted her husband. "If he'd bleed her a little, all that nonsense would go out of her. We were debating about it just when you knocked at the door, Señor soldier. But maybe you can help—she has asked for you several times. 'Where is the big soldier with his sword?' she said."

"It is not good to have her here", said his wife. "A mad girl. You don't know what she will do next. She may sneak up on me when I am sleeping and cut my hair—or my throat. And I absolutely forbid you to call the physician, Mateo. When he bleeds her, she will fly into a rage and kill us all. Everybody knows that the possessed have all the strength of their demon."

"It is not very—agreeable", admitted Padilla. "We are no longer young. . . ."

"Speak for yourself", snapped his wife.

"Well, not as young as we used to be, and all this excitement . . ."

"Lead me to her", said Uli drily.

The room was near enough. Padilla opened the door just wide enough to let Uli enter and then closed it behind him very quickly, when he saw the girl turning round.

Prepared as he was for the sight, it gave Uli a shock all the same. The slim creature staring at him had little in common with the girl he remembered. This was a dark-eyed, dark-haired boy of sixteen with a pale, pinched face.

"They told you, of course", said the outrageous creature. "But if they hadn't, would you have known it's me?"

"I'm not so sure even now", said Uli.

The creature sighed. "Thank the Virgin, you've come back. I thought I was going mad."

"They", Uli jerked his head back, "think you are."

"I know. Do you?"

"I don't know", said Uli truthfully. "Why did you do that—cut off your hair and—put on that dress?"

"It is better so."

"They say you won't eat."

"Is that a sign of madness?"

"N-not necessarily. But they say you talk to yourself all the time."

"Not all the time, but I did. I was praying. Must one be mad to do that?"

"And you wouldn't speak to them."

The girl thought that over. "That is true", she admitted. "I didn't say much. I couldn't."

There was pain in her voice.

He tried again. "Why is it better to have your hair cut off and dress like a boy?"

Her eyes avoided him now. "They might have come back", she murmured. Her little face was taut, and she pressed her lips together in a grimace of disgust.

He nodded thoughtfully. "They might at that", he admitted. "That's why I came to have a look."

"I wanted to go away", she said in a forlorn voice. "But I didn't dare. They could have been waiting outside...."

She was trembling. For a minute he had thought that there was nothing wrong with her. Now he was no longer so sure.

"Perhaps they would not have recognized me", she went on. "Perhaps they would have thought I was a boy. But if I had seen them again, I ..." She began to cry quietly.

"That's better", said Uli. "Wash it all out."

But she had already stopped.

"I want to go away", she said fiercely. "Far away."

"Where do you want to go?" he asked.

"To Barcelona, I think", she said after some hesitation. "Mother is there."

"Now that", said Uli, "is a very sensible idea. But how are we going to get you there?"

"I don't know", she admitted.

"Well, how did you get here from Barcelona in the first place?" he enquired.

"Aunt Mercedes brought me here, in her *carreta*. She—she—" She began to sob again.

Uli was thinking furiously. It was no good leaving the girl here. The old people wanted to get rid of her anyway. But how could one get her to Barcelona? If he took her to the alcalde ... but that worthy had other fish to fry with an army occupying the town. A priest? He didn't know any. Perhaps the girl did. But what could he do? It was not exactly agreeable for a priest to be burdened with a sixteen-year-old girl, even if she was dressed as a boy. But he might know somebody who could take charge of her or take her to a convent, where the nuns could look after her, till some respectable female was found who was traveling to Barcelona. But all this had to be done very quickly—he could not let his transport wait forever.

"Listen, little lady", he said. "Do you know a good priest here? Or a convent where they can take you in?"

"I know only Padre Gómez. He is very good. When I confess to him, he giggles. He is ninety-one."

The idea of having to explain to a ninety-one-year-old priest why he should take charge of a sixteen-year-old girl made Uli wince.

"What about a convent?"

"I don't know any here", said the girl.

Well, perhaps the Padillas did.

"Come with me", he said.

The girl's eyes began to sparkle. "Oh, thank you", she said enthusiastically. "I knew you would help me. I knew it all the time. I have been waiting and waiting, and always when I thought you wouldn't come, I closed my eyes, and then I knew you would come. And when we reach Barcelona, Mother will . . ."

"Hi", interrupted Uli. "Not so fast, little lady." He began to scratch his head. "I can't take you to Barcelona—I'm a soldier. I've got to obey orders. What I wanted to say was: come with me. I'll talk to the people here. Perhaps they know a convent that could take you in.

The girl's face fell. "They don't like me", she said. "They think I'm mad. I don't know what they will do when you go away."

He saw the fear flickering in her eyes.

She was not wrong, either. When he returned to the anteroom, with the girl half a step behind him, he found the Padillas standing there stiffly and sullenly, in an attitude of finality. They did not want a mad girl in their house. They had seen a soldier lingering about in the street—it was not safe to have her here. Certainly, a convent would be a very good solution. There was a Franciscan convent just outside the city; the nuns there could look after her.

"May I keep this suit?" asked the girl.

She could, of course she could. Alonso had outgrown it anyway. But there was little possibility that the good nuns would let her run about in it.

They had made a small bundle of the clothes in which she had come, and here it was.

The girl refused to take her clothes, so Uli stuffed them into the bundle hanging from his pike. He had the uneasy feeling that he was taking on a responsibility he could not really carry. But the convent the Padillas spoke about was

69

right on his way out of town, so it would be only for a very short while.

When the Padillas saw that they were getting rid of her they relented a little. It would all work out very well, assuredly. The nuns were very good and could look after her; they had their own physician who came to see them, and she would be safe there till her relatives could send for her. They were quite voluble in their good wishes and so piteous in their all too obvious relief that Uli cut it short. But he heard the girl say, not unkindly, "I thank you for the suit and for all that was meant well."

Then they left, and behind them the Padillas closed the door and locked it.

"Now listen to me", said Uli gruffly, as they walked away. "You have chosen to become a boy, and a boy you will be till we reach the good nuns. Don't mince. Walk. Take longer strides. Don't make pretty movements with your arms and hands, either. Just let them hang about or treat them as practical things. Yes, that's better. We are joining my men for a short while, and they need not know you are a girl. What is the matter with you?"

"I don't know—I feel so—strange. . . ."

He seized the half-fainting girl by the scruff of her neck. "Hold on. I know what's wrong with you. Hold on, I say. Fainting is for girls. You're a boy now, but a starved one. Have a bite of this." He produced a sizable piece of bread from one of his many pockets and a carefully wrapped piece of spicy cheese from another.

"Eat", he said, as the girl took a deep breath. "Slowly. Chew every bite carefully, or you'll get the belly cramp."

A third pocket produced a small skin of wine.

He loosened its aperture deftly and held it to the girl's lips. "Three sips will do", he said.

The coarse wine gave warmth almost instantly, and she attacked the remaining piece of bread and cheese with gusto. A faint flush returned to her cheeks.

"Can you walk now?"

"Oh, yes—yes—"

"Then come on."

The nuns would take some persuading. Suddenly he began to chuckle.

"I don't even know your name", he said.

"Juanita—Juanita Pérez."

"You will have to be Juan, till the nuns take you. Can you walk a little faster now, Juan?"

It made her smile, and somehow that first smile made him wonder, as he had many times before, what stuff girls and women were made of.

But the smile died as quickly as it had come, and she said in the tone of a disappointed child, "I don't want to go to a convent. I want to go with you."

He shook his head. "Big boys like you mustn't talk like that. Keep your voice low. And don't *mince*."

The litter was nowhere in sight. Well, he had been away much longer than a quarter of an hour. They had simply obeyed his orders.

Nevertheless he became a little restless, and he strode along so that the girl had a hard time keeping pace with him.

Passersby looked at the unequal pair with some curiosity, but Uli could see no indication that they penetrated the girl's disguise. She did look like a boy.

Then he saw the litter, carried by four of his men. The other two were probably in front. Yes, they were. So all was well.

It took Uli and the girl a few more minutes to catch up, and by then they were nearing the last houses of Pamplona. Where was that Franciscan convent the Padillas had talked about?

Ah, there it was. He drew a breath of relief. For a moment he had seriously believed that the panicky old couple had lied just to get rid of him and the crazy girl.

But this fairly large white house with its strong, whitewashed wall was a convent beyond doubt.

"Come with me, Juan", said Uli. The litter carriers looked at him, but he beckoned them to go on.

The girl was obviously very reluctant. Well, he could not help her. This was where she had to go.

Uli rang the little bell.

"I don't want to go to the convent. . . ."

"Sh . . . you'll obey orders."

He hated himself for it, but what else was there to do? These nuns were slow. He rang the bell again.

"Let me go with you. . . . I promise I'll obey orders. I'll walk as quickly as you want me to. I can cook, too."

"The nuns will appreciate that."

But there was still no sign of any nuns. This was getting awkward. He rang for the third time. The bell seemed to wail under the impact.

Nothing happened.

Out of the corner of his eye he saw the beginning of a hopeful smile on the girl's lips. Angrily he gave a fourth ring, a whole series of rings, loud enough to alarm the entire community even if they were all fast asleep.

But he knew they were not sleeping, and there was no singing coming from the chapel. And he knew the convent was not deserted; there was a thin wisp of smoke coming from a narrow chimney. They were cooking their midday meal, and they did not seem to need the girl's help for that.

He had not been so helpless when he stood before the rampart of the citadel the day before. But no cannon had the right elevation for a convent wall. And the good nuns had seen his pike and his two-hander and had decided not to take any risks.

He turned away abruptly and saw that his men had stopped and put the litter down. They were all looking at him. They were probably curious. It was not surprising.

He began to walk toward them, the girl Juan trotting behind him like a little dog.

A ruddy-faced, red-haired soldier with a beaky nose asked hoarsely, "Were you thinking of taking the veil, Sergeant?"

The others laughed.

"Up the litter", Uli barked. "Follow me."

A glance into the litter showed that the Spaniard was asleep.

Uli took the lead. The girl Juan followed. She kept her chin high, and she did not mince. He saw the quiet mirth in her eyes.

He did not have to explain her presence to the men. A sergeant is a sergeant. And at least so far they did not seem to have discovered that she was a girl. Just as well she was skinny.

He would have to get rid of her at the next opportunity, of course. But until now she had had it her own way.

*She* isn't crazy, he thought grimly. I am.


CHAPTER EIGHT


THE JOURNEY TOOK LONGER than Uli had anticipated, but he had to admit that it was neither the girl's nor the Spaniard's fault. Juan behaved as if he had never been anything but a boy. A dreamy, quiet, frail-looking boy, but a boy all the same and accepted as that by the men. He cooked their meals, unless they spent the mealtime in a village inn (and he cooked rather well), he was quick in running little errands, and he was astonishingly good at something none of the men knew much about: looking after the needs of the wounded Spaniard.

Boys were nothing rare in an army. Most of them were used as drummers or trumpeters. Thus there was nothing particularly unusual about Juan's presence, although he did not seem to be the usual type of army boy, recruited from the poorest of the poor, who were glad to get rid of one more mouth to feed.

Uli saw to it that no unnecessary questions were asked.

If Juan did not have to cook, run an errand, or look after the Spaniard, he had to stay at Uli's side.

At night, whether they camped in the open field or rested in a village inn, the boy's place was with the wounded man.

It was all very simple and perfectly natural.

Some of the men thought that he was a relative of the Spaniard, others that he had been ordered to accompany them as a male nurse.

The Spaniard behaved in the best tradition of the hidalgo.

During the entire journey no one heard him utter a single exclamation of pain, although it was clear enough that he suffered greatly. The continuous movement of the litter was not exactly the best treatment for wounds still raw; they even started bleeding again, and Juan had to renew the dressings several times. Uli watched him doing that and saw tears in his eyes at the sight of the terribly mangled flesh of the right leg. It was broken, and the leeches had set it and put it into a wooden contraption which must hurt him constantly, but it was impossible to take it off without endangering the process of healing. The left leg had only received a flesh wound and was doing fairly well. The boy had tears in his eyes—but not the patient. He did not even allow himself to wince when the dressings, stiff with blood, were taken off; all he did was to clench his fists, the only expression of pain the code of a knight permitted. But he never omitted thanking the boy most courteously for his services.

In Ozaeta they had to stop for a whole week. The Basque roads, all up and down hills, proved too much, not only for the patient but also for the litter bearers. It was a strange country. Wild precipices, small valleys of a weird, deathly stillness, with here and there a thatched hut, poised dizzily on a rock, the only sign of human habitation. Then again wide fields or small stretches of forest, chestnuts, oaks, and beeches mostly.

Ox carts creaking along the dusty road, driven by sharp-faced, silent men. Uli tried to speak to them, but they answered only a few words in Basque—they might as well not have answered at all and would have probably preferred it.

It was enemy territory, of course, but the attitude of the people was neither hostile nor friendly. They seemed to take no interest in them at all.

In Ozaeta it was different. It was no more than a hamlet, but the people there knew the wounded man. Women came with flowers for the little room they had put him in, in the house of an elderly couple, and there were always groups of silent, sullen-looking men who seemed to keep watch over him, though they were not armed and showed no sign of hostility.

It was there that Uli had his second talk with him.

So far the Spaniard had limited himself to greeting Uli with a little nod, coldly polite, to a few occasional explanations about the road to be taken or a short though still polite bulletin about his condition when he was asked for it. And the Swiss was not particularly eager to make conversation.

Great gentlemen did not care much for talking to a simple soldier, even one who had risen to the rank of sergeant. And there was the fact that, after all, he was responsible for the man's wounds.

It was a strange thing, he thought. If he had not shot that cannon, he would have been hanged. Instead he had been given twenty-five—no, twenty-six—golden ducats, had been made a sergeant, and was allotted the task of looking after the very man he had shot. Poetic justice, said the general— whatever that meant. There was nothing poetic about smashed legs, and as for justice: this Iñigo de Loyola y Something-or-Other was the only brave man they had had in that citadel, and he paid for his courage with a couple of wounds and might well be a cripple for life. What was just about that?

It was a chain of thought that came up in his mind time and again, and he always ended it with a shrug. Poetry and justice—there was precious little of either in the world, and certainly none in war and politics.

But here in Ozaeta, after a week of enforced rest, Juan came up to him.

"He wants to see you."

Uli frowned. "What is the matter? A relapse?"

It would be very unfortunate. Only yesterday there had been hopes that the journey could soon be resumed.

"No, he is quite well today."

"What is it then?"

"I don't know."

Perhaps it was the opposite, thought Uli, making his way to the Spaniard's room. Perhaps he wants me to leave. If so, we'll fall in with his wish. It is not much fun escorting a litter across half the mountains in Spain. If only they were mountains like those back home, snow topped, glowing in the setting sun.

"You should see the mountains we have at home, Juan",
he said. Only then he saw that she had not followed him.
Funny, how one got accustomed to talking to that—boy. Not
that it happened often, with the men within earshot. It was
her presence rather than anything else. Like that of a faithful
little dog. She had been tired a few times, he had seen it
clearly enough, but she would have bitten her tongue out
rather than say so. Maybe she had learned that from the Spaniard. Maybe one could learn a thing or two from him. And
here he was. In the semidark of the room Uli could not see
whether he looked better or not.

"There is something you wish, sir?"

"You will be kind enough, perhaps, to answer a few questions, Sergeant von der Flue?" He pronounced the outland-
ish name with great care. Nothing could be more barbarous
than to address a man with a phonetic caricature of his name.

"Certainly, sir, if I can."

"I have been in this room most of the week. Have there
been any troops passing by?"

"No, sir."

The Spaniard closed his eyes.

Now why had he asked that? Why should he think of
troops passing by here, at this miserable little village? Of course,
it was on the road from Guipúzcoa to the Ebro River and to
Saragossa. But now came the next question.

"Have you sent any of your men away?"

"No, sir." This was stranger still. Why should he, and why
should the Spaniard care if he had?

"And finally, I have been unconscious a few times, and I
have been feverish. I hope I have not disturbed you with too
much talk in my feverish state?"

"Never heard you say a word, sir", said Uli quite truthfully.
"That is, unless you are in a feverish state now. Are you, sir?"

"I am quite well", was the calm answer. "I think we can proceed with the journey, if that is agreeable to you."

Whichever of the famous ninety-nine shades this was, it sounded definitely like an order rather than a suggestion.

"Very well, sir", said Uli phlegmatically. He went to find Juan. Why on earth these questions? Suddenly he stopped and began to whistle softly. Of course. Don Iñigo was thinking of Basque troops who might march to the help of the Spanish viceroy in Logroño. They could have passed through Ozaeta, or near it. And he wanted to make sure that none of the Frenchmen had been sent back to report such troop movements. And he was worried that he himself might have given something away by talking in his sleep, when he was feverish. That was it. That fellow would cease to be an officer only when someone smashed his head to pulp, rather than his legs. In three questions he had got everything out of Uli that he wanted.

Uli began to chuckle. This man was not much older than he was himself, but he was the stuff generals were made of. Maybe one day he would be a second Frundsberg, and people would tremble when his name was mentioned.

You never know. And here was Juan.

"Tell me, does Don Iñigo talk in his sleep?"

What enormous eyes the boy had!

"Very little. It's usually a name."

"What name?"

"I thought at first he was talking of his sister—the word sounded like *hermana*—but then he called her his queen. It's Queen Germaine, of course."

"What has he got to do with her?"

"Oh, he told me, when I asked him. He was her page when he was very young. She must be very beautiful. I think he loves her."

"Is she the queen of the Basques?"

Juan gave him a reproachful look. "You don't know who Queen Germaine is?"

Uli grinned. "I haven't been in Spain very long, you know. All I know is that she can't be King Charles' wife."

"Indeed she isn't. She isn't a queen at all."

"Just a minute. You said she was one. You just reproached me for not knowing her . . ."

"She *was* a queen. She married King Ferdinand of Aragon, when Queen Isabella died. Then King Ferdinand himself died, and then she married again, the margrave of Brandenburg, who is the governor of Valencia."

"You know a lot about royalty, don't you?"

"Oh, yes. Aunt Mercedes always told me about . . ."

She broke off. He saw the shadow hovering over her eyes and said quickly:

"Don't forget that you are a boy, now."

A slight tremble. The pitiful ghost of a smile. Then she said, "I won't forget."

"That's better." It was not all over yet. "I wonder where he can have met that Queen Germaine of his? What do you think?"

"In Madrid. He went there just when she arrived from France. She was a princess de Foix."

He began to laugh. "That means she is a relative of my general. Well, that's how it goes with kings and queens and princesses. They can only marry each other, and in the end all the courts of Europe are related. And then they have to fight each other, and a simple man has trouble sorting out which is which, and who is on what side."

"I think he loves her very much", said Juan again and for a moment did not look like a boy at all.

"Did he tell you that?"

Juan was shocked.

"Well, how else do you know that he loves her?"

"The way he mentioned her name in his fever. It's quite different from the way he talks about her when he is awake."

Uli shook his head. Juan smiled.

"Do you still think I'm crazy?" she asked softly.

"He loves a queen", said Uli gruffly. "The queen is a Frenchwoman, but married to a German nobleman who is a Spanish governor, and her cousin is just now invading Spain. I'm a Swiss fighting for the French who are fighting for Navarre. We are all crazy—why should you be an exception?"

This time her eyes were clear, and her smile was no longer a ghost.

He gave her a slap on the shoulder.

"We're leaving now", he said and started bellowing for his men.

CHAPTER NINE

IT WAS VERY QUIET. It was unbelievably quiet. Only the pain sang, and a pulse hammered at his temples.

The shuffling of feet that had punctuated the endless journey was no more; the quick, rasping talk of the litter bearers, their coarse jokes and even coarser curses—all that was gone, a thing of the past.

They had been waiting for him at Anzuola: his brother Pero López, the priest of Azpeitia; and Martín de Iztiola, the doctor; and at the old Loyola bridge at Azcoitia, Magdalena de Araoz had joined them with her daughters and young Beltrán—he had grown—and together they had made the last bit of the way to the castle. It seemed endless, this last little bit of a long journey, and yet the worst was still to come—the jouncing as they passed the narrow gateway and the steep stairway to the top floor, where Magdalena had the room with the canopy prepared for him. The journey across the sierra had been nothing in comparison. Every step brought fresh pain.

To lie here now was like—like a moment's respite in purgatory.

Magdalena had seen to it that he was given it; it was rare that a woman was both intelligent and good. She had taken the doctor with her. She had felt that he needed to be alone for a while.

There was no need to tell her anything about what to do about the French soldiers. She knew what to do. They would be given food and wine and everything they needed.

He would have to talk to Magdalena about them later nevertheless.

But not now. Not now.

This was Loyola, at last. He had smiled a little when he saw the massive, grim old building on the little hill overlooking the Urola River, with the strange, graceful little turrets perched on it.

And this was the "room with the canopy", as they had called it when they were children, the main guest room with its low ceiling of heavy beams and its two windows of Moorish brick: one window on the north overlooking Izarraitz with its marble quarries and oak trees, the other on the east, toward the valley and the gardens of Azpeitia, with the shrine of Our Lady of Olaz and the parish church.

He wanted to see all that again.

But now garden, shrine, and church were invisible, hidden behind the spreading foliage of an enormous oak.

A slight breeze brought the fragrance of sweet-smelling apple trees.

He took a deep breath. Then his lips tightened a little, and he stretched out his hand for the silver bell Magdalena had put on the table next to the bed.

She came at once, and with her the doctor.

"Where is Martín?" he asked.

Martín was his eldest brother, the head of the family and Magdalena's husband.

"His last word came from Logroño", said Magdalena.

He nodded thoughtfully. Logroño. That was where the viceroy was now. That was where he himself would have been, except for his hasty decision to join the men in the citadel.

"Where is Pedro de Zabala?"

"The council of Azpeitia has put him in charge of the militia. He left three days ago."

"How strong is he?"

The doctor began to murmur a protest, but it sounded rather weak; he knew the Loyolas too well.

"Eleven hundred", said Magdalena quietly.

Eleven hundred. And Martín had 3,500 men. But no artillery. Still, cannons were not everything. Maybe they would be one day.

He began to calculate. By this time the duke of Najera would have drawn all the garrisons of the vicinity together. There was the contingent of the Marqués de Lara ...

But the figures began to fight his brain. They would not allow themselves to be added up, and for a moment or two the room spun around.

"Now, really ..." said Doctor de Iztiola.

82

Don Iñigo held up his hand. "The French", he said with some effort. "The French who brought me here . . . see to it that they are given guides . . . who do not lead them where they can encounter our troops . . . on the march. They must see nothing . . . they can report, when they return."

"Of course", said Magdalena. "They have treated you well?"

"Yes. They did their best. Especially their leader and . . . the boy. Now, Doctor, I am at your disposal. . . ."

Then he fainted.

## CHAPTER TEN

Two more doctors were called in, when de Iztiola decided that an operation was imperative. The French had made a very bad job of it, doubtless through ignorance rather than intent, as de Iztiola magnanimously declared. The leg would have to be broken again and reset.

Don Iñigo gave a courteous nod. He refused to drink the wine mixed with poppyseed that they wanted to give him. That was for women.

He stared at the wooden beams on the ceiling and dug his nails into his palms, as the butchery began.

"The main thing", he said, "is for there to be no deformity."

The learned physicians looked at each other, then murmured that they would do all they could.

"No deformity", repeated the patient coldly.

After that he spoke no more.

Outside, Magdalena was waiting, with Padre Pero López.
It was always better to have a priest ready in such a case.
Not a sound came from behind the heavy door.

## CHAPTER ELEVEN

THERE WAS NO NEED for Padre López after all.

Four days after the operation the doctors were far from satisfied. After a short conference with his colleagues, de Iztiola returned to the sickroom.

The patient was fully conscious, but feverish.

The sharp face of the Basque doctor was void of expression. "Don Iñigo, it might be advisable to receive the Viaticum."

The patient gave him a stony look.

"Is it certain or only probable?"

"It is not certain, Don Iñigo."

The patient nodded. "Send for my brother Pero."

He received the last sacraments with the courteous reverence of a knight for the supreme sovereign.

As so often happens, after that he seemed to get better. Then the fever mounted again, but his thinking was still quite clear, its speed increased rather than diminished by the heat of his blood.

King Charles—it was incomprehensible that he had not reacted to the many messages of the duke of Najera, messages mounting in urgency. As emperor he had to listen to the troubles of the whole world, of course, and there were many, especially in Germany, where a mad monk by the name of Luther had set himself up as a judge over the Church and was made use of by the princes.

But it could be fatal for the emperor to forget that he was first and foremost the king of Spain. He was young, true. But he had good advisers, like Adrian of Utrecht, who had been watching over his education.

Messenger after messenger, and no answer. And the French came nearer and nearer and by now they would know about the *comuneros*, the seditious, militant movement against the privileges of the nobles. It was quite possible that there was a secret alliance between them and the French. It was even probable, as the duke had said himself.

It was a terrible shame that the viceroy had had to leave Pamplona. It was a flight, even if he said that the string of an arquebus had to be drawn back before its missile could be released. This was not the time for witticisms; it was the time for action.

Only a week earlier Iñigo had pleaded to be allowed to get reinforcements from Guipúzcoa, and the duke had given him permission. He had roused the countryside: 3,500 men followed him and Martín—to arrive outside Pamplona only to find the viceroy had fled.

Worse still, the town was already parleying with the French. Of course, there were not even two thousand troops holding it. So doubtful was the loyalty of both town and citadel that Martín insisted on withdrawing his men. Perhaps he had been right; nothing could have been worse than to be caught between two fires. And yet it was intolerable, intolerable.

Martín was the head of the family. Martín was the commander of the Guipúzcoans. But he could not refuse Iñigo the two hundred volunteers he asked for.

The town was wavering. Most of the people were for the French, for their puppet king; Iñigo knew he could easily be caught before he even managed to get into the citadel.

So he raced through the town at top speed, visor lowered, shield on one arm, naked sword in the other, and his two hundred behind him. Their very entry into the citadel was bound to give fresh courage to the defenders, and it did— though not for long. Two hundred men, and the French were twelve thousand and more. But they had to listen to him; they had to consult him at least; he was the viceroy's envoy.

"Defend the citadel or die!"

It was not quite clear to Don Francisco Herrera whether that was the viceroy's own order or not, but he did not press the point, wisely. Herrera was a fox and had the cunning of a fox.

But a fox defends his hole, doesn't he?

Should a Spanish fortress fall to the enemy without firing a single shot?

Not if Iñigo was one of the defenders, not if he was the least of its defenders. Defend the citadel or die. Defend the citadel or die.

How they shouted! But they grew silent when they saw the assault columns approaching. There was no end to them, and the ladders, the ladders must be pushed back, get on with the job, you—don't you see they are coming up?

Down with the ladders.

Something was hissing like a hornet, like the devil's own hornet; someone was screaming, "Look out!" and then the wall seemed to fall to pieces, and the pain . . . They must not lower the flag; are they mad?

But this was Loyola. The room with the canopy.

De Iztiola gave him something to drink, cool . . .

He was on fire. There must be no deformation. There must be no deformation.

Why did they all look so worried?

The countryside must be roused, every man who can carry arms. Let the king know.

I will serve my lady, my beautiful queen. I will lay my deeds at her feet.

I must ride. Get my horse. Don't you hear me? My horse!

This time three men were sitting around him, three physicians, their faces solemn and grave.

Don Iñigo de Loyola looked at de Iztiola.

"Is it still not certain?"

The physician answered without even a trace of hesitation. "If you do not improve by midnight, it is certain, Don Iñigo."

The patient looked out of the window. The sun was high. He could hear, very faintly, the sound of church bells.

"Why—the bells?"

"It is the Vigil of the Feast of Saint Peter."

Saint Peter . . . the patron saint of the Loyola shrine.

Saint Peter, the patron saint of knights, who drew his sword in the defense of the King of kings.

He had an ally. He decided to defend the citadel.


CHAPTER TWELVE


"I WISH WE COULD have seen him once more, before we left", said Juan.

"They said he was unconscious." Uli grunted. He was looking ahead, where the two Basque guides on their mules were taking another turn to the left. This was definitely not the way they had come.

Juan sighed deeply. "You don't think he will—" He did not dare to release the last word.

"Maybe he'll die, and maybe he won't", said Uli philosophically. "We all have to, and what's the difference of a few years more or less?" After a while he added, "It would seem a silly waste to have carried him all this way, only to have him die a few days after his arrival."

Perhaps the way the guides took was shorter, as they said it was.

"I wish I had been better about looking after his wounds", said Juan. His lips were pale and trembled a little.

Uli laughed. "You looked after him like a little mother, my boy. Don't you remember what the good lady said?—Doña Magdalena they called her. It was flattering enough, I should think."

The boy flushed. The lady with the strong, aquiline face had taken both his hands in her own: "You have been good to a wounded man, Señorito. Don Iñigo has told me all about it. God will not forget it, and we too will remember it always."

"They are wonderfully strong people", said Juan thoughtfully.

"And not exactly given to long speeches", added Uli drily. "Which makes it sometimes rather difficult to know what they think. Frenchmen are easier to understand."

The guides were out of sight now, but that was only because they had passed around a hill that blocked the view.

"They thanked you, too", said Juan. There was an undertone of reproach in his voice. "And they gave us food and guides and everything."

Uli nodded. "They've been decent enough, especially considering that I shot the man."

Juan stopped abruptly, staring at him with wide open eyes. "You? You shot him?"

"Yes. It was a cannon shot, but I trained it."

"But—you never told me—"

88

"Why should I? My dear—boy, even you must have heard that in a war people shoot people nowadays. And don't let anybody tell you that it was any better before they invented cannons, because it wasn't. It isn't so much what hits you but where you get hurt that matters. Our Spanish friend got his in the legs. There are worse places than that, believe me."

"Do you think he will ever walk again?"

The guides were back in view now, making straight for a forest, looming up behind the hills.

Uli grunted something unintelligible before he replied.

"It depends upon the leeches, I suppose. Most of them are butchers. But even if they are good, I don't think he will lead men into battle again. It may be just as well. . . ."

"What do you mean?"

"He's the kind of man who becomes a general sooner or later. I've seen a good many. And for every general there will be a few thousand dead. Only the best—the very best—know how to win a battle without a few thousand dead. Well, maybe he would have become one of those few; you never know. Now he'll become a country noble instead, that's all."

He began to grin. "It's the first time that I've bothered to think of what may lie in store for a man I put out of action. And why should I bother whether the Spaniards will or will not have a good general in a dozen years or more?"

Juan looked at him attentively. "Because you may have to fight against him—again", he said.

He laughed outright. "Or under him", he said with a shrug. "How do I know who'll hire me then? I've served with the French and against the French, with a duke who was a rogue against a count who was not much better. I served the good city of Cologne when she had a quarrel with the good city of Mainz, and I even took part in a campaign against the Turks. . . ."

"But surely that at least was a good thing", said the boy Juan frowning. "To fight against the infidels ..."

"That's what I thought." Uli nodded. "I was very young, and very stupid. And they did preach so beautifully about a new crusade and a holy war, in the good city of Landshut. The duke had been promised fifteen thousand ducats if he got two thousand men together against the Grand Turk. So he got them together, and I was one of them. An imperial envoy arrived and made a wonderful speech. That was not very important. But he had brought the fifteen thousand ducats, and that was important, because the duke had run out of money. As soon as the imperial envoy left, the duke got himself the new mistress he wanted—you have no idea how expensive some ladies are, my boy—and we were promptly disbanded."

"But—but that's fraud", cried Juan aghast.

Uli shook his head mournfully. "It is, when *you* do it, or *I*," he said, "but when a duke does it, it is a matter of expediency."

He spat.

"Then—then the little people are really better than the big ones", said Juan thoughtfully.

"I doubt it." Uli laughed. "There are so many of them; you can't check up on them all. But from what I have seen, most of them would behave just the same or worse, if only they could. When a man is good—or a woman, Juan, my boy—it is often enough only because he didn't have an opportunity to be otherwise. Or because he didn't have the courage to do what he really wanted to do. Or because he was too lazy, too indolent, to be greedy. And when one of those little people rises ... phew. He's worse than the highborn duke every time. He takes out on the other little people what he has suffered when he was one of them. And he knows all the tricks, too."

Juan shook her head. "Is there no good in people then? Father always said there was—and everybody loved him, dukes and little people alike. And you are good yourself. If it weren't for you ..."

"I? Good?" Uli was mildly amused. "Because I knocked that pig Garroux over when he was after you?"

She blanched a little, but recovered quickly.

Getting over it at long last, he thought.

"It isn't only that", said Juan. Her voice was fairly steady. "You came back to look for me."

"I never like leaving a job unfinished", said Uli drily. "But I'm no better or worse than anyone else, and why should I be?"

After a pause she said, "Father was a poet. And he used to say that poets were like sparrows and like God—no respecters of persons. And he said it was good to have something in common with God."

"I suppose it would be." Uli shrugged. "If God would let us. But I don't think he cares. Don't look so surprised, Juan. If he cared, could the world be what it is today? Look at it. Christian princes fighting each other instead of fighting the Turk—town fighting town—and greed and hatred among the little people wherever you go. If God cared ... would he let all that happen?"

"But he does care", said Juan. "He sent you, when I ... He does care."

"I happened to pass by when a certain little lady came running out of her house", said Uli. "But do you think that always happens? I used to think the way you do, but I've seen too much since. We are left to our own devices, and maybe there's justice in that. I don't know."

"But—but Our Lord", stammered Juan. "Surely you believe in Our Lord Jesus, who came to save us."

Uli looked grave. "Right", he said. "And what did they do to him?"

"But he founded his Church on earth...."

He nodded. "And what has become of it? I served in the papal guard. All the Holy Father could think of was building magnificent buildings and hobnobbing with the kings and the politicians. A very elegant man, the Holy Father. If Jesus came back to pay him a visit—I don't think he would find time for him. Perhaps that's why he doesn't come."

"You mustn't say things like that", cried Juan.

Uli laughed. "I said them in Rome, my boy. Not exactly to the Holy Father—he wouldn't speak to a simple soldier like me—but loud enough to be heard. That's why I had to leave the guards. I was eighteen then. I didn't know then that a man mustn't say what he thinks if he wants to get on in life. That's just it, don't you see? I can believe that the Lord Jesus wanted us to have a chance. But then he left it to mere men, and they botched it all up. I don't understand it quite, because after all he is supposed to know all things, so he would know that we *would* botch it up, but still—there it is."

"Aunt Mercedes", said Juan in a quavering voice, "Aunt Mercedes told me about a man in Germany, I forget his name—he refused to obey the Holy Father and stirred up the people to follow him instead—are you—do you think—?"

"You mean Luther, I suppose", said Uli thoughtfully. "I've heard of him. No, I'm not one of his men, and I don't think I ever shall be. He's sincere enough, from what they say about him—those who know him. But he also is only a man, and no man however sincere can take over where God has walked out. Besides, he broke his word."

"Broke his word?"

"He used to be a monk. He made vows. And he broke them. A man must stick to his word. A soldier doesn't learn much, but he learns that. When I swear the oath of fealty I must keep it even if I hate the guts of my master."

"But why did you become a soldier?"

Uli's face became hard. "It's as good as anything else. And if a man has to choose between being hammer or anvil, I'd rather be the hammer."

"But—what do you believe in?" insisted the boy.

"Doing the right thing, as I see it. In my reason—my horse sense—and when necessary in Little Hans here." He patted the two-hander. "Oh, well, there is a little more to it, I suppose. Even if God has walked out on us, at least he once took the trouble to share our life. It's a good thing to re-member, like remembering one's parents. He chose himself a mother, too, they say. It's a lovely thing to think of. I like to think it's true, because it is so lovely. It's good to be able to believe in one woman at least. . . ." He rubbed his fore-head. "Blessed if I know why I'm blathering about all this", he rasped. "You're asking a lot of questions today, Juan, my boy, when I'm the one who should ask them—no, not of you—of those guides of ours."

He stomped off.

Juan had tears in his eyes. This had been the longest talk she had ever had with the Swiss, who usually only spoke when he had to, and then in as few words as possible. And what he had said was something Juan had never heard be-fore. No one had ever questioned the faith in Mother's house in Barcelona, and as for Aunt Mercedes, the merest men-tioning of anything against the Church was unthinkable. How could a man go on living when he thought that God had forsaken the world?

The girl Juanita had eyes in her head—and ears—she had seen and heard enough to know that not every priest was a saint, to say nothing of the way some lay people behaved.

93

Everybody knew there were sinful people, and no one was quite without sin, including the girl Juanita—even if Padre Gómez sometimes giggled at what she said in the confessional. He did not always giggle, though, and once he had said quite sternly, "Remember, my daughter: grave sin estranges us from God as long as we do not repent in our heart."

Could it be that God had become tired of the world, that he had given it up as hopeless? The whole world?

He had saved her. Only a few weeks ago he had saved her through the very man who believed that he had deserted the world. But then, he had not saved Aunt Mercedes—and Silvio—and Ana. . . .

The girl Juanita—not now the boy Juan—thought of what Uli had said about the Mother of God, that it was good to be able to believe in one woman at least.

He must have been hurt very much, thought the girl Juanita. "I wonder who she was, who hurt him so much. . . ."

The six soldiers, now free of the litter they had hated, came up chattering among themselves.

The boy Juan always kept away from them as much as he could, and much to his relief they did not seem to seek his company either. He did not know that their sergeant had taken them aside on the first evening of their march to Loyola castle. "There's one thing I want to have quite clear: leave the boy Juan well alone. He's the youngest nephew of the general, and the old man wants him to gain experience, so he's allowed to travel with us. It's a confounded nuisance, but I can't help it. He's as tender footed as a young girl, and he'd do better strumming a guitar or dancing with the ladies at court. But I don't want to be bawled at by the commander because you gave him the rough side of your tongues or made fun of him. The order is: leave—him—alone. That clear?" It was, and entirely ignorant of his social rise, the boy Juan was left in peace.

94

Uli in the meantime had reached the guides just before they entered the forest.

"Through here?" he inquired. "Why not take the main road?"

The answer, in broken Spanish, was that this was a short cut. Uli had heard it before.

"Very well. But give me that mule of yours for a while. You'll get it back, never fear."

"The mule, Señor Sergeant?" The Basque did not seem to relish the idea.

"That's what I said. And be quick about it."

The two guides exchanged a few hasty sentences in Basque. Uli began to play significantly with his two-hander.

The guides were unarmed. Again a short exchange of Basque words; then one of them climbed down, and Uli mounted his mule. He waited till the boy Juan and the soldiers had come up.

"Follow the men as before", he ordered. "I shall be back shortly. I've lost a valuable locket, and I think I know where." He had spoken loud enough for the guides to hear him, and he thought he could see a faint smile of relief on the face of one of them. He turned the mule and rode back.

A few minutes later he stopped behind a group of trees. His men had disappeared from sight. He rode the mule off the road and up the hill. It was steep, even for a mule, and it took the better part of half an hour before he reached the summit.

From here he had a glorious view across the Basque country and down to the faraway Ebro and Spain proper, all gilded and bronzed by the rays of the afternoon sun.

But what he saw did not satisfy him. He did not gaze at the blue-green splendor of the forest, at the peaceful cattle grazing in the meadow, or at the spire of a church rising gracefully between two smaller hills.

His eye followed the main road, the road they had not taken because the ride through the forest was a short cut.

The dusty white of the road was interrupted over there by what seemed to be a long, long brown snake, crawling along so slowly as to appear almost immobile.

Fifteen hundred men, about three hundred horse, he thought grimly. Then he turned the mule and began the descent. When he reached the road, he let the mule fall into a trot. After a few minutes he came to the forest. The trail was easy to follow, and half an hour later he caught up with them.

"Did you find what you had lost, Señor Sergeant?" asked one of the guides.

Uli shook his head. "It's gone for good", he said sadly. "Here's your mule."

The guide looked at the animal, covered with sweat from its exertion, but he did not say anything.

By nightfall they reached the last Basque village and found quarters at the only inn.

Uli seemed to wish to drown his loss; he ordered wine for everybody and saw to it that the guides had their proper share.

The boy Juan was dead tired and went to bed at once. The bed was no more than a palliasse of straw with a rough cover, but he had become accustomed to that by now and fell asleep in the middle of his prayers.

He awoke suddenly and gave a muffled cry. There was a man standing beside his bed, shaking his arm.

"Quiet, Juan", whispered Uli. "Get dressed as quickly as you can. We leave in five minutes. No time for questions now."

The Swiss was fully dressed, two-hander, bundle, and all.

Numb with sleep, Juan gazed at him.

"Leave—now?"

"Yes, come along. Quickly."

"B–but I can't get out of bed as long as you're here. . . ."

Uli gave a short laugh. "I clean forgot that you are—such a timid boy." Clanking in his arms, he left the room.

The boy Juan jumped out of bed and struggled into his clothes. Still half dazed, he came down the stairs, only to be shushed fiercely by Uli, waiting for him at the foot.

It was pitch dark, and a cold wind came in through the open door.

"Not a sound", whispered Uli, taking the boy by his arm and leading him out of the house.

Juan gaped with surprise when he saw a large *carreta* waiting. The six soldiers had boarded it already. The next moment he felt himself lifted up bodily and placed squarely on the seat beside the driver's. Uli followed, took the reins, and gave a low, clucking noise. The mules began to move. There were two, and despite the darkness the boy Juan thought that they looked rather familiar.

"Hold tight now", said Uli. Bending down, he produced a whip and let it crack. The mules began to trot.

"Sorry I had to disturb your sleep", said the Swiss, chuckling. "But the news I have must travel quickly if it is to arrive in time."

"Aren't these our guides' mules?"

"Certainly. They were the only ones I could find in this godforsaken village. The *carreta* had to be stolen, too. I couldn't help it."

"But they were so good to us at Loyola and . . ."

"Not the guides. They've been trying to slow us up and lead us on all sorts of bypaths so that we couldn't see what's going on. Put your tender conscience at rest, though. I left six ducats on the table for them, and if the innkeeper doesn't pinch them, they will get their due and more, the rascals."

97

"But what news have you got that cannot wait at all?"

"News for the general."

"Are we going to Pamplona then?"

"No, to Logroño. And now keep your little mouth shut."

Juan did.

Uli cracked the whip again. The mules laid their ears back and began to gallop.

"Hi, Sergeant", cried a frightened voice. "Do you want us all to break our necks?"

He gave no answer. He had his hands full. The mules were used to being ridden, not to pulling a *carreta*, and he had to force them into obedience. So far they trusted the firmness of his hand, but let one of them make a single false step and stumble, and they would stop and dig their hooves in. Every muscle, sinew, and nerve in him was on the alert and stayed on the alert. The road was as bad as it could be, uneven, stony, full of holes. The *carreta* swung wildly from left to right and back again; the men were jerked about in their seats, but their curses and yells were drowned in the thundering of hooves and wheels. Up and down and sideways they bumped, and at least some of them would have fallen out, had they not clung together with the strength of desperation.

Pale with fright, Juan threw her arms round Uli's waist and hung on for dear life.

Several times they bumped over something that was not stone—a weasel, a cat, or a rabbit.

Then something like a long, whitish band loomed up in front—the main road to the south.

Uli did not slow down. The *carreta* raced ahead, the whitish band broadened, they were there, they were on it, and now it seemed to stretch ahead of them into infinity.

He cracked his whip again.

Somewhere behind them crawled the long, brown serpent, fifteen hundred men, three hundred horse.

## CHAPTER THIRTEEN

"FIFTEEN HUNDRED MEN, three hundred horse, sir", said Uli. "They'll be here in about five to six hours."

André de Foix leaned back. His white perfumed hand began to play with the ends of his beautifully curled mustache.

"Hear that, my Lord of Elgobarraque? And you, my Lord Bishop? They are Guipúzcoans, of course. And the road on which they are traveling is not the only one. They seem to have waked up at last. We shall have the whole swarm of Basque hornets about our ears."

The fighting bishop paced up and down the roomy tent and halted abruptly before the long, lean figure of the Swiss.

"How do you know?" he asked truculently.

"I counted them, sir", was the modest reply.

The bishop snorted. "You counted them—yet you say they'll arrive only in five or six hours. That leaves three logical possibilities. One: they are crawling like snails. Two: you have flown here on the wings of a bird. Three: you are a liar. Which is it?"

"They didn't seem to be in a particular hurry, sir", said Uli calmly. "And if your Lordship will take the trouble to send a man back the way we came, he will find the bodies of four mules where we left them. I was lucky to find a couple of horses for the last part of the way, or I wouldn't be here now. It took us thirty-four hours to get here."

The bishop saw the man's hollow eyes, his pallor, and the dirt on his face, hands and clothes.

"It looks to me", he said, "as if I had forgotten a fourth possibility: you're a good and faithful soldier. How did you come across that enemy column?"

Uli smiled faintly. "My task was to take a wounded officer home, a Don Iñigo de Loyola. When that was done . . ."

"Will he recover, do you think?" asked André de Foix with mild interest.

"Surely," said the bishop, "after such an almost miraculous survival he is not going to die from his wounds? The man is in the hands of God."

"I left him", said Uli blandly, "in the hands of three Spanish surgeons. We were given guides on our way back, and they seemed so keen on keeping us off the main roads that I decided to have a look at what was going on."

André de Foix nodded. "I made you a sergeant of my artillery last time I saw you, because you seemed to be wasted on the infantry. Now I'm not so sure whether you won't do better as an agent."

"I served under Frundsberg, sir", said Uli in the tone of a father explaining something to a somewhat backward child.

"Which means that you are a paragon in all things military, I suppose." The commander-in-chief was amused. "Well, in any case I am grateful to you for a piece of work well done. Did you pay for those mules?"

"For two of them, yes, sir. I regret to say that I stole the other two—and the horses."

"My Lord Bishop will give you absolution." André de Foix laughed.

"This", said the bishop somewhat stiffly, "is a military matter, not a spiritual one. I will refund you for what you paid out, Sergeant."

"Thank you, my Lord."

"And I", said André de Foix, "will buy those two stolen horses from you for twenty ducats and give you another ten for a valuable report. Let's pay him now, my Lord Bishop, lest the little matter is forgotten by the treasurers—I never trust those pen pushers, whether in war or in peace. Here you are, Sergeant. Faith! You have earned it."

Pleasantly enough the bishop too drew out his purse of purple velvet and added a dozen ducats to the pretty little heap in Uli's cupped hands.

"War is war," the bishop said drily, "but still I'm glad that you paid at least for the first two mules, poor brutes."

The gold disappeared quickly in Uli's roomy pockets. "Thank you, my Lords", he said, grinning. "I'll pass on some to my six men, if I may."

"Take that for them", said Lord Elgobarraque, and he threw another purse at the Swiss, who caught it deftly. "And get out." He had not said a word before but had shown every sign of impatience.

"Just one moment, my Lord Elgobarraque." The commander-in-chief sounded a trifle irritated. "I have not yet quite finished with our friend the sergeant. Now then, Sergeant: you have shown me that you can do more than fire a gun, with all due respect to your ballistic talents. I need a good man to deliver a letter for me, rather an urgent letter. The address is—somewhere in Spain. You will have to think of some suitable disguise. Think you can do that?"

"Surely, sir", said Uli phlegmatically. "Under the condition ..."

"Are you making conditions now?" exclaimed André de Foix, frowning.

"Under the condition", went on Uli, "that I receive a slightly more explicit address for the letter than somewhere in Spain."

The commander gave a short laugh. "Cheeky rascal. Wait outside in my secretary's tent. He will give you the details in due course. Off with you now."

When the Swiss had left, Lord Elgobarraque said hastily, "We have lost a great deal of time over that fellow. I need not tell you what the news means that he brought us, and we must . . ."

"You need not tell me anything, my Lord Elgobarraque", said de Foix sharply. "And we have lost not a minute more than necessary. It is perfectly obvious that we must raise the siege of Logroño and return to Navarre. The intelligence reports of the last two days are clear enough: both the constable and the city communities have raised troops. There are about a thousand men on the march from Valladolid alone, and we can be fairly certain that there will be contingents also from Segovia, Medina, Salamanca, and Toro, perhaps also from Burgos. Together with the men from Guipúzcoa, that is a sizable force, and I have no intention whatever of being caught between them and the garrison of Logroño—that would be just what the duke of Najera would like. We are quite safe today, though . . ."

"With the Guipúzcoans only five or six hours away?" Elgobarraque interposed.

"Yes. Fifteen or eighteen hundred men cannot risk an attack. They must wait till the other forces catch up with them, and they have farther to go. We shall leave at night without breaking camp. Najera won't know that we've gone until we are miles away. The offensive is over, my Lords. Now we shall take up fortified positions in Navarre and wait. . . ."

"Wait for what?" asked the bishop.

André de Foix smiled. "For the effect of the letter our good sergeant will deliver to a place somewhere in Spain."

## CHAPTER FOURTEEN

"THIS WAY, SERGEANT", said the orderly.

"Hold on a moment", said Uli, and he seized the heavy linen flap of the tent to keep himself from falling.

"What's the matter with you?"

"Nothing much. My bones are as soft as dough, that's all."

"Too much dissipation, I wager", said the orderly reproachfully.

Uli laughed. "Guessed it the first time. Wonderful opportunities, where I've been lately." He leaned against the tent, breathing laboriously. "Air," he said, "that's the best invention of them all. Air and water."

"Bit touched in the head, are you?" asked the orderly.

"Sure, brother. My head is delicate, not massive like yours. Getting better now."

But he staggered like a drunken man on his way to the secretary's tent and the orderly had to support him.

"I have enough air", he said. "What I need now is water."

The commander-in-chief's first secretary, a rubicund little man with a cheerful little button for a nose, saw at once what his visitor required. He yelled orders right and left.

"Water is no good alone", he said, filling a mighty goblet.

Uli emptied it in one long draft and held it out for more.

"Not too much", warned the secretary. "Half a goblet, no more."

"Fill it up, friend", said Uli. "I've never been one for half measures. That's better. And if you have a piece of bread . . ."

"We can do better than that", chuckled the good-natured little man. "Hi, somebody. Get me some cold meat and cheese and half a loaf. We can't let a good man starve."

The food came soon enough and disappeared even faster. The secretary looked on, his pudgy hands folded around his protuberant belly. "Not bad", he said. "Not bad at all. But you'll need a few hours' sleep before you can leave to—where you have to go."

Uli stared at him. "What do you know about that?"

The little man laughed. "It's my business to know these things. I've been with the commander eleven years. He hates long explanations, so my post is just outside the door, and doors are thin in a tent."

"I see." Uli chuckled. "You're right. I need some sleep."

"He's writing the letter now. It won't be long. And I don't think you will have to leave straightaway, not before midnight. That gives you eight hours. Is that enough?"

"More than enough. How is the siege going?"

The secretary's eyes became shifty. "Better leave that to the general, Sergeant."

Uli chuckled again. "Good advice."

"You just sit back now and take it easy. You'll get your letter in an hour or so." The little man rose and wobbled away into the adjacent section of the large tent, where half a dozen men were busily writing. Uli saw that it had a special entrance on the other side, leading straight to the tent of the commander-in-chief.

Well organized, he thought. But organization was not everything in war. And the general was no Frundsberg.

Frundsberg would have made use of the news about the Guipúzcoan column at once. He would have sent a quick-moving force, double the size of the Basques, and dispatched them within twenty-four hours, before they could join up with the besieged in Logroño or with any other force coming to the help of the Spaniards. He would not have gone on sitting on his elegant behind. And the siege was going badly.

Bah, what did it matter? A man swears an oath and does the bidding of his master, whether it is playing governess to a wounded enemy officer, bringing back a useful report, or delivering an important letter "somewhere in Spain". At least the general knew how to keep his mouth shut, even though his secretary listened to the discussions in his tent.

And he was generous. Neither the good bishop nor Lord Elgobarraque would have paid up so nicely, if he had not given them such a good example.

He fished Elgobarraque's purse from his large pocket and opened it. Twenty good gold ducats. Three for every soldier, with two to spare. Those would be for the boy, and with a dozen or so more he would have enough money for a journey to Barcelona—if somebody reliable could be found to accompany him. If not, there must be a convent in Logroño that would not close its door when a man knocked. Thunder and lightning, no! The convents were in Logroño proper, and Logroño was under siege, and it did not look at all as if it were going to be taken. But to leave him here with the army was sheer madness. And to take him on a mission like this was madder still.

He blew out his cheeks. When a situation was completely hopeless, something always turned up. Anyway he was too tired to think now. The chairs in this tent were simple, stiff, and hard, but at least they did not jerk wildly about, and there were neither horses nor mules to be coaxed, argued, whipped, and bellowed into greater speed. Somebody appeared with another plate of cold meat, and Uli grinned. "It never rains but it pours." It was roast chicken, and he had one bite of a leg. Then he fell asleep with the chicken leg still firmly in his hand, like a tiny club shielding his head that had sunk on his chest.

That was how the secretary found him. Smiling, he touched his shoulder, and at once Uli was up, the chicken leg dropped on the floor, and he grasped the hilt of the two-hander. "Yes—here I am. Where are they?"

"Easy now, easy." The secretary smiled. "And wipe your hand before you touch the letter, or it'll be as greasy as a moneylender's palm."

Uli wiped his hands carefully on the seat of his trousers before he took the letter. It was small. There was no address on the envelope.

"Order of the general", said the secretary quietly. "You will leave the town at midnight in a southwesterly direction. When you have reached Cadera—it's a small village—you may open this letter. It contains another envelope, with an address. That address you will learn by heart. You will then remove the envelope and destroy it very carefully, and you will deliver the letter to the person whose name you found on the envelope. Is that clear?"

"Very", said Uli attentively.

"That is all, then", said the secretary.

"Not quite", said Uli. "How long is this journey of mine supposed to last?"

"I don't know, my good Sergeant. A few weeks, I should think."

"In that case", drawled Uli, "I would like to have a little money for traveling expenses."

"You've only just got a whole stream of gold", snapped the little man. All the good nature had drained from his rubicund face.

"The reward for services rendered", said Uli with gentle reproach. "How much did the general tell you to give me? I didn't listen, so I have to take your word for it—till I meet him again."

"Eating, drinking, and grabbing gold, that's all you soldiers can do. Here, take this, and sign for it."

Uli weighed the purse in his hands. Then he opened it and looked at the contents. It was filled with silver.

"Perhaps you expected diamonds and rubies?" asked the secretary venomously.

"I never expect more from an ox than a piece of meat", said Uli cheerfully. "This will do. Where do I sign?"

"Can you write?"

"I'm full of hidden qualities", replied Uli modestly. He took the quill from behind the secretary's ear, dipped it in ink, and very carefully wrote his name on the paper handed to him. With his tongue between his lips he added, "40 pieces of silver received". Then he stuck the quill, still moist with ink, back in its place behind the secretary's ear. "My handwriting is a bit close", he apologized. "It may be difficult to add a zero to the figure. Being an honest man, you won't mind that, I'm sure."

"Are you quite finished now?" snapped the enraged secretary.

"Almost", nodded Uli with a friendly smile. "Just one more question. When I have delivered the letter, where shall I find the army?"

"I'm no prophet", muttered the little man. "Somewhere in Spain, I should say."

Uli chuckled. "I'm afraid you're right that you're not a prophet. Never mind. Listening behind the tent curtain is almost as good. My respects to the general, and thanks for the chicken and the wine."

"I hope and trust you will arrive safely at your destination", said the little man slowly. "But I won't mind if they catch and hang you on your way back."

"It's been tried before", said Uli pleasantly. "But it seems my neck isn't the right size for the rope. Thanks anyway."

He stalked out. Maybe the little man was right and soldiers were all alike, more or less. So were secretaries. Perhaps there was one who did not try to pocket his master's money rather than paying it out as he was ordered to. Nothing was impossible.

It was cooler now, and for a moment Uli watched the Ebro flow with lazy majesty past the besieged fortress.

He saw a number of men bathing in the river. They were well within cannon shot, but apparently the gunners of Logroño did not wish to waste their ammunition on so small a target.

A little farther upstream were clusters of boats attached to rough moorings. Perhaps the general planned to try an attack from the riverside. It was not a bad idea, but there was something desolate about those boats; Uli got the impression of an idea rashly conceived and just as rashly rejected.

Most of the soldiers he could see were without their armor. A good many were dicing, without interference from their officers. Now if the besieged made a sortie . . . but they would not. They were bound to know by now that reinforcements were on the way. They would wait for them.

Something dead about the whole thing, thought Uli. Was the general really doing nothing about those reinforcements? Nothing except sending a letter to somebody somewhere in Spain?

It was impossible. What would Frundsberg do?

Stupid question. To answer it one would have to have Frundsberg's brilliant mind—though he always insisted that all his generalship was mere common sense. Was he right, and was the real difference between him and lesser men that he could put a common-sense idea into immediate action? "Do it at once", was his favorite expression, and he had no use for men who vacillated or hemmed and hawed.

Common sense said that even a much lesser mind could not afford to let things go and do nothing. Perhaps de Foix also was expecting reinforcements? He could scarcely hope to conquer all Spain with a little over twelve thousand men.

Why didn't he at least try one more energetic attack against the fortress before the enemy grew stronger?

Well, it was not Uli's business, and thank God for that. But there was a stink in the air, not the honest-to-goodness stink of the battlefield, but the heavy, musty, dank reek of impending disaster, or at least of something that had gone seriously wrong.

Maybe I'm lucky, he thought. They haul me up the rope, and yet they do not hang me. They're running into something foul, and they send me away just before it happens.

He gave a bitter laugh. Uli von der Flue—lucky.

Now where was that tent where he had left the boy and the men?

On the way he had to pass groups of Gascon infantry. They too were dicing, and few looked up.

"Ah," said a hoarse voice, "what do I see? The half-hanged wonder of Pamplona is with us again."

Garroux.

He decided not to answer and to walk on, but the burly Gascon sergeant planted himself in the way, arms akimbo, angry lights in his porcine eyes.

"Let me pass, Garroux."

"So you've been traveling about whilst decent soldiers did the fighting for you, eh?"

"You don't mean yourself by any chance, do you?" There was something so irritating in Garroux's tone that Uli could not help hitting back.

"Sure I mean myself. I don't go and play the nurse when fighting's to be done."

"You have done some fighting? Must be quite a change after murdering women."

Garroux laughed. "Everybody knows how much you like going around telling lies."

The men had stopped dicing now. This sounded like a nice juicy quarrel in the making, and a quarrel or a skirt were the only things that were even better than dice.

Uli saw the crowd thickening.

"Orders of the general", he said gruffly. "Will you let me pass or not?"

"Orders of the general", repeated Garroux with mock reverence. "And what orders have you given him, my fine friend?"

"Butcher women", said Uli. "Force yourself on poor girls, steal people's cutlery—but don't try to be witty."

Garroux smirked. "You don't care very much for women, they say. I'm told you have been traveling about with a boy and . . ."

He got no further.

Uli rammed his pike into the ground, swung his leg up, and kicked him in the stomach. In the next moment the huge two-hander blinked in his hands.

"I'm on my way in the general's service", he said. "Anybody else who wants to stop me?"

They stared at him sullenly. Garroux was feared for his great physical strength, yet there he was, writhing on the ground and mouthing obscenities. Perhaps it was that rather than fear of the general which made them recoil slowly, as Uli walked on, leisurely, the pike in one hand, the two-hander in the other.

"We'll meet again, you . . ." bawled Garroux.

Uli turned. "If we do," he said coldly, "it'll be an unlucky day for you."

He walked on again, unhurried; he knew any sign of hurry would make them rush him at once.

After a while he relaxed his viselike grip on pike and sword. What's the matter with me? he thought. What Garroux had said was the kind of thing men of his ilk would say almost as a matter of course. Why should it make him so angry? It was absurd anyway. And it was good that Garroux had not discovered who the boy Juan was. Yet he was angry.

It's because I'm tired, he thought. Well, he could still have a few hours of sleep before midnight.

And here was the tent, and his six men were sitting before it on their haunches and dicing, too, but they rose as he approached them.

"Where is the boy?" he asked.

"Inside, sleeping", said the redhead who usually was the spokesman.

Uli lifted the flap of the tent and looked in. The boy Juan was fast asleep. He looked absurdly small and absurdly young. His hair had grown a little, and a few dark wisps fell across his forehead.

Uli dropped the flap. "All right, boys", he said. "I suppose I shouldn't have told you that he is the general's youngest nephew, but I did, because I think you're men and can keep a secret. His uncle seems to think that, too, so he's given me three ducats for each of you. Put them under your tongue—it'll keep you from talking too much. Here they are."

They pocketed the gold pieces with alacrity, grinning all over their faces.

"Any time you want us again for a special job . . ." said the redhead. "Though I'd rather carry a damned litter across the whole Pyrenees than ride in a *carreta* with you as the cabby."

"That'll do", said Uli. "You can rejoin your unit now. And don't forget: there have been seven of us on this little trip. Seven, no more. Good evening."

Six contented men strolled away.

Uli went to the back of the tent. There was the *carreta*. The horses, a black and a roan, were grazing quietly. They had been given water; a bucket still half filled stood near the *carreta*. The boys have earned their three ducats, he thought.

He went back to the tent. Juan was smiling in his sleep, poor little mite.

Not with a single word had she complained about the exertions of the last days, as many a real boy might have done. Time and again Uli had looked at her anxiously, while the *carreta* bumped over a bad stretch of road, only to receive a reassuring nod or a brave smile.

But something had to be done about her—about him. They could not go on like this. And Uli had to think of it quickly. But not now. He was too tired.

He laid the pike down in another corner of the tent, so that he could use the bundle attached to it as a pillow.

But then he hesitated.

He had never slept in the same room with Juan before. Somehow it did not seem right that he should. It was quite idiotic, of course. The boy Juan was the boy Juan, and that was all there was to it. But it did not seem right.

There was nothing he could do about it. He had his pockets full of gold; he could not possibly sleep outside, where they might club him over the head and rob him. He had to sleep here, and why shouldn't he?

The boy's breath came quietly, regularly. He slept with his little fists before his face, like a baby.

It was hot in the tent. Uli passed a weary arm across his forehead. He grunted something unintelligible. Then he drew out all the golden ducats in his pockets and pushed them cautiously under the bundle of straw the boy was lying on, took up his pike and bundle again, and walked out. Just outside the entrance of the tent he sat down, with his back against the flap, and closed his eyes. After a while he stretched himself a little and fell sideways. He was asleep before his head touched the ground.

A good deal has been said and written about the untroubled sleep of the just man, but nowhere has it been suggested that he should be awakened by a kick in the rear.

Uli jumped up. About him was darkness.

"General alarm", said the gruff voice of an officer. "Wake the men in that tent and join your unit. Be quiet about it."

Rubbing his eyes, Uli saw the officer walk on to the next tent, to repeat his order. It could not be midnight yet; he would have waked by himself at midnight, as always when he set a mental time limit to his sleep. The moon was still up, a coppery crescent.

A hubbub of voices from afar and the tramping of men. The camp was coming to life everywhere.

General alarm, eh? So the general had thought of something after all. An attack?

He looked about. The boats were still attached to their moorings. And that column over there was marching north. It was not an attack. It was a retreat.

Well, what did it matter what it was? He had his own orders to carry out. He yawned hugely, went to the back of the tent, took the half-filled bucket, emptied it, and ran with it to the river. Shedding his clothes was a matter of half a minute. Then he waded into the water. The current was not too strong so near the bank, but the water was icy. He came out with his teeth chattering, dressed again, filled the bucket, and returned at a run.

The camp was busy as a beehive now, and there was a great deal of noise, despite all the efforts of officers and sergeants to keep the men quiet.

"Hi, Juan, wake up."

The boy sat up, bewildered—and instinctively crossed his arms before his chest.

Uli laughed. The gesture was curiously incongruous. Juan had been sleeping in his clothes.

"Here's some water", he said. "Wash quickly and get ready to leave."

"L-l-leave? Where to?"

"Does it matter?" asked Uli. "Anyway, everybody is leaving. Can't you hear them? I'll get the horses ready. When I come back, you must be ready too. Get going."

He came back after little more than five minutes and found the boy staring at half a dozen golden ducats in his hand.

"Look what I found", he said.

Uli laughed. "You haven't looked closely enough. Wait."

He pushed the straw aside and began to collect the golden coins. "This is the land of the elfins and hobgoblins", he said. "Didn't you know that? Keep those you found. I'll keep these. That's all of them, I think." He seized the bucket. "Let's go."

"But it's still quite dark", said the boy as they left the tent.

"It's about midnight, yes. What's the matter with you? You've traveled by night with me before, haven't you?"

Horses and *carreta* were ready. The roan whinnied softly.

"There's water for you", said Uli, putting the bucket before them. "Up with you, my boy. We have a long way to go—I think. Stop pushing your brother, Blackie, there's enough in the bucket for both of you, and it's large enough. That will do now." He kicked the bucket aside, mounted, and took the reins.

"But the soldiers?" asked the boy.

"They're not coming with us this time."

"Only we two?" asked Juan with a slow smile. "Good."

"I don't know about that." Uli grunted. A pull at the reins, a clucking noise of his tongue, and the horses began to move.

Twice on their way out an officer tried to stop them. It was natural enough; they were driving in a southwesterly direction, and the army was moving north.

"Order of the general", said Uli, and they let him pass. They thundered across the camp and beyond till they reached the main road. Uli seemed to have owl's eyes. He chose with unerring certainty a fairly small road branching off the highway but still leading in a southwesterly direction.

"I'm sorry," he said, "but I cannot put you on the road to Barcelona yet. I'll do it at the earliest opportunity."

"There is no hurry", said Juan in a low voice. "I—I like traveling with you."

"You do, eh?"

"Yes. I feel safe with you."

Uli gave an angry little laugh. "I don't know about that. There may be a great deal of trouble ahead."

"Why?"

"Who taught you to ask so many questions? The less you know, the better for you."

"As you wish", said the boy submissively. "But I wish you'd take those ducats back. I don't know what to do with them, and I have done nothing to earn them."

"They are yours", said Uli curtly.

"Thank you very much", was the polite answer. "But can't you keep them for me, then?"

"You are a big boy", declared Uli. "You're expected to look after your own money. Remember that, if you please."

"Aunt Mercedes said she didn't think I would grow any more. I'm glad I'm big enough for you."

"Above everything, remember that you are a *boy*", snapped Uli. "Or I'll leave you at the first convent we pass, and if they don't open their gates, I'll throw you over the wall."

Juan hunched up his slender shoulders and said nothing. After a while he dared to ask, "But who am I?"

"You used to be the general's youngest nephew." Uli grinned. "But where we are going, you mustn't so much as breathe about that. Neither you nor I have anything to do with the general or the army, understand? I'm a Swiss, looking for a relative of mine, somewhere in Spain. And you— you are my younger brother. It's a comedown for you, but I can't help that."

"I'd much rather be your brother than any general's nephew", said Juan firmly.

"In that case," declared Uli, "you are crazy after all."

"Maybe I am", the boy said softly.

Uli said nothing. He gave the horses the whip, and they thundered along, deeper and deeper into Castile. After an hour or so they crossed a small river. The little wooden bridge under the horses' hooves sounded like the deep, grumbling laughter of a giant.

Far ahead a few lights became visible, the lights of a village.

Cadera, thought Uli. And there we shall know more about it all.

It was foolish, of course, to spend the rest of the night there, but he had to find out in what direction he must proceed. He halted the horses when they had reached the village, produced the letter, and tore off the first envelope. He began to whistle softly.

"Juan . . ."

"Yes?"

"What was the name of that lady our wounded Spanish friend seemed so fond of?"

"Queen Germaine."

"That's right. But you said she was no longer a queen."

"Because King Ferdinand died, and she married the margrave of Brandenburg, the governor of Valencia."

"And her maiden name was French, wasn't it?"

"Of course. She was Germaine de Foix. Why do you ask all that?"

"Never mind."

He began to tear the second envelope into tiny pieces. He looked extremely puzzled.

The boy Juan saw that the third and innermost envelope showed neither name nor address. Uli put it carefully back into his doublet. "This will be a long journey", he said thoughtfully.

"Are we going to Valencia, then?" asked the boy, with eager eyes.

"No. First we must get to Burgos, and then—never mind. I told you not to ask questions. Let's go."

He drove on, but more slowly. And Juan saw a strange expression on his face, the expression of a man who was trying hard to find the solution to a riddle knowing all the time that the answer was beyond him.

BOOK TWO

# CHAPTER FIFTEEN

DOCTOR DE IZTIOLA closed the door of the sickroom behind him. He smiled as he saw Magdalena de Araoz' anxious face.

"He is out of danger", he said.

She crossed herself. "Thanks be to God and his saints", she said. "Martín will be so pleased. I wish I could let him know."

"I must say I'm rather pleased myself." The physician chuckled. "There was a moment when my noble colleagues both thought that mortification had definitely set in, but I contradicted them quite sharply, as certain symptoms were missing."

"You have done wonders, my dear Doctor, wonders. . . ."

She was far too intelligent not to know that even a devout physician did not like to have the whole credit for a successful operation given to supernatural forces.

De Iztiola smacked his lips. "We did our best", he declared cheerfully. "No man can do more. But what a constitution, noble lady, what a constitution! Believe it or not, the wound is almost completely closed now. And if . . ."

He broke off. "You have a visitor, I believe, noble lady. I just saw a man on horseback passing the castle."

Magdalena de Araoz rushed to the window. Could it be that her husband . . .

"I can't see him."

"He was riding too quickly—a chestnut, I think. He must be at the gate now."

Martín's horse was a piebald. Her heart sank.

But from downstairs came the voice of her elder daughter:"Mother, Don Pedro de Zabala has arrived."

She blanched. Zabala was with her husband's troops. If something had happened to Martín . . .

She flew down the stairs, and de Iztiola followed her, puffing and murmuring soothing words she could not possibly hear.

De Zabala bowed to her, his strong white teeth gleaming in a joyful smile. She concluded at once that he could not have bad news. Erect and with dignity she returned his smile.

"You are very welcome, Don Pedro."

"Faith, there's good reason for that, Doña Magdalena." De Zabala laughed. "Greetings from your husband—and we have beaten the French in a decisive battle."

Her eyes sparkled. "The saints be praised! You are doubly welcome." She turned to the physician behind her. "Don Pedro brings us news of victory. Don't you think Don Iñigo should hear about that at once? It will do him good; it is bound to do him good."

"Excellent, excellent—your servant, Don Pedro—by all means. It is an indisputable fact that good news has a wholesome effect on a patient when he is at a certain stage of recovery."

They all ascended the stairs, but when de Iztiola arrived in the sickroom, de Zabala was already sitting beside the bed.

". . . so the duke decided to follow the French as quickly as possible. We had just joined him, and a day later reinforcements arrived from all sides, Valladolid, Toro, Burgos, and even Segovia."

"Did you cut him off the road to Pamplona?" asked Don Iñigo calmly. But his eyes were gleaming.

"That's exactly what the duke did. We forced him to give battle just about a league south of the town. And what a battle it was. . . ."

"One league south", said Don Iñigo. "That means the heights of Noain."

"That's right. And the Guipúzcoans had the vanguard. And the vanguard of the vanguard was the company of Azpeitia under Captain Juan López de Ugarte, 102 men, and every one a hero. The attack was made with such vigor that we pierced the French lines and captured the whole of their artillery, every gun they had, twenty-nine of them."

"My leg is avenged", said Don Iñigo with the ghost of a smile. "Go on, friend."

"We captured André de Foix himself," exulted de Zabala. "And he had to pay ten thousand ducats' ransom. De Beaumont accepted his sword."

"I think I see it", said Don Iñigo, closing his eyes. "You must have bypassed them at Esquiroz. How many of them escaped to Fuentarrabia?"

De Zabala bowed his admiration. "About half. But how did you know . . ."

"It was the only thing they could do, in the circumstances", said Don Iñigo with a slight shrug. "The first place where they can hope to reassemble. About half of them. The war may not be over yet."

"I think it is." De Zabala laughed. "You should have seen the rout. They fled in complete disorder. And while I am talking to you the duke is entering Pamplona in triumph."

"The citadel", said Don Iñigo, smiling again, "will be surrendered a second time, but this time by the French. The stain on our shield has been washed off." He took a deep breath. "This is better than all the medicines in the world, Don Pedro. It would call me back from my death-bed. . . ."

He closed his eyes again.

De Iztiola gave a warning sign to de Zabala, who obediently rose and tiptoed out of the room, followed by Magdalena and the physician himself.

But he was wrong in his assumption that the news had overexcited the patient.

Don Iñigo had closed his eyes because he wished to be left alone. And he wished to be left alone because he wanted to recapitulate the battle of Noain in his mind from the beginning to the end. Fuentarrabia—that was the sore spot in the entire matter. Fuentarrabia was at the very frontier between Guipúzcoa and France, and it was a fortress. The French could not hope to take it on their flight, but if they reassembled in that region, Fuentarrabia would be the first object of their counteroffensive.

The duke of Najera would now think of his triumph, of marching into Pamplona. He was a Castilian, not a Basque.

But Martín was likely to think of Fuentarrabia, and if he did, he would have to send troops across Guipúzcoa to the frontier. That meant that they would pass nearby. It meant also that Martín himself would pass here in a few days. As the leader of the vanguard in the battle of Noain, he would have to take part in the triumphal entry into Pamplona, but then he would come. In two days he would be here. Not sooner, but scarcely much later.

Good enough.

Two days later Martín García arrived, greeted by the clanging of the church bells, the barking of the hounds in their kennels, and the joyous shouts of the family.

Only the nearby convent of Saint Francis remained silent. There was a feud between the convent and the family of Loyola. It was a trifling thing, really, but Basque obstinacy prevailed on both sides, and the matter had gone to Rome for the decision of the Pope himself.

When he had looked after the needs of his piebald and greeted his wife and children, Martín mounted to the top floor and entered the sickroom.

For over an hour the two brothers discussed the battle and its consequences. Fuentarrabia was mentioned frequently.

"What about that leg of yours?" asked Martín then. "May I uncover it?"

"If you wish", said Iñigo calmly.

Martín frowned as he saw it. The wound was healed, and the bones had already begun to knit, but just over the knee-cap was now an ugly lump, caused by the overlapping of the reset bones.

"I am not satisfied with it", said Iñigo. It was as if he were speaking of the plan of a house or the cut of a coat just delivered by a bungling tailor.

"Leeches are leeches", said Martín. "But it's your own fault, brother. You should never have joined the citadel. You should have stayed with me and the Guipúzcoans. You could have acquired all the glory you wanted at Noain."

"That is easy enough to see—now", said Iñigo. "Then it was different. And I would do the same again."

Martín looked at him. "I believe you would, too."

The brothers looked a good deal alike: the same high-domed forehead, the same imperious nose. The shape of their eyes was similar, too, though Iñigo's lids were a little heavier. And while Martín's short, pointed beard was black with a few early touches of gray, Iñigo's, though of the same cut, only looked black when there was not much light in the room. It was of the deepest brown with a reddish tinge to it. Alike they were also in the restrained dignity of their movements.

"Well, never mind the leg", said Martín. "You have done very well as it is. Herrera is again in command of Pamplona, and he will write to the king, of course, if he has not done so already. There is no doubt that he will mention what you did."

"Perhaps he will", said Iñigo, with a thin smile.

"This opens vistas, of course", pondered Martín. "Especially as the duke thinks very highly of you, as you know. You may get a good lieutenancy somewhere. In Flanders, maybe, or in Italy. They may even want you to go to the Indies. What would you prefer?"

"I do not know", was the slow answer. "But it is pleasant to think about. I have started to think, but there is plenty of time for that. I must get rid of this first." And Iñigo pointed disdainfully to the lump on his kneecap.

"Get rid of it?" Martín stared at him. "How?"

"By having it opened again, of course."

"Brother! Are you mad?"

"It would be madness", said Iñigo phlegmatically, "to think of a career of the kind you mentioned with a deformity of this sort. I would have too many duels with those who felt inclined to laugh at my knee. And they could not help seeing it, especially when I ride. No, the lump must go. I have asked de Iztiola to bring his instruments."

Martín shook his head.

"You've only just come back from the very mouth of death. And this lump is made of bone. Do you realize what pain that means?"

"The operation will be painful, yes—" always in the same cool, even tone—"and there will be about six rather disagreeable weeks to follow. It is better than thirty years of humiliation."

"Well, I know I couldn't go through it", said Martín. He rose, as Magdalena came in with the physician.

She had great difficulty in hiding her anxiety. "Iñigo, I have just heard that you want another operation. I cannot believe my ears. That is tempting God!"

"Surely not." Iñigo looked at de Iztiola, who seemed somewhat ill at ease, as a man will be when he has promised to keep a secret and then has allowed himself to be questioned just a little too penetratingly by a lady accustomed to finding out what she wishes to find out.

"It is only a matter of correcting a mistake, Doña Magdalena."

"I will not permit this butchery in my house", declared the outraged lady.

Martín looked startled, but Iñigo said only, "In that case I shall have to be transported to the house of de Iztiola, Doña Magdalena, and that may be a better solution. I have given you so much trouble already. . . ."

"As if I meant that", she cried. "Oh, Don Iñigo, how can you say such a cruel thing! I just can't bear having you in danger and in such pain again . . ."

"You are most kind", said Iñigo courteously. "But it must be. I have explained it all to Martín, and he will tell you. Now if you will be kind enough to excuse us, I would like to talk to de Iztiola."

"Give it at least another week, Don Iñigo", pleaded Magdalena as her husband led her to the door. "Talk it over with him, de Iztiola, I beg of you."

"I will, noble lady, I will."

When the door had closed behind them, Iñigo asked, "You have your instruments?"

"In my bag, yes . . ."

"Then start cutting."

127

# CHAPTER SIXTEEN

THE DAYS OF CLENCHED FISTS followed again, of feverish nights and sudden intolerable bouts of pain, grating, biting pain as if in the jaws of a wolf.

He escaped from them by plunging into vistas much more grandiose than the more prosaic mind of Martín had been able to conjure up.

Herrera could not be trusted to give much credit to the action of a man inferior to him in rank—especially when that man had done what he himself should have done. But the name of Loyola opened every door, including that of the emperor's study, and an audience with Charles the Fifth could be of decisive consequence.

Flanders? Italy? The Indies? What mattered was that laurels could be won to be laid at the feet of a great queen.

She would always be a great queen, although she had condescended to marry a simple margrave after her first husband's death. Nothing could take away an iota of her inimitable dignity; she was royal, royal of her innermost nature as well as in her appearance. Who could stand in her presence without feeling it?

He would have to go to Valencia first, to tell her what he was going to do in her honor.

The thoughts, the words had to be found by which he would address her when he was ushered into her presence.

And no one would titter behind a hand because of the knight's deformity. There was no more deformity. What was all the pain in the world before that thought?

He could stand before her without shame, a knight she could be proud of, even she, of the purest blood of France, the niece of Louis XII, who had shared the throne of Spain with the widower of Isabella of Castile.

Martín would never understand such thoughts. He was happily married to a good wife, and when he was not soldiering he rode with his hounds or busied himself with controlling the household, even down to writing the most accurate and painstaking inventories of all his possessions.

It was strange how different brothers could be.

Martín never wrote poetry, had not written a single line of poetry in his life. He scarcely even bothered to read a book. He had glanced through *Amadis of Gaul* and could not see the realm of splendor that it opened. And yet Amadis was the most shining example of knighthood ever described by the pen of man; his love for Oriana was the very symbol of knightly love. One never tired reading of his adventures; one could spin them out, add to them in one's mind, till they encompassed everything ever achieved by that most masculine of all phenomena—the spirit of a true knight.

There could be no higher task for a man than to serve Beauty. There could be no higher aim for a knight than to have as his lady the last great queen of Spain.

Pain—what was pain to a man with such plans and ideas? He had fainted when de Iztiola's saw grated on the bone. A man had no control over that, but he had not screamed, not once. And he had not spoken for twenty-four hours, because he wanted to be quite certain that his voice would be steady when he spoke.

Amadis of Gaul . . . It would be good to read them again, those glorious adventures.

Like calling upon the help of a brother in imagination, a fellow poet, in the hour of need.

It would take his mind away from the Machine.

The Machine was an ingenious device of which Doctor de Iztiola was extremely proud. They were using the likes of it in Toledo, he said, but he had bettered their crude ways.

The tendons of the wounded leg had shrunk. The leg had to be stretched back to its original length, or he would limp heavily for the rest of his life. That was what the Machine was supposed to do for him. It was a complex and formidable apparatus which immobilized him, stretched the leg, and pulled it, all at the same time. An Inquisitor might have welcomed the Machine, as its very aspect was enough to frighten a prisoner into confession.

Hemmed in, stretched and pulled, navigating in a sea of pain, he called for *Amadis of Gaul*.

"But it's all lies", exclaimed practical Martín. "Or most of it. There probably never was such a man. Anyway, I haven't got that book."

"Then what about *Sergas de Esplandian*?"

Martín did not have that either. "I shall talk to Magdalena", he promised. "I—I think she has a volume or two about something. I'm not much of a reader myself."

Courtesy forbade even a smile at this understatement.

In the afternoon Magdalena came with two heavy, richly bound tomes. She was most embarrassed.

"These are all we have in the house," she said, "but you may like at least to look at them for a while. They are not knightly tales, though."

She saw him look with amused respect at the title of the uppermost volume, *The Life of Christ*, and then at that of the other, *The Flower of the Saints*. He nodded graciously.

"As I cannot hear Mass on Sundays yet, Doña Magdalena, this will serve very well as a substitute."

She could never be sure whether or not there was an undertone of subtle irony, natural enough when a man is given books usually read only by women, or read to them.

When she had gone, he fingered the first volume carelessly. It was really a beautiful thing, the first book to be printed by the printing press of Alcalá, a wonderful new invention—there might be a book or two in many thousands of castles soon. Then he saw the name of the man who had translated it from the Latin of the author, Ludolph the Carthusian, into Spanish: Fray Ambrosio Montesino.

Montesino. That was a link with the past. As a page of Queen Germaine he had read some of Montesino's poems to her, and her musical ear had become reconciled to the harsher sounds of Spanish words through these winged stanzas.

Smiling, he opened the heavy tome. There was a picture, beautifully drawn, of the translator on his knees, offering his book to King Ferdinand and Queen Isabella, seated on their thrones. Beneath it a large shield of a united Spain was shown. And here was the preface, in fine Gothic lettering in black and red as in a missal.

It was a glowing panegyric to their majesties, praising their piety, their zeal for justice, the peace and order they had brought to Spain, the great triumphs on land and sea, the great discoveries beyond the Atlantic. Spain's golden age . . .

Montesino was eloquent, admiring the courage and the constancy of the royal couple, "in having wrested the kingdom of Granada from the Saracens, who were wont to die rather than surrender, thirsted for Christian blood, and defended their wicked, foolish, profane and most abominable sect, and all their cities, towns, and castles, which were so powerful and impregnable, that it was beyond belief they could ever be taken".

Then more praise "for having resisted time and again the fierce and bloody hand of the Turks and infidels who waged cruel war by land and sea with mighty armadas and numerous armies", and "for the excellence and virtue of their persons, as well as fortunate and blessed by glorious victories, and by discoveries of various lands and islands in distant seas, in the Indies as well as among other barbarous peoples . . ."

It was true enough. Such was the golden age of Spain, and such was the spirit of its rulers. And there was no need to regard it a matter of the past. Not if he could help it.

"You provided all the churches of your kingdom with proper and very excellent prelates for their administration," wrote Montesino, "having more concern for their spirituality, virtue, and learning than for the nobility and influence of their lineage. For you regarded conformity to the will of the Most High and to canon law more important than the affection of ambitious and importunate men. You considered that the prelates should serve the churches, and not the churches the prelates. . . ."

The reader nodded. That had been one of the most difficult feats of all and must have created legions of ambitious enemies. What a satisfaction to go ahead nevertheless, not to give an inch . . .

It was a great thing to be a king, if one remained a knight, after kingship was attained.

"You also have reformed most of the religious orders in Spain, which had lost most of their founders' primitive spirit."

The golden age. Iñigo remembered an old priest in Arévalo who used to say that in the eyes of God a country was as good as its monasteries and convents.

It was logical. Just as a country was as powerful as its army in the eyes of an enemy.

Men had their several functions. But a king's business was to see that all of them achieved the highest standard.

"Your Majesties have advanced and reformed learning in the schools and universities of these kingdoms, so that their students might be no less proficient in divine and human studies than these same kingdoms are fertile and abound in temporal blessings. You have constructed throughout Spain, and even at Rome and in the holy city of Jerusalem, temples of religious and magnificent splendor for the service of God, endowing them with wondrous riches and ornaments of gold, silver, and precious stones. You have erected castles and fortresses for the greater ennoblement and defense of your lands and domains."

To understand such thoughts and to share them meant that a man possessed that spark from which the flame of kingship was kindled. Such a man could well raise his eyes to the highest in the land, and indeed nothing less than the highest would satisfy him.

Ferdinand and Isabella had gone, and Queen Germaine was no longer ruling in Madrid. And since then there had been nothing but disturbance and unhealthy tension in Spain, under a young king who had no time for his own country, who was not even a Spaniard, strictly speaking, but an Austrian, and cared more for the empty dignity of emperor than for close relations with his subjects.

His tutor, Adrian of Utrecht, was supposed to be one of the wisest and most learned men of the time. But he was Adrian of Utrecht, not of Alcalá, Salamanca, or Toledo.

Iñigo weighed the book in his hands. Much could be done in Spain and for Spain, as much as and more than Amadis had done for the kingdom of Lisuarte, for his queen Oriana.

He could not help smiling when he opened the second book.

*The Flower of the Saints* also had a prologue, and that too was written by a man he knew, having met him at King Ferdinand's court six years ago: Fray Gauberto María Vagad, the Cistercian.

Queen Germaine had listened to his sermons at the palace chapel, and Iñigo had sat behind her, fingering his rosary and staring at his lovely lady's graceful neck rising from the lace of her dress of black and gold.

Montesino and Vagad—both of them links with the past, links with her . . .

A golden thread, infinitely fine, finer even than the lace on the dress of a queen.

He decided to read both books.

CHAPTER SEVENTEEN

"ONCE WHEN HE CAME to Rome on pilgrimage he exchanged garments with a poor man and stood before the Church of Saint Peter among the poor and begged and ate quite willingly as they did."

That was horrible. There was nothing more horrible in the world than filth, dirt, vermin, the stench of unwashed limbs, the disgrace of the man whose whole body showed his wretched helplessness—feed me, for I cannot feed myself, feed me with the crumbs from your table, with the foul remnants of what was once a meal, with that which you despised to eat, noble sir, noble lady, the bitten-off crusts, the gristle, the bones on which there is perhaps a little meat left, greasy and dirty . . . You might as well eat the very vermin in your tattered clothes.

Go away, Francis, go . . .

"And he did this often without permitting shame in the presence of his acquaintances, or the devil who kept after him, to draw him away from the good road he had begun to follow. . . ."

Was that courage of a sort, or was it madness?

What did it matter what it was? It was alien, brutish; it was unworthy of a knight even to dwell on it. There was no shine to this sorry courage, no noble rush against the enemy—it was pitiful.

The Indies. Penetrate the jungle among a thousand dangers, crocodiles and snakes, the poisoned arrows of the savage tribes. Vanquish them all and with the heathen gold build a cathedral for the King of kings, come home in triumph, lay its jeweled keys at Queen Germaine's feet.

A man must risk his life for his ideal, not sink into abject humiliation.

"And then there came a man with a claw hand, a leper, and though naturally he felt some repugnance, yet remembering what that voice had said to him: 'Francis, take the bitter as sweet and despise yourself if you desire to know Me', he ran after that man and began to kiss him."

Monstrous. But—monstrous courage. The little beggar hit back at him here, for what he had just thought.

Could *he* do it? He, Iñigo de Loyola y Licona?

This was a challenge. He had been challenged before, in Madrid, in Arévalo—yes, the situation at Pamplona had been like a challenge accepted. But kiss a leper?

The blood went to his forehead. A dancing, smiling, impudent little friar looked at him from printed pages and challenged him as he had never been challenged before. No use feeling for his sword, shouting for his horse and armor. What this little man fought were ulcers, stinking sores . . . leprosy.

That must be the bitterest of all battles. The only way to win was for Iñigo to fight Don Iñigo de Loyola and to vanquish him, as Francis had vanquished Francis.

The only way to cross swords with a saint was to take up the cross.

He buried God's smiling little beggar with fifty pages of the heavy tome and found himself in the life of Saint Onuphrius, the Savage Saint, a man of princely origin who had decided to live in the solitude of the Thebaid desert "eating nothing but herbs" and fighting "the enemy of human nature". The devil. Satan.

Now this was fighting. Not against armored men, not against the king's enemies arrayed on the battlefield in beautiful strategic order, not against the monsters and dragons of knightly tales, but against the archetypal monster itself, the embodiment of the seven capital sins, the enemy of the King of kings himself, trying to destroy creation.

But he was subtle, the demon. Often enough he adopted the nature and manner of a woman. The nature—for like her he was weak and received strength only through the weakness of his opponent. And the manner, too—for like a woman he lost courage quickly when resisted, but no beast on earth could match him when he waxed strong as soon as he found that his opponent feared him.

To set up the standard of God against the standard of Satan, like the captain general of the heavenly forces, like Saint Michael himself . . .

But a man had to be trained for such warfare. It could not be waged from a smooth bed, with loving relatives looking after the least of his needs.

He must be trained, and he must be armed with new arms—such a man.

136

Now here was Saint Dominic. "And each night he disci-
plined himself with an iron chain: the first time for himself,
the second for the sinners in the world, and the third time
for the souls in purgatory."

Iñigo had been at Caleruega, where the saint was born; it
was very near Arévalo. He had visited his churches of San Pablo
and San Gregorio in Valladolid with the whole court three years
ago, when young King Charles took the oath at the Cortes.

The knights of God.

But he was not trained for that kind of fighting.

Rise in rank. Be made a count, a grandee of Spain, the coun-
cillor of the king. Win the king's battles as the Jefe of his armies. Present Queen Germaine with the spoils of victory. . . .

Her husband was a margrave. A grandee of Spain was the
equal of anyone but the king. If he achieved such rank (and
though it was not easy, there were those who had attained
it), he could meet the margrave in any field, including that
of single combat.

And then . . .

## CHAPTER EIGHTEEN

MARTÍN CAME with astonishing news. Despite his glorious
victory at Noain, the duke of Najera had been relieved of
his rank as viceroy of Navarre.

"They've chosen the count of Miranda in his stead. And
they are sure that the king will confirm it."

Iñigo frowned. He had seen before what happened to a
man when he fell from power—and the higher the position,

the deeper and harder the fall. There was Velásquez, the treasurer of Castile, to whose family he himself had been attached so many years; there were others.

Martín, meanwhile, was pacing up and down in the sickroom, bellowing with fury against those who had brought about the duke's downfall.

"You can be sure they've told all manners of lies about him, Iñigo. Nothing will surprise me. Now, if Queen Isabella were still alive, I'd saddle my horse this very hour and ride straight to court. But there's young Charles instead, and he in some godforsaken place in Germany having it out with the *luteranos*. The plague on them; can't they let a king govern his kingdom? And that's not all . . . you were right about Fuentarrabia, Iñigo. Something's brewing in the neighborhood. They say there are new troop concentrations near the frontier. Not under de Foix. Under Admiral Bonivet. But you are not listening . . ."

"Forgive me", said Iñigo. "It is indeed grave news."

"You look much better", said Martín. "But why do they bother you with those heavy books? Reading pious stories to you or something? Let me get rid of this stuff."

"No, no", said Iñigo hastily. "I—I glance through them myself from time to time."

Martín snorted.

"De Iztiola is most satisfied, you will be glad to hear", he said. "He even says you may be on horseback again in a month or two, if all goes well. Just in time, too, I should think. I very much fear we shall have to call up the militia again. Told Vergara that, and Juan de Eguibar and Ugarte. When the French strike, they strike quickly, as we know. Well, if they do, we shall use their own damned artillery against them. I'm off now. Must talk it over with Ortiz de Gamboa and the lord of Lizaur. If there is anything you wish to convey to them . . . ?"

"Nothing," said Iñigo after a while, "except my respects and best wishes."

When Martín had gone, he sank back into a reverie.

He was sorry about the duke of Najera, naturally. He was interested in Martín's news, again most naturally. But . . .

"But what?" he asked himself sharply. Surely it ought to matter to him very much that his old protector and friend was no longer viceroy. It ought to excite him, spur him into action, at least of the mind, if not of the wretched body, that the French were obviously out to avenge Noain and regain Navarre.

But it did not. And it was not because he was weak. He was no longer weak.

This was the second strange fact he had come across in the last twenty-four hours.

The first fact was really much older than twenty-four hours, but at first—and for quite some time—he had not realized it, and even now he was not sure of its full implications. Which was intolerable.

It was something that was going on in him, that had been going on in him for weeks. He was thinking about two different things, and each of them caused a whole chain of thoughts, and they were alternating in his mind.

The first thought chain was the planning of his future career, his rise to power, his rise to honors and to a position in which he could look boldly at his great lady's lovely face. All this I have done, and I have done it for you. It was a chain of glittering, sparkling thoughts; it was all a knight could desire, and he had tasted it again and again. And the more often he tasted it, the less it became. Its sparkle had gone dull, its glitter cheap. It was as if he had gained for himself, for a deed of incredible valor, the Order of the Golden Fleece, and he had walked on clouds. But a second deed of equal valor earned him the matchless Order for a second time. Then a third, and fourth and tenth—and it all looked strangely absurd, as if the court fool had looted the king's box in which the orders were kept and hung them all around his own neck. He could still think of it with pleasure—but only as far as the deeds themselves went. And even they left a feeling of dissatisfaction, of hunger not appeased, of hopes remaining unfulfilled in their very fulfillment.

The second thought chain saw him on the road to the Holy Land. The knight not of a queen, but of God. There was no glitter here, and no sparkle.

Going barefoot to Jerusalem, eating nothing but herbs, mortifying the flesh in a hundred ways to subjugate it and firmly establish an iron rule over that which Friar Francis used to call "Brother Ass". Climbing the narrow footpath to God's own fortress in the skies, as Dominic did and Onuphrius, careless of jeers and jibes, jeering and jibing himself at the temptation of Satan.

And here no bitter afterthought remained, no disappointment, no weary discontent.

All the glitter of the first thought chain became habitual— and ended in boredom.

But this new path could bore one as little as could God himself.

Why was this so?

Now that he knew it as a fact, he had to have an answer.

With the sharpness of a knife he dissected it.

If something desirable left a stale taste in the mouth, could it come from a good source?

Was it possible that Satan was the author of his ambition, of his dreams of greatness for the sake of an earthly queen who was someone else's wife? And if so, was the purpose of such dreams to drown that other voice, urging him to imitate the saints?

He sat up in his bed. He could do so without difficulty. "Yes", he said coldly.

In the next moment he realized that this affirmation by itself solved also the second riddle—his lack of interest in what had happened in the affairs of the duke of Najera, and even in what was brewing at the frontiers of Spain.

Francis, Dominic, Onuphrius: none of them had cared for worldly affairs.

The battleground of the knights of God was the soul.

The soul that had to be wrested away from the enemy and won for God, his own first, those of others later.

But who was he, to think of such things?

What qualifications, what credentials had he for joining the company of the saints?

None. Absolutely none. Whoever heard of a saint who had spent his time in gaming, dueling, and the courtship of women? It was absurd.

Or—was it?

Again his mind cut deep into the confusion of his thoughts. What was the true situation on the battlefield?

He smiled grimly. The very fact that he was thinking about the issue showed that the battle had already begun.

Intelligence reported that the enemy occupied a great part of the field.

The enemy's move was an attack on the grounds that any serious resistance was futile because he occupied most of the field.

But if it were not for that fact, there would be no battle! General Saint Augustine and even General Saint Francis had to deal with a similar situation when they first gave battle to the enemy.

This indeed was the meaning of this kind of battle; no, it was the battle itself. By asking for his qualifications and credentials the enemy suggested—capitulation.

It was a treacherous attack. For it tried to make use of the very virtue of humility. "You are not worthy of such an aim. Give it up." But a Christian said, "Lord, I am not worthy", and then went on to receive the Lord all the same!

And the man who had first said, "Lord, I am not worthy", was—a soldier, a Roman officer.

The battle is on, he thought, with an entirely new kind of eager satisfaction. No, it had always been on, but so far he had been a very bad general. He had neglected his army and its equipment. He had let the enemy filter in where he could have been repulsed.

Now at long last he had recognized the state of affairs—no, he had begun to recognize it. There would have to be the most thorough inspection of both men and material; there would have to be changes, new equipment, methodical training. And every single one of such measures was in this strange new kind of fighting a sort of battle by itself.

There was no glow in him, no jubilation over such a flood of cognition. He did not rejoice. He knew now that the urge of the saints for penance was a sort of military necessity.

There was no virtue in kissing a leper, as long as he himself was a leper.

He began to examine and test all thoughts welling up in him for their true origin. There must be a way to find out where they came from, whether from God or whether from Satan. There was.

When Magdalena de Araoz entered the room the next time, he asked her for paper and ink. He had found the formula, and he did not want it to slip from his mind. He wrote, "In those who proceed from good to better the good spirit

142

touches such a soul gently and softly as when water drops upon a sponge, and the evil spirit strikes it sharply and noisily, causing disquiet as when water drops upon a stone."

He liked what he wrote. He decided to go on making notes. Also there were passages, both in *The Life of Christ* and in *The Flower of the Saints*, that he wished to have with him in writing, without having to carry the two heavy books around. He would get a notebook and copy them out.

A great deal of such simple work would have to be done.

He was not only the general, commanding the army. He was also the humblest foot soldier.

The whole thing was a huge task, far bigger than the defense of the citadel of Pamplona or of Fuentarrabia. It was a full-scale war, and he had to do everything by himself.

## CHAPTER NINETEEN

HE COULD NOT SLEEP that night. It was August now, and the day had been very hot, but it was not that. De Iztiola had let him get out of bed for the first time, and he had walked, actually walked up and down in the room, limping a little but not very much. De Iztiola thought that he would need only a couple of weeks more, and a tight bandage on leg and foot, to be replaced later by a special sole in the shoe which would make his limp almost imperceptible. This, of course, was good news. A very short while ago it would have made the difference between life and death.

It still made some difference. There was something undignified about a limp, something that evoked ridicule. But

Francis might have said it was better to limp toward heaven than to gallop toward hell.

The lump on the kneecap was gone. But it could well be that in the future no one would ever see his knee, except he himself.

Anyway, he could walk. Shakily, using the bedpost, the edge of a cupboard, the back of a chair to support himself. He had been up only a few minutes, and even they had seemed too long. It was a relief to go back to bed.

And now he could not sleep. It was not the heat, and it was not the excitement of his first outing, though the heat was oppressive.

Perhaps there would be a thunderstorm soon.

Perhaps the man who invented the cannon had been led to his invention by the flash of lightning and the crack of thunder? Some way of imitating one of the creative aspects of God.

He could not see whether clouds were gathering; it was too dark, and there was no moon. Perhaps he could see, if he went to the window, but he could not face leaving the bed again, not before tomorrow.

He had prayed as usual.

He had always done that. A hidalgo could not afford an act of discourtesy toward a lady or toward God.

The *Pater*, the act of fealty to the supreme Sovereign, the acknowledgment of vassalship, of dependency.

The *Ave* to the Queen of Heaven, the supreme human being, the link with God, blessed among women.

If it were not for her, chivalry would have no meaning; it would never have come into existence. The Moors and all Moslems despised woman, made her a plaything and a chattel, and a plaything and a chattel woman was everywhere where Mary was not. It was her spell that ennobled every woman and made man doff his cap and bow his head before her.

Why, if it were not for Mary, even Queen Germaine ...

Frowning, he began to analyze again. What—or who— was it that made him fix his love, his devotion on the lady who some years ago had been the queen of Spain?

More than once, ah, a hundred times he had told himself that it was madness to choose as his lady one whose social position was far too high for a simple knight; only occasion- ally he had talked himself into believing that through some great deed he might be able to achieve a rank that narrowed the abyss between them.

Now suddenly he knew that the madness had been the only good thing about it—that madness to aspire for things too high. But he had not aimed high enough, still not high enough.

No one could be his lady but she who was full of Grace, she of the Shrine of Olaz, of Aránzazu, of Montserrat, she through whom he was related to God himself.

And without her all his planning, all his tactics and strat- egy were in vain.

He had to do everything by himself. But nothing that he did by himself could be done without her help.

He did not think this, not consciously. He simply knew it as if he had been told so by infallible authority.

No word was spoken to him, but the knowledge was a flower rooting in his heart and branching out into his mind in one instant.

For this was the Shrine of the Blessed Virgin, and she was holding the Child Jesus.

And the words of Fray Ludolph the Carthusian, passed on to him by Fray Ambrosio Montesino, rang in his heart, loud and clear as the treble of bells: "Virgin of Virgins, glorious Mary ... Thou who first of all women made a vow to observe virginity and offered so glorious a gift, though untaught by word or example of any mortal to do this new thing. And thou who wast pleasing to God, adorned with this virtue and all others, and hast left all an example to live, I beg of thy immense bounty, direct thou all my life and obtain for me from thy Son the grace to imitate all thy virtues and example as far as in me lies, and, Lady, grant me that thy grace may ever be present. Amen."

She did not smile, but he received the fullness of her glance. The distance between them was as wide as the heavens and yet as near as God.

And the Child who was God did not smile, but he gave the fullness of his glance to his Mother.

When heaven passed away and earth returned, Iñigo lay very still, very calm, his hands folded over his chest, as is the custom with one who has died and has been cared for by those who loved him.

And he knew that indeed he had died to his past and all images of the past had been obliterated from his soul.

Quietly, without effort, he slipped out of bed and stood and walked to the door.

A vow was required of him, and there was no moment to lose.

Martín awoke with a start.

The candlestick on the table beside his bed was dancing a mad dance.

When he stretched out his hand to put it down firmly he felt his bed move, and not only his bed but all the furniture in the room was moving.

From Magdalena's room came a stifled cry.

He jumped up, but the floor shook under him, and he almost lost his balance.

He staggered into her room. She, too, was out of bed, and she stared at him, her mouth half open. He could see the white all around her eyes. He took her into his arms.

"It's an earthquake."

But it was all over.

They listened. All they could hear was the beating of their hearts.

Then there was some movement and noise in the servants' rooms, downstairs.

"It's all right", said Martín gruffly. "Nothing to worry about. Just a *temblor*. I better go and see whether there is any damage."

"Don't—don't leave me alone."

He shook his head. "You have been through a *temblor* before, haven't you? I must have a look. You can come with me, if you want to. I'm just going to put a cloak round my shoulders."

"I'll be ready in a moment, too."

They went down the stairs to the first floor, where the servants were sitting, huddled together and wailing softly. Martín told them to go back to their beds.

"It's all over. And it wasn't a very bad one either."

But they went on sitting where they were, and he could hear their teeth chattering with fright.

Shrugging, he left them and joined his wife in the narrow corridor. "I suppose I'd better have a look at the stables."

"What about Iñigo?"

"My dear, he is bound to be all right; nothing has happened. I don't think so much as a window is broken. All right, let's have a look."

When they had climbed up to the second floor again, Martín saw that the door to the little chapel was slightly ajar.

He walked up to close it, but Magdalena heard him gasp in astonishment and saw him stand strangely rigid and taut, as if pressed back by some invisible force.

She was a strong, energetic woman of a courage far above average, but often the strong rather than the weak and sensitive resent it to their very core when the solid earth ceases to be solid. She had been frightened of the *temblor*, and she felt fear gripping her again now. What was wrong in the chapel?

Despite her fear, her legs carried her toward Martín, and shielded by his body she looked over his shoulder like a terrified child.

Iñigo was kneeling before the picture of the Blessed Virgin. It was the panel of the Annunciation—Queen Isabella had given it to Magdalena when she was a lady of honor at court.

"How did he get down the stairs?" whispered Martín. "And he is kneeling ... his knee ..."

She could not answer.


CHAPTER TWENTY


"ÁVILA", said Uli, pulling at the reins. "My, what walls and turrets. Well, it's not so long ago that they had to defend it against the Moors."

"It is beautiful", said the boy Juan. "I like it much better than Segovia."

"Bah, everything is the same in this country. At least everything has the same colors. Gray, brown, olive-green; everything is gray, brown, and olive-green. Sad colors. You ought to come to Switzerland one day, Juan."

"You forget the sky", said the boy, smiling. "And the cathedral is shining silver."

"They certainly have cathedrals here", admitted Uli. "If only the people . . . never mind. I know what's wrong with the colors of this country. There's no red. And it's the red that makes a landscape live. You should see the red glow on my mountains every morning, every evening. . . ."

"Brown is black and red mixed", insisted Juan. "Father used to say, 'There is red blood in every crumb of the good earth, and it is God's own blood. If it weren't nothing could ever grow. We live of him.'"

"He must have been a remarkable man, your father."

"Oh, he was, he was. He was a poet. . . ."

"Yes, I know. He was a remarkable man all the same. Well, we've done it, Juan, my boy. This is the end of our journey. Burgos—Segovia—Ávila. We've seen something of Spain."

Juan looked at him with a twinkle in his eyes.

"Are we going to find the Lady Germaine here then?"

He looked past her. "I never said we were going to meet any particular person", he said severely.

"No, you didn't, but I can guess. I was never so surprised in all my life than when you asked me about her at Cadera. Don Iñigo's great lady! He didn't talk much, but when he did it was about her all the time."

"Boys", said Uli, "are not as a rule so interested in such things."

"Oh, but they are. I know you're not, but I have heard boys talk."

"Have you?" It sounded very indifferent and casual.

"Yes, I have. I heard them talk in Barcelona, in Doña de Méndez' house. She had a little girl my own age and two older daughters—one was eighteen and the other twenty—and boys would come to their windows and talk to them. Dolores and I laughed and laughed; it was so funny how they rolled their eyes and made pretty speeches. And they gossiped about other boys' girls and other girls' boys all the time, and the duenna did not mind because she liked gossip too."

"That was in Barcelona, eh?"

"Yes, and in Pamplona too."

"You were the only girl in your poor aunt's household, I believe." His tone was just as casual as before. "I suppose the boys came to your window there and rolled their eyes and made pretty speeches. . . ."

"Two did", she said. "But Aunt Mercedes chased them away before they even had time to roll their eyes. I was very angry at the time, but she told me that a girl is thought of as marriageable from the time when the boys come to her window, and if I allowed them to come when I wasn't yet the right age, people would talk about me as of an old, old girl in a few years, and then no one would come to my window at all, except the really wicked ones whom a girl should not even look at."

"Your Aunt Mercedes was a very intelligent woman", said Uli. He knew with what severity and caution young girls were brought up in Spain. That serenading at the window was about the only liberty allowed them, and even then some lynx-eyed duenna sat within earshot.

Time and again he had marveled at the natural way she had accepted this journey—a thing of enormity, a fantastic, incredible outrage according to Spanish customs. But she was still a child, and he was her father or a very old brother.

Well, obviously.

She was his little brother on this journey; he had told dozens of people so.

He had told himself so, whenever there was the need for it. Thoughts and feelings could run curiously astray at times and had to be reined in like horses.

A younger brother was a younger brother.

One didn't think of him more often than necessary, even if he was a touching little figure when he prayed in the enormous Cathedral of Burgos, a tiny frail creature, all wrapped up in God and the Blessed Virgin, and looking very much like a girl, with his sensitive face and his long lashes.

He looked very much like a girl, too, when he fell asleep in the *carreta*, with his head on the bundle, helpless, and graceful as a fawn.

And that was no good at all.

In the cathedral it didn't matter; a man has other things to think of there, and if he's disturbed he can always go back to them.

But in the *carreta* it was different.

A man had to resort to all kinds of tricks to keep his eyes off a sight that could make him forget the little brother stuff.

Hum the old songs to himself, the holy ones and the peppered ones, the ones the Bavarian devils sang when their duke sent them out to loot someone else's villages, those French rhymes that could make a blacksmith blush or the one they sang when they marched against the Turk.

Or a man could talk to the horses, silly brutes, dragging the *carreta* along because somebody made clucking noises, turning left, right, at the pull of the rein. You don't know where you're going, but you are going there anyway. That's because you're poor silly brutes. A man always knows where he's going and why, doesn't he? And that makes the difference between a man and a brute. Or does it?

Anyway, when a man feels he's got a brute in himself, let him talk to the brutes, and he'll be in better company than they are.

The inns at night. "I want a room for myself and one for my brother here. You only have one? No, he never sleeps in the room with me. Because he can't sleep then at all. Neither could you. I snore like seven devils with their noses stuffy with pitch and sulphur."

He chuckled grimly.

A brother was a brother, and that was all there was to it.

And now the young brother said, "It's a lovely view, but I think I am getting hungry."

Uli nodded. "Right. Feeling a bit hungry myself. The horses had a breather. In half an hour we'll be in Ávila."

The *carreta* had a couple of new wheels, the horses had new irons, and Juan had a new suit, bought in Segovia for half a ducat. The tailor, confound him, wanted to take his measure. He had small, experienced hands.

"I'll have no fancy stuff for my brother. Just show me something that's ready. We're in a hurry."

The only suit ready was one for a young boy in the neighborhood, and he was to come for it that afternoon.

It took a bit of arguing, but the tailor finally gave in.

Segovia. That's where they heard about the battle of Noain.

The town was full of it, everybody shouting and yelling in the streets, and the innkeepers having a glorious time. There were toasts to the king, to the duke of Najera, to the victorious soldiers from Segovia, who had done the main work in the battle.

He had shouted with them and drunk with them.

Later, alone on his bed, he did some serious thinking. Even allowing for the usual amount of boasting and exaggeration, it looked like a serious defeat. They said that the

French commander had been captured. That could be any-body: Elgobarraque, or the good bishop of Couserans, or André de Foix himself.

But even if it was de Foix, such a gentleman could always buy himself off. It would make a mighty big hole in his pocket, but he had ways and means of filling it again. There were always towns and villages he could bleed just a little more.

Of course, if the battle had been as decisive as the good Segovians thought, the war was over, at least for the time being.

But was it?

Too early to judge. But rather no than yes, at least as long as the king was not back in Spain. When the cat is away, the mice go dancing.

The mice had been frightened off the cheese, but a good mouse comes back soon enough. And France was strong.

He had been right, though, about the smell in the air, that night when he left the army. Dank, musty stink of defeat.

And his question to the fat little secretary: "Where shall I find the army, when I come back?"

Somewhere in Spain, the little man had said.

Bah, it was not much of a triumph to have a finer feeling for a thing like that than a pen pusher.

And there was only one thing to do: to go on, as if noth-ing had happened.

To Ávila.

And there they were now. The turrets and walls were grow-ing. In half an hour he would knock at a certain gate and ask for a certain lady and get rid of a letter that by now might well be meaningless—or dangerous. It could not be helped. It had to be risked. But not with the boy. He had to work that out.

"Look", said the boy Juan suddenly.

"What?"

"These children . . ."

A boy and a girl. Nicely dressed. He was about ten, the girl no more than six, but it was she who was walking in front, her determined little chin in the air.

"What about them, Juan?"

"What are they doing here, so far away from the town? We haven't passed a village for over an hour. Where are they going?"

He grinned. "You're right. I'll ask them. Hey!"

They had heard him, but pretended not to. The boy seemed to hesitate, but the little girl took him by the hand and marched on.

Uli stopped the horses and jumped down.

In a few long strides he caught up with the children, who looked at him, the boy sullenly, the girl with open defiance.

"Good evening, Señor and Señorita", said Uli politely. "May I ask where you are going?"

The little girl shook her head. "It is a secret."

Juan, who had joined them, sat down on his haunches.

"You can tell us", he said. "We're very good at keeping secrets. We have a lot of them, too. What's your name?"

"Teresa", said the little girl and curtsied. "Teresa de Cepeda. And this is my brother Rodrigo. I have many more brothers, but they don't know. Only Rodrigo knows."

"I'm Juan", said Juan. "And this is my brother Ulrico. He is my only brother. Now do tell us where you are going."

Teresa gazed at him for a while. "You won't tell anybody, will you?" she asked gravely.

"Of course not", said Juan.

"We're going to the Holy Land", declared the little girl solemnly. "We are martyrs."

"Oh", said Juan, and he bit his lip.

His brother Ulrico turned away a little, and his back heaved strangely.

"Your brother's crying", said Teresa. "Rodrigo cries too, sometimes. All my brothers do. I don't cry."

"I'm sure you don't", said Juan. "But Ulrico is only coughing. He has a bad cough. You will have a bad cough too, if you go on. It will be night soon and very cold. You wouldn't like that, would you? Cold and dark."

Teresa thought about it.

"Perhaps it won't be so cold", she said then. "And we must get to the Holy Land. We are martyrs."

"Yes, I know", said Juan. "But you are awfully young for martyrs, you know. It'd be much better if you grew a little more first. Then you could be really big martyrs."

"That's what I told her", said little Rodrigo suddenly. "But she says we can't wait."

"Can't you?" asked Juan, his eyes on Teresa. "Why not?"

"Because when I grow up I'll be wicked", said little Teresa. "I know I will. And then I won't want to go to the Holy Land. I'll want to do wicked things, and I'll go to hell when I die. So you see, I must go now and be a martyr right away. And Rodrigo, too."

Juan's mouth trembled a little. And it was obvious that his big brother's cough was very bad indeed.

"I see", said Juan. "You've thought it all out, haven't you? There's only one thing you have forgotten—if you want to go to the Holy Land you must start very, very early in the morning so that you get there in time."

Teresa said nothing. Juan saw the first shadow of uncertainty in the large, dark eyes of the child. He said quickly; "Let's all go back now and try again in the morning. You won't be so very wicked until tomorrow, so there's time enough."

155

"Yes, let's", said Rodrigo eagerly.

Teresa did not take the slightest notice of him. She was still thinking.

"In an hour or so it will be dark," went on Juan, "and then you'll miss your way and get to the wrong place— someplace where they won't kill you at all, and what good would that be? Come now, we'll all get in our little *carreta* and go back, and tomorrow you set out again, quite early."

She took the child by the hand and led her to the *carreta*. Before she lifted her up, Rodrigo had already climbed in. Uli brought up the rear, wiping his eyes.

As they were nearing the gate, a rider came up on a mule. He was a lean, distinguished-looking man in his early forties.

"Por Dios", he exclaimed. "Teresita! Rodrigo! What are you doing here?"

"Uncle Miguel!" cried Rodrigo.

Teresa looked at Juan and laid a tiny finger to her mouth. "You promised", she whispered.

Juan nodded reassuringly.

"I am Miguel de Cepeda", said the rider. "I hope the children have not inconvenienced you, Señores...."

"Not at all", said Uli.

"It is very wrong of you to go outside the walls", said Don Miguel reproachfully. "I shall talk to your mother about this. She will be most upset."

"It's all her fault", complained Rodrigo, pointing to Teresa. "She made me do it. Just because she thinks she's going to be wicked when she grows up, why should I be a martyr, too? I'm not wicked."

"Oh, dear!" said Juan, shaking his head.

Teresa said nothing. But as her uncle lifted her from the *carreta* and put her down before him on the mule's back, she gave her brother a look of sovereign contempt.

"What is all this about being martyrs?" asked Don Miguel.

"Climb up behind me, Rodrigo, up with you. There. Now will you tell me what all this is about, Señorito?"

But Rodrigo had caught Teresa's look.

"Perhaps your new friends will explain", said Don Miguel.

Juan said quickly, "We found the children and asked them to come back to town with us, and they did."

"I am most grateful to you for that, believe me, and so will Doña Beatriz be when she hears about it—my sister-in-law and the mother of these two unruly little good-for-nothings. She must be extremely worried by now." Don Miguel ruffled little Teresa's hair. "But I don't understand this business about martyrs and being wicked. Does it mean anything to you, Señor?"

"I am not at liberty to tell you about it, Don Miguel", said Juan with the utmost gravity. "It is a great secret."

"Oh, it is, is it?" There was a twinkle in Miguel de Cepeda's eyes. "Very well then, I won't press the point."

Juan gave a little bow, but his eyes rested on Teresa, whose serious face was just visible behind the long ears of her uncle's mule.

And Teresa ceremoniously returned the bow.

Brother Ulrico suffered another coughing spell.

They had been moving toward the gate and now passed through it. A few guards gave Don Miguel a sleepy salute.

"A beautiful town", said Uli. "The big building over there on the left is the palace of the duke of Albuquerque I suppose."

"It is."

"The duke", said Uli innocently, "has a very illustrious lady as a guest, I heard."

"He had", corrected Don Miguel. "Our former queen, you mean, don't you? A very lovely lady. She stayed in Ávila several weeks."

"She has left?" asked Uli indifferently.

"She returned to Valencia a few days ago."

## CHAPTER TWENTY-ONE

IÑIGO WALKED across the meadows between Eguibar and Azpeitia. He walked on crutches, and they bit deep into the soft earth.

He knew every inch of the ground; he had played here as a child. He had played here when his legs had not yet the strength to carry him far, and now it was the same thing all over again.

Later he had raced across it this way and that, when he was Amadis of Gaul, out on his ride through wild country, to liberate the princess, to slay the dragon.... Was it so long ago?

Though now he could only hobble along, his thoughts were racing far faster than Amadis' horse, across whole countries, across the sea to the Holy Land.

Much had to be done, but the pilgrimage to the Holy Land came first. This decision was the final result of his walk, and he analyzed carefully by what method he had reached it. It might be worthwhile to write that method down in his large notebook, when he got home.

Many of the excerpts he had made from *The Life of Christ* and *The Flower of the Saints* he knew by heart, certainly the passage in the former that had started him on his meditation.

"It is indeed a holy and pious exercise to contemplate the holy land of Jerusalem, where all the churches of Our Savior are never empty. For that sovereign King of ours, Christ, dwelling therein and enlightening it by his word and doctrine, at last consecrated it with his precious Blood. And since this is so, it is even more pleasing to behold it with bodily eyes and meditate upon it with the mind, for in each of its places Our Lord wrought our salvation. Who can number the devout who visit each place therein and ardently kiss the earth, reverence and embrace the places in which they know or hear that Our Lord visited, taught, or performed some work? And these at times strike their breasts, at times shed tears and groan, at times sigh to heaven with sorrowful gestures and yearning devotion. Often their outward manifestation of their inner contrition moves even the Moor. Surely we ought to groan and bewail the idleness and indifference of the Christian princes of our day, who, having before them so many examples, are so weak and unconcerned for its conquest out of the hands of the enemy, for Our Lord consecrated it with his precious Blood."

The Holy Land came first. Everything else later.

Slowly he hobbled on toward Azpeitia and Loyola.


Martín had come back from the battlefront only half an hour ago, haggard and weary and parched with thirst. There had been no need for him to tell his wife that things had gone badly. One look at him told her enough, and she urged him to have some wine and then to lie down for a while.

He had accepted the wine, but refused to lie down.

"I can't close an eye. You don't know what has happened, and I don't know how to begin to tell you."

Magdalena had been married to him too long not to know that she must conceal the pleasure, the infinite relief she felt at having him back safely, even if it was not for long, safe and without a wound.

Seeing Iñigo slowly approach, she took it as a welcome opportunity to divert her husband's mind at least for a few minutes from the things he was brooding over. A defeat was bad, but sometimes a defeat brought about peace quicker than a victory did, though such heresy could never be uttered to a soldier like her husband.

She began to whisper to him about Iñigo, and he listened, but what he heard did not change his mood. He frowned heavily and cut her short.

"I'll talk to him. Here he is now."

The brothers embraced courteously.

"Does your leg still give you much pain?"

"Very little. A few more weeks and I shall not need crutches any more. I can get about in the house without them now. How do things fare with you?"

"Badly, *por Dios*. If you will be good enough to come with me to my room . . ."

In his room, Martín closed the heavy door behind him and beckoned Iñigo to sit down. He himself remained standing. "We are beaten", he said bitterly. "Stupidly, treacherously beaten."

"Fuentarrabia?"

"Has fallen. The French brought up their artillery, not light pieces of the kind we captured at Noain, but heavy monsters that hit us all the way from Gasteluzar, more than twenty of them. It wasn't a fight at all. It was just sitting in a hole with rubble falling on our heads all the time. It is dreadful what war has come to! Diego de Vera held a council of the *Parientes Mayores*. He spoke, I spoke, and many others. But by then we had repelled a general assault—did quite well, too. Only the water supply was short. Too many men in the fortress."

Iñigo listened patiently. Martín could never tell a story in the correct sequence, he thought. First came the assault, then the council. Confusion of thought was bound to lead to confusion of action.

"It's always either too many or too few", Martín went on grimly. "The water shortage was serious. We had to cook our meat in cider.... As long as we had meat—and cider. Then they bombarded us again, and the militia lost heart. It's not their way of fighting. Give them good, open terrain and they're all right, but not stuck in a hole, hit by an invisible enemy and thirsty and hungry to boot. I am sorry to say there were desertions. Many desertions."

The militia. Guipúzcoans. Poor Martín. This was terrible for him.

"The council was on the sixteenth", said Martín. "By the eighteenth even the leaders began to yield. It was infamous, Iñigo, infamous. Do you know, I could not tell Magdalena about it; I was so ashamed.... I tried to stem the tide, and so did Juan Ortiz and a few others, but it was like—like an epidemic. In the end it was all rubble and a handful of us, not enough to resist an attack—any attack. So I marched them out like soldiers rather than have them steal away under the cover of darkness. And the French marched in."

"The king has lost a fortress", said Iñigo.

"What? Oh, yes, I see. Well, of course it's not the end of everything. But it is a stain, Iñigo. *Dios de mi alma*, have you no blood left in your veins? The shame of it!"

"What measures have been taken?" enquired Iñigo.

"The regency has been transferred to Vitoria. We are fortifying San Sebastián as quickly as we can. And Diego de Vera has been superseded by the duke of Albuquerque; he is taking over today, as general of the frontier. Guipúzcoa is going to be defended."

"There may be no attack", said Iñigo, his eyes far away. He knew the French and their way of thinking. They had to do something to extinguish the memory of Noain. Now they had done it. If this were part of a far more ambitious plan, they would not give the Spaniards time to fortify San Sebastián; they would pounce on it quickly. It had been known for some time that King Charles as the emperor had made an alliance with King Henry VIII of England, and there had been rumors about Milan being threatened by imperial forces. King Francis I of France might soon need his troops elsewhere than for a military adventure in Spain.

He saw all this quite clearly, in a moment or two of concentration. Guipúzcoa was a dear place, but a small one, a small issue in the politics of the great lords of Christendom.

But then again the great lords of Christendom were of very small importance themselves. All their petty ambitions, all their struggles for prestige, their quibbling and fighting, were like the tinny noise of children's war games.

He thought that and then felt a little frightened that he could think it. Looking from the outside at both his thought and his fright, he smiled.

Martín saw the smile and took it as an answer to his words. "*Cáspita*", he said angrily. "I don't know what's come over you lately, Iñigo, but whatever it is, I don't like it."

"It has not harmed you", said Iñigo quietly.

"Not so far", admitted Martín. "Except that talking to you now is almost like talking to a stranger. I'll say this for you: you gave good advice, and it led to the settlement of our trouble with the good nuns. It was a stupid affair, and we were all too deeply involved to see it. You did see it, and now it's all over. Right and good. You are still suffering from an honorable wound and can't take your share in the fighting—right and good again. But your mind doesn't fight any longer either; something's happened to it."

"Whatever happened to it," said Iñigo slowly, "it is still fighting."

"I wonder now", said Martín. "You've sent one of our servants to Burgos, haven't you? Carlos. What for?"

Iñigo said nothing.

"I know what for", pursued Martín. "You have asked him to go to Miraflores to get you information about the Rule there. Miraflores—that's the Carthusians. Monks. I couldn't believe my ears. A Loyola a monk. One of the king's most promising officers spending all his time wiping the floor with his knees. *Dios!* I'd rather see them both shot off by another cannon ball. A Loyola a monk—one in a crowd with the sons of merchants and craftsmen. Faith, it's enough to make one puke. I know even Pero won't like it, and Pero is a priest."

Iñigo checked the answer ready on his tongue. Many of the sins of the past he shared with his brother Pero. Pero was a priest. He was not a good priest. But it was not Iñigo's business to give judgment. He remained silent.

"I know what it is", exclaimed Martín suddenly. "I see it now. It's the duke. The duke of Najera. You are a member of his household; he's the man who was to help your career, and he has fallen into disfavor. You never said much about it, but I know it was a great disappointment to you. You did magnificently at Pamplona, and you were never even thanked for it properly. You resented that. Take all this and your long illness, all that cutting and scraping by the damned leeches—and this is the result. You're running away from life, that's all."

Iñigo put his hand into his pocket and produced a letter, which he quietly handed to his brother.

The duke of Najera wrote that he had been very pleased with the exploits of Don Iñigo de Loyola, that he hoped he would be fully restored to health soon and come and see him about a command, as it was not meet that an officer of such ability

163

and courage should be wasted on a subaltern position. He added that he had just received most welcome news as well as praise from his majesty the king and that he felt it his duty to pass on such praise to a man who had acquired great merits in the defense of the king's fortress of Pamplona.

Martín's face reddened a little.

"I was wrong about this", he said, breathing heavily.

It was a difficult thing for him to say. Iñigo smiled a little. Martín gave him back the letter, which he pocketed. For a while there was silence.

"What about the Carthusians?" asked Martín finally. "Will you promise me that you are not going to bring disgrace on our name and join them?"

"I will not disgrace our name", said Iñigo coldly. "I have not come to a decision about Miraflores yet." He rose.

"That's better than nothing, but it isn't much", said Martín. "I am the head of the family. You will have to do better than that to satisfy me."

"I am fully aware that I have to do better."

Martín eyed him with suspicion. "You're a fox", he said. "The devil knows what you're thinking."

"If he does," said Iñigo, "he doesn't like it."

Few people were able to detect a sense of humor hiding behind a layer of ice, and Martín was not one of them.

"What do you intend to do then?" he asked abruptly.

"To get well."

After a moment he added, "To pay a visit to the duke of Najera."

Martín's face brightened.

"That's better."

They bowed to each other as they invariably did at the end of a discussion, and Iñigo limped back to his own room, on the floor above.

He sat down at his desk and began to make a fresh entry in his notebook. Pages and pages had been filled with his extremely accurate and careful handwriting. There were excerpts from his books, especially from *The Life of Christ*, with the words of Christ written in red ink, and the words of his Mother in blue. There were also notes of his own.

"A prelude toward making a decision", he wrote. "In every good election, as far as it is in our power, the eye of our intention should be single and pure, to consider the end for which we were created, namely, for the praise of Our Lord God, and for our own salvation. Wherefore these things alone are to be chosen which conduce to this end. Since, in every case, the means is in subordination to the end and not the end to the means."

He underlined the last sentence.

He began to think about it. The point was clear enough to him, but would it be clear to every man who might one day read it? He decided to give an example or two, to clarify it.

"It so happens that many err, who in the first place marry, which is a means; and in the second place in the married state desire to serve God, which service is an end. Similarly, there are others who in the first place wish to take ecclesiastical offices, and afterward in them to serve God. Such as these, therefore, do not rightly aspire after God, but wish rather that God straightway should incline to their affections, and consequently they make a means of the end; and that which ought to occupy the first place holds the second place."

That should be clear enough.

His aim was to serve God. For that reason he wanted to go to the Holy Land. He did not want to go to the Holy Land and take it as an opportunity also to serve God.

But his brother was worried about him. He thought that he might join the Carthusians, which would be regarded as a disgrace to the family. As Iñigo had not made up his mind yet about the point he had said so. Well and good. He had told him he was going to pay a visit to the duke. This was permissible only because such was in truth his intention, although it was not the whole of his intention. It would have been wrong, quite decidedly, to tell him a lie, even if it was only to comfort or humor him.

He wrote, "All things which fall under election must necessarily be good in themselves, or certainly not evil."

The means had to be subordinated to the end.

But the end did not justify the means, if the means were evil.

Surely that was now all clear and could never be twisted or perverted by fools, knaves, or enemies.


## CHAPTER TWENTY-TWO


"Report", said Martín curtly.

The beefy squire before him turned his cap in his hands. "We set out on the last day of February", he began.

"Of course you did", interrupted Martín impatiently. "I saw you all off."

It had been a goodly sight, too. At long last Iñigo was himself again. Came down the stairs as in the old days, his limp scarcely visible, and elegant enough in his yellow hose and blue cloak, the dagger in his embroidered belt and the sword at his side. He mounted his mule without help.

"We set out on the last day of February", said the squire again. He was perspiring profusely.

Martín opened his mouth to give him a piece of his mind, but then gave in. No use hurrying a man like Juan de Landeta, and the other fellow, Andrés de Narvais, was worse, and yet they were the best men he had been able to spare for the task.

"We were four", went on the squire. "Don Iñigo, Padre Pero López, de Narvais, and I."

Just a little more patience, thought Martín, grinding his teeth. In the end he is going to tell me something I do not know. Just a little more patience.

"Padre Pero López wished to visit his sister at Oñate," said de Landeta, "and Don Iñigo was most courteous about it, although he seemed to be in rather a hurry. But when we came to Aránzazu he forgot about being in a hurry and wanted to perform a night's vigil at the shrine there, and now Padre Pero López seemed to be in a hurry and wanted to go on."

Martín suppressed a grin. Of the two brothers Pero was the priest. He had been ordained at least, and of course he did say his Mass, but that was about all. A whole night's vigil at a shrine was not his favorite pastime.

"Don Iñigo persuaded him to it, though", said the squire. "And— and us, too."

"Well, it can't have done you any harm." Martín grunted. "Go on."

"Next we came to Oñate, and Padre Pero López remained there. He said he needed much sleep and then much food, and Don Iñigo reminded him that it was Lent—very politely, but Padre Pero López said he had known about Lent before Don Iñigo was born, and Don Iñigo said that perhaps that was why it was necessary to remind him of it, as we tend to forget things that are far back in time."

Lord and squire looked at each other diffidently. It was one of those sayings of Iñigo that were difficult to fathom.

"So we three took the road to Navarrete," de Landeta went on, "and when we arrived, Don Iñigo went to Santa María la Real ..."

"Church again", said Martín sullenly.

"Yes, my Lord. And he sent us to the duke's treasurer with a note, and the treasurer read it and was angry and said to tell Don Iñigo that he had no money."

Martín nodded. No treasurer paid out money at once. They always said no first.

"So we went back to him at the *posada*—"

"I thought you said he was in church?"

"Yes, but he had told us to wait for him at the Posada del Rey, and he met us there after a while, and we told him, and he said nothing except that we should tell him when a visitor came, and he went to his room. And then ..."

"Out with it", said Martín gruffly. "Don't you dare to hold back on me, de Landeta."

"We had the room next to his", said the squire, and he looked about and shifted from one foot to the other. "And we heard noise."

"What sort of noise?"

The squire gulped. "It didn't sound good to us", he quavered. "But we knew he had locked the door from the inside, and nobody had come to see him—we would have heard that. So we let it be. But in the morning, when Don Iñigo had left the room, de Narvais went in, and he saw bloodstains on the rug."

"It's his leg again, I suppose", said Martín.

"Yes, my Lord", said the squire hastily, and Martín knew that he lied to please him, but he let it be.

"Then a *caballero* came", said de Landeta. "Don Estebán de Guelvas. He came from the duke, and as it was an official visit, Don Iñigo bade us stay. Don Estebán was most cordial, most cordial indeed. He came to present his grace's compliments and a bag of ducats, and he said his grace said even if there wasn't any money in the treasury, there was always money for a Loyola, and there was a good lieutenancy too if Don Iñigo was willing to accept it."

A quick flame flickered in Martín's eyes and went out.

"Go on", he said.

"Don Iñigo thanked Don Estebán and gave him his respectful compliments for the duke."

"And?"

"He said nothing else, my Lord, and Don Estebán departed."

Martín murmured something between his teeth.

"Then what happened?"

"Don Iñigo gave us two ducats each and asked us to deposit some of his money with his compliments to the Manrique family. He said he was indebted to them. But the main part he gave to a hermitage we had passed when we entered Navarrete. There was a statue of Our Lady there, and it was without adornments, and Don Iñigo said he could not tolerate it."

Martín did not comment on that. After a while he said; "Is that all?"

"Practically, my Lord. Except for two things."

"Faith, must I extract every word from you with the tongs of the torturer? Which two things?"

"Well, first Don Iñigo was in a hurry all the time, despite the night we spent at Aránzazu. He said he wanted to avoid the new Pope's progress."

Martín nodded. Cardinal Adrian of Utrecht had just been elected Pope *in absentia* and was now on the way to Rome. He would pass Navarrete and then proceed to Barcelona. There were many Basque nobles with him, and of course they all knew Iñigo. Iñigo did not want to be seen. Worse and worse.

"Two things, you said, de Landeta."

"Y-yes, my Lord. When Don Iñigo sent us away, he said . . ."

"Out with it."

"He said he was going to Montserrat on pilgrimage."

Martín's face became stony.

"That is definitely all?" he said hoarsely.

"Yes, my Lord. If my Lord wishes to interrogate de Narvais . . ."

"No. I have heard enough. Thank you, de Landeta."

"Your Lordship's servant."

The squire withdrew.

Martín stared into the void. Then he called for Magdalena.

"Iñigo is visiting every shrine and every church he passes by. He has taken to flagellating himself at night. And he's going on pilgrimage. To Montserrat."

Magdalena raised her eyebrows.

"Montserrat. It could have been worse."

"He has not accepted a lieutenancy offered to him by the duke", said Martín.

"He has probably vowed not to accept any honors before he has made his pilgrimage. He'll come back and accept the post then."

"I hope you're right", said Martín. "But you never know with him. He's a deep one. I wish you'd never given him those books. He'll disgrace the family yet; you'll see."

"I wonder", said Magdalena.

"What do you mean?"

As with the squire, he again had to urge and insist, till she yielded, almost grudgingly, "Remember the night of the earthquake."

"I remember", he said. "What of it?"

"You couldn't understand how he managed to climb down the stairs, and to kneel, on that knee of his. Neither could I. Neither can I."

"I don't know what you are talking about", said he scornfully. "It has nothing to do with it. I don't like it."

But she knew that he had understood what she meant. He always blustered when he did not want to follow a certain line of thought. His next words confirmed it.

"He's my brother. He is Pero's brother. I've known him all my life. Why on earth should he, of all people ... Bah, why discuss it. You will see; he'll do something disgraceful. He's the most obstinate man I know. I don't like it. He'll disgrace us all, I tell you."

"Maybe", said Magdalena indulgently.


CHAPTER TWENTY-THREE


IT WAS UNUSUAL for a *caballero* to travel without servants, but that was a small matter, and it was necessary to shed, bit by bit, the links with the past.

Iñigo had left Martín and Magdalena at Loyola, Pero López at Oñate, de Narvais and de Landeta at Navarrete.

It was part of a necessary strategy.

He knew something about strategy; he was well aware that it was an innate talent of his. But he had never led large concentrations of troops, he had never led an army, and now he found that to be a soldier of the King of kings meant to be a general.

He had been worried about an old and powerful enemy, the flesh. That was why he had stopped and performed a vigil at Aránzazu. There he had built a fort against that enemy. He had made a vow of chastity for the rest of his life.

Wealth he had never particularly cared about. Even so, as quickly as possible he had got rid of the money the duke had sent him, keeping only what little money he had taken with him from Loyola to deal with the expenses of the journey.

From Montserrat onward he would have no more need for money.

So far it had been simple. But then came the first real task, the cleaning out of all undesirable elements, the shedding of his sins in thought and word and action during his entire life in a general confession. It was an army of sins, and he had to eliminate it. It was a battle against specters, ghosts, bat-winged foul creatures hovering all about him and extending over almost thirty years in time.

A relentless pursuit was necessary over mountains and across rivers, nooks, and crannies of the soul.

He had set himself a task far bigger than anything he had ever undertaken in the service of King Charles the First.

He was a recruit, a raw private in the forces of heaven, but there even a private was in command of a large army.

To serve God was—to rule.

A few days earlier he had passed Logroño. Keeping on the right bank of the Ebro, he had left Calahorra and Alfaro behind him, then Tudela, Cortes, and Mallén, and he was now approaching Pedrola.

In a few days the newly elected Pope would travel the same way. In Logroño they had said that they would greet him with a salute fired by all the cannons conquered from the French. A good and holy man and a learned man. If he kept his name, he would be Adrian VI.

Perhaps Iñigo would meet him one day. But most certainly not now. He had kept up the utmost speed to make quite sure that he would not be drawn into the rapids surrounding the Vicar of Christ, consisting of half the nobles of the kingdom, countless people he knew and who knew him and would ask questions he did not wish to answer.

Every evening his foot was swollen very badly, and he had to cool it with water and vinegar to be able to mount his mule again in the morning.

His back hurt, too, from the discipline applied to the mutineers, rebels, and deserters. No cooling was applied to it. The pain did not impede his progress.

It was good to travel alone. It was good to think that he was now really on his way to the Holy Land.

Moors, Turks, Saracens, Arabs. It was a never-ending field on which to work, and ...

He stopped. He stopped not only his thoughts, but also his mule, uttering a sharp exclamation.

A Moor. A Moor on a donkey had overtaken him.

It was only a very small Moor, and he was riding a very small donkey.

From the height of his mule Iñigo looked down on a large white turban and a flowing green dress like a strange flower being carried by a donkey.

The Moor had heard him exclaim and turned in his saddle. The flower suddenly had a face, a fleshy, brown face with almond-shaped eyes and a full, pink mouth, adorned by a little, black mustache and supported by a little black beard.

He probably thought that Iñigo's exclamation had been a greeting, for he stopped his donkey, lifted a pudgy brown hand to his chest and forehead, and said: "Peace be with you."

It was his habitual courtesy that saved Iñigo from acute embarrassment. Obviously he had to reciprocate a polite greeting, and while doing so he could get some order into his thoughts. He had not been suddenly transferred to the Holy Land, as might have happened to a knight in some wondrous tale—or even to a knight of God, if it pleased God, who after all was almighty. He was still on the road near Pedrola. This was Spain. But it was also Aragón, and there were still a good many Moors in Aragón.

The Moor had greeted him after the manner of his people, although he had used the Spanish tongue. And in Spanish this greeting sounded very much like the one used by the Lord and his apostles: Peace be with you.

Perhaps it was a sign after all.

By now he had reached the little man, who was still bowing, with his right hand on his chest.

The little man was smiling, too.

"You are most kind, my Lord, to greet me as I passed you", he said. "In fact I was a little worried, as there are some who do not like to be bypassed on the road, just as they do not like to be bypassed on their way to fame. And indeed the road they ride on may well be their road to fame."

"Not in my case", said Iñigo. "I am a pilgrim, although the holy place I am going to visit is the most famous of all."

The little Moor, riding beside him now, had again become a curious kind of flower.

"That is a habit of my people too," he said, "and one very much blessed by God. We go on pilgrimage to the holy places of Mecca and Medina, of Djidda and of El Kuds, which the Christians call Jerusalem. God preserve me, I have never been there and probably never shall be, unless it is written in the Book of Life."

"Jerusalem", said Iñigo, "is a holy city."

The tactful implication that the same could not be said about the other places he had mentioned seemed lost on the little Moor, who began to sing the praise of Jerusalem, until Iñigo said, "I am going to Montserrat."

"I have heard of it", said the little man. "It is very beautiful, they say, and there lives the spirit of the lady who was once addressed by the Archangel Gabriel."

"You believe that?" asked Iñigo, astonished.

"All good Moslems do", said the Moor, looking up at him. "It is in the Koran."

Iñigo winced a little.

"She must have been a very holy lady", said the Moor benevolently. "Or else Allah would not have chosen her to become the mother of a great prophet."

"You believe that, too, then?"

"Oh, yes, naturally. It is in the Koran. I have thought about it often, and I can well believe also that she was a virgin despite having conceived a child. It is not in the Koran, but it is possible all the same, for there is no limit to the power of Allah."

"Well said", acknowledged Iñigo. "She is Virgin and Mother. And she is the Queen of Heaven."

"I do not know about heaven", said the Moor modestly. "I have never been there, and Allah only knows whether I shall ever go. But I well believe that she was Virgin and Mother. After all, that is the natural sequence."

"Ah, but she remained a virgin all her life", exclaimed Iñigo. "If you know so much, you should know that, too."

"All her life?" asked the Moor incredulously. "How can that be, as she gave birth to a child?"

"You yourself said that there was no limit to the power of God", Iñigo reminded him.

"It is true, it is true. And I also said that I could believe that she remained a virgin although she had conceived, which is a great miracle. But once she had conceived, what further need was there for another miracle?"

"Her virginity is eternal," said Iñigo, "as is her purity." There was severity in his tone now.

"A little ahead of us the road forks out", said the Moor noncommittally. "I must take the way to the left then, to a farmhouse, where I have business."

"There can be no doubt whatever about it", insisted Iñigo. "Eternal virginity. Eternal purity."

The little Moor hung his head, which made him become a flower again, and remained thus while Iñigo amplified his theological argument.

When he had to pause for breath the Moor looked up again with a shrewd smile.

"This is all most beautiful," he said, "but it cannot be true."

Iñigo stiffened, and the little Moor hastened to add, "I know you are quite sincere in your belief, my Lord, but you have forgotten something, or maybe it is not realized by Christians. Isa, the lady's son, was a great prophet, as well we know. And he was the lady's firstborn. But after him there were other children. Does he not speak himself of his brothers and sisters in the holy book of the Christians? Now how could he have brothers and sisters and his mother still be a virgin?"

"It is an error", declared Iñigo. "Our Lord had neither brothers nor sisters. The word for 'brother' and for 'sister' in the original language of the Bible is the same as for 'cousin' or 'relative'. He had relatives, not brothers and sisters. Every Christian child knows that."

"Never having been a Christian child," said the Moor, "I didn't know."

"Well, you know it now", said Iñigo sternly.

His hands had become heavy on the reins, and the mule began to prance.

The Moor's little donkey grew nervous, its long ears stiffened, and it looked worried.

Its master seemed to share its feelings. Nevertheless he said courageously, "I only know what you tell me. Allah forbid that I should go the way of those who err. Anyway, what does it matter? A woman is only a woman, and that is not very much."

"How dare you say that!" thundered Iñigo, his eyes ablaze.

Moor, mule, and donkey recoiled in fright.

The mule, who had never heard its master raise his voice before, rose on its hind legs.

The little donkey threw its ears back and fell into gallop.

It was as if the two animals had decided that this was the moment to end the theological debate.

An experienced rider, Iñigo forced his mule to a standstill. He saw the Moor riding ahead rapidly and disappearing round the bend of the road.

He was stirred to his depths and thoroughly dissatisfied with himself. Had he done his duty? Could he allow the Moor to get away like this after what he had said?

The knight of the Queen of Heaven—could he allow her to be insulted by a benighted infidel and let it go unavenged?

Yet the little man had been kindly enough and very near the truth.

What was the right thing to do?

His hand ached for the hilt of his dagger, strike, strike for the Queen of Heaven. But he realized that this was his desire, the urge of his blood, of his fighting spirit.

Was it the will of God?

He rode on slowly to give himself time for a decision.

But he did not come to a decision. He could not bring order into the voices crying out in him.

He rode round the bend and came to the fork of the road the Moor had mentioned.

On the right the highway went straight on. On the left a secondary road led to the farmhouse the Moor had spoken of and to the town of Pedrola. It was a good, wide road.

He stopped, still undecided, exhausted by the argument and counterargument in his mind.

What was the will of God?

He turned the mule, rode thirty paces back, and turned again. He dropped the reins.

"Go", he said.

The mule began to move.

He would let it go whatever way it would. If it took the way to the left, the way the Moor had gone, he would follow him and kill him. If it went to the right, he would bypass Pedrola and go on to Montserrat that way.

Now the mule reached the fork.

He sat quite still, his mind a blank, his muscles relaxed. May God's will be done.

The mule took the fork on the right.

Quietly he took up the reins again and rode on.

The matter was solved. He gave it no further thought.

## CHAPTER TWENTY-FOUR

Fray Juan Chanones of the Order of Saint Benedict received the elegant nobleman with the same grave courtesy as he had accorded the man preceding him, who was a tax collector from Saragossa. For the Benedictine Rule prescribed that every guest must be received as if he were Christ.

The men who came to Montserrat were all pilgrims, and penitents, and such are usually ill at ease and tense. But none of them (a few fugitives from the police excepted) refused to give his name.

The nobleman did.

It did not seem likely that he was a fugitive from the police. But if he was, it was not the affair of the monastery or of Fray Juan Chanones.

Besides, the nobleman did not seem to be particularly tense, and he was not ill at ease. He wished to make preparations for a general confession and asked whether there was any book that might be helpful to him.

The Benedictine gave him the *Exercitatory of the Spiritual Life* by García de Cisneros, which the novices usually read, and he rather liked the way the penitent accepted it, closing his long, aristocratic fingers around it as if he had been given something that was worthy of veneration.

He went with him to the hostelry and saw to it that he was given a cell without having to inscribe his name.

Then he left him alone, and Iñigo began a most painstaking, relentless, and merciless military operation.

There was little need for Cisneros to tell him how severely God could punish sin, to remind him that Lucifer had been hurled forever from heaven for one single sin, that Adam had been cast out of paradise for one single sin.

He was determined to bring all his sins to the surface, every single one of them, like the boy in the wondrous story who had been commanded to shoot every bird in the forest and to catch every fish in the lake.

He shot them off on the mountain crags and cliffs of pride and vanity, in the flat plains of complacency, and in the abyss of ignorance. He pursued them into the innermost recesses, probing here and there with his lance; he scraped them off the cells of his memory, picked them out like lice and other vermin, ran his sword through them for the monsters and dragons they were. He dove into the waters after them, wresting them from the seaweed of forgetfulness, scratching them off the coral banks of habit, and he followed them into the ultimate, slimy depths no longer consciously known.

And he did not rest until they were all stretched out before him, an amorphous mass, jellylike and putrefying, weakly twitching and blinded by the light of his cognition.

All this was his; by all this he had increased the weight of the divine Cross; every one of these sins had driven the nails deeper into the hands and feet of his Lord.

Grinding his teeth, he compounded a list of them all, overlooking nothing. He did not allow any to wriggle away, to hide themselves, or to put on embellishments.

The very angel of judgment could not have been more exacting.

The bell rang for the midday meal, but he stayed still. He had a loaf of bread and a pitcher of water in his cell. That was enough. In a few days' time he would regard so much as luxury.

He shared in the Vespers and Compline of the monks, but returned to go on with his battle.

From midnight to six in the morning he slept. Then Mass. And the battle was resumed.

It lasted altogether three days.

Other pilgrims saw him cross over to the main building to look for Fray Juan Chanones—they saw a slender man with the fashionable little pointed beard; with long, beautiful hands; elegantly dressed and with a slight limp; he carried a heavy volume and a notebook.

The good Benedictine had heard confessions by the thousand. Never before had he heard a man read off the sins of his past with such uncanny precision, such ice-cold attention to detail.

He forgot what he heard as soon as the penitent had left him after the absolution, as he invariably did. There remained only one impression, and he would never lose it: that this was the only absolutely complete confession of a man's entire life he had ever heard.

He was summoned to the abbot later in the day.

Abbot Pedro de Burgos was a little worried. A pilgrim who seemed to be a Basque nobleman had asked for permission to donate his mule, his arms, and his dress to the monastery. He would have been glad to accept such generous gifts, but the donor refused to give his name, so what was he to do?

Fray Juan Chanones set his mind at rest. He thought it would not be risky to deviate in this case from the custom of refusing anonymous donations.

"Very well, very well, if you think so. But not the dress. The mule we can use, indeed we can, and the arms can be an *ex voto*—I think such is the man's intention—but what would we do with a nobleman's dress here? We can't possibly give it to anybody; it would only be a cause of embarrassment."

Fray Juan Chanones made his obeisance and left the presence. A few minutes later he informed Iñigo of the outcome of his talk.

The mule became forthwith the possession of Saint Benedict. Never again would it chase blaspheming infidels.

Iñigo watched a sacristan hanging his Toledan sword and dagger on the grille which separated the Virgin's chapel from the main church. They shared the place of honor with the heavily silvered shoes of a little child the Virgin had saved from drowning, the scimitar of a Moorish prince who had been converted to Christianity, and countless plaquettes in gold, silver, and bronze with expressions of gratitude, fiery or humble, engraved on them by their donors for mercies and graces received.

Then Iñigo thought he recognized two acquaintances of his family in the church, and he returned to his cell in a hurry. After darkness had set in, he emerged again and left the monastery. With him he carried four things: a tunic, made of ordinary sackcloth, rough and prickly; a pair of sandals; a gourd; and a staff.

A couple of thousand yards from the gates of the monastery was the thatched hut of a beggar.

He asked the astonished man to let him change clothes in his hut and gave him his suit. He went away then in his tunic of sackcloth, pursued by the wine-sodden voice of the poor old fellow, crowing his gratitude.

It was quite dark now, and the night was starless.

Only in the vast church the light of countless candles burned, a smaller universe replacing the one outside, hidden by the clouds of an early spring.

It was the twenty-fourth of March, the vigil of the Annunciation, then the Feast of the Archangel Gabriel.

Iñigo walked up to the grille before the Virgin's chapel and knelt there at the edge of the candlelight.

The archangel's wings, black and tremendous, filled the whole church.

Clusters of pilgrims murmured their prayers from far away.

The organ prayed, too, touched by invisible fingers.

Iñigo rose. His knee would no longer support him, and he gave in to it, because it would have work to do tomorrow. He stepped back into the shadows, where the light of the candles no longer touched him, and there he stood, immobile, staff in hand, head bowed.

He had shed his sins. The evil burden was no more. But what was there instead—except the longing to be filled?

*Soul of Christ*, he thought, *sanctify me.*

He was alone. It was still the archangel's day, and angels were so different, so utterly different from man. God alone could create a bond between the two worlds. Angels were winged intellects, flying will power. They had no bodies. He was frightened.

*Body of Christ*, he thought, *save me.*

When a man came to think of it, could he ever cease to be thankful for the Word having been made flesh? It was only then that man could say "Father" to God, because the Son of God had taken to himself a body.

God had become man. And man had killed that Man.

How strong it was in man, the desire to kill. Only two or three mornings ago he himself had desired to kill a man, and there had been a moment, a moment very closely akin to lust, and thus he had known that he could not rely on his own judgment but would have to leave it to God.

To God, who had shed his own Blood for him, the precious Blood, the very stream of Life—that was what a man must long for, the wine of salvation, divine drunkenness.

*Blood of Christ*, he thought, *inebriate me.*

Poured forth on Calvary, from the right hand and the left hand; from the right foot and the left foot; from the forehead, torn by the crown of thorns; from the broad wound in his side, opened by the spear of Longinus.

Thus it was shed. And he was already dead when Longinus pierced his side. Not only his Blood flowed out, but also Water. The cleansing of the world, the fountain of eternal life.

*Water from the side of Christ*, he thought, *wash me*.

He was newborn. He had shed everything: his name, his title, his sword, his dress, his wealth. All the petals of the flower were gone, and he felt naked and cold and very weak. He would suffer. But that was not the thing to fear—that was what would unite him with the suffering of Christ.

*Passion of Christ*, he thought, *strengthen me*.

Was he heard? Was he really heard? Or was he just mumbling to himself, as a child whistles in the dark?

*O good Jesus*, he thought, *hear me. Hear me*.

And at that moment there was a deep, metallic sound that seemed to come from high heaven.

The bell ringer sounded the mystic summons on the great bell.

It was midnight.

The monks had risen from their beds and assembled in the choir. They intoned the Invitatorium of the Annunciation.

A tremor went through the tremendous black wings of the archangel. The moment had come again for the greatest of all messages, and mankind listened to it in Mary.

The fullness of time had come for all races, all men, and it pierced first a tiny cottage in Nazareth.

Men at peace and men at war, men in sorrow and men in joy, men in health and others in sickness; men born and men dying; men talking, blaspheming, reviling each other; men smiting and killing and rushing down to hell.

Yet over them the Blessed Trinity had woven the golden thread of destiny, and in Mary it touched them.

And mankind in Mary made the greatest of all elections. Of her free choice she accepted. She was offered the crown of high heaven, and she said she was the handmaid of the Lord: "Be it done to me according to thy word."

And the Word was made flesh and dwelt among us from this moment onward.

Iñigo stood quiet, staff in hand, head bowed.

There was a great stillness about him and in him.

It was over before he was aware of the passing of time, and once more the monks came and intoned Matins and Lauds and the salutation to his Queen and Lady.

"Ave Stella Matutina."

He sang it with them.

Once more stillness descended, and with it came thoughts welling up in him which filled his whole being, thoughts he would never reveal to anyone—except by living them.

## CHAPTER TWENTY-FIVE

THE CONSTABLE could not believe his eyes.

Old Diego was a well-known figure around Montserrat, and everyone knew what his wardrobe consisted of: a pair of patched trousers that had once been green but now shone in practically all the colors of the rainbow; a shirt with so many holes that it would take half an hour to count them; and a kind of beret, so dirty that it was impossible to say where it ended and where the filth he called his hair began.

The pilgrims were good to him, and he could have had a decent dress if it had not been his habit to carry every coin he received straight away to the inn to exchange it for *aguardiente*.

And now here was old Diego, positively flamboyant in a yellow doublet of the finest French wool, yellow hose, and a finely woven blue cloak. His stubbly head was adorned with a gaily-colored cap, and he strutted about in all this finery like an ancient crane at mating time.

When he saw the constable, he turned and tried to vanish behind the shrubs.

The constable climbed after him, and, as he was younger and more accustomed to the clothes he was wearing, he caught old Diego after a minute or two.

He had been given all this by a pilgrim? A likely story. He would have to think of a better one when he met the procurator.

Old Diego, however, stuck to his story with astonishing obstinacy.

The procurator rubbed his chin. The man was a drunkard, though he had not stolen before—but what did that prove? There was always a first time.

Old Diego whined that he was an honest man and that it was not his fault if a noble pilgrim had made him a present of clothes fit for a king. He had not even solicited the gift.

"What was the man like?" asked the procurator.

Well, it had been fairly dark when he came, and there had been only a little piece of candle burning in his hut, but nevertheless . . .

The procurator received a fairly accurate description of the eccentric donor. What was more, old Diego had seen him pass by this very morning, on the road to Barcelona.

"But he is not dressed as a nobleman now, Vuestra Merced", croaked old Diego. "He is wearing an old sack and sandals, and a staff."

The procurator looked at the constable, but found no help in the blank, oxlike face.

"When did the man pass by here?" he asked.

"An hour ago, perhaps, Vuestra Merced. It is not my fault, is it, that a noble is a little touched in the head? I did offer him my own trousers and my shirt, but he wouldn't take them. He wanted his sack. What can I do? I never ..."

The procurator waved him to silence.

"We shall see", he said. "Constable, you'd better follow the man and find out what this is all about. He cannot have got very far."

The constable scratched his head. It was a nice, cool morning, and the road was downhill. But he had to come back, and then it would be no longer nice and cool, and the road would be uphill. "If I could get myself a mule or a horse", he said.

"It's perhaps better", agreed the procurator. "The good fathers in the monastery have a new mule in their stable; it was given to them by somebody. Ask them whether they will lend it to you. And don't come back without full information."

The constable hurried off. The brother who looked after the stable gave him permission to take the mule, and a few minutes later he was riding down the road to overtake the pilgrim. He was in a hurry, because after a while the road forked out a few miles ahead, and how would he know which way the madman had taken?

He caught up with him soon enough. A man with a bad knee, walking on sandals for the first time in his life, does not proceed very quickly.

Iñigo paled when the constable asked him pointblank whether he had given his clothes to a beggar.

"What is all this?" asked the policeman. "Who are you anyway? What is your name and your nationality? Where are you going?"

"I will answer only one of these questions", said Iñigo. "I have given my clothes to a beggar, yes. And I regret very much that my gift has caused him this trouble."

The constable looked at him sharply.

The man could not be an associate of the beggar. His dress was absurd, but he had clean, well-kept hands, and his hair and beard, too, were well kept. He had tears in his eyes. Well, he was probably a little mad. But why didn't he want to give his name? The procurator wanted full information. Should he take him back with him? Bah, he had given the testimony that really mattered. No good making too much fuss about it. Perhaps the man had made a vow to conceal his name.

He nodded, gave a perfunctory salute, and turned his mule.

Iñigo walked on, his eyes still filled with tears. He had not recognized the animal. All he could think of was that he could not even do good to his neighbor without also bringing harm to him.

It never occurred to him that no one had seen him cry for many years, not since his early boyhood.

A short while afterward he was overtaken again, this time by a cavalcade of men in rich dress. They passed too quickly for him to see whether he knew any of them, but he began to suspect that there would now be many such cavalcades. The progress of the new Pope was catching up with him after all.

This must not be.

They had not paid any attention to him, but any moment now he might find himself face to face with somebody he knew; letters would go to Loyola, to Martín and Magdalena, to the duke of Najera. . . .

He took the next road leading away from the highway. It led to a town he had never seen before, a small town. He had not even heard of it.

A gray-bearded man told him that he was in Manresa and showed him the way to the hospice of Saint Lucy, where the poor could find a bed and perhaps a plate of soup.

It would be a good place to stay a few days till the Pope's progress had passed. He could write down the things he had thought of at night, during his vigil in Montserrat. But first he had to do what Saint Francis had done, what Saint Dominic had done—that thing that was so terrible to the man he had been. It was not easy even now.

He left the hospice and walked down the next street. At the corner he stopped. He leaned against the house. He felt quite faint, but it was not from hunger.

He had fought in many a battle, in many a duel.

Never had his arm performed a more difficult task than this. He had to force it to stretch out, palm upward.

His voice would not obey him at first.

"Bread", at last said Don Iñigo de Loyola, commander of the king's cavalry, member of the household of his grace the duke of Najera, a noble of Spain. "Bread, of your kindness. For the love of God, a piece of bread for a poor man."

A florid woman, apple cheeked and ample bosomed, heard him and stopped. "Go to Saint Lucy's", she said sharply. "They'll give you soup there."

She went on.

"A piece of bread, for the love of God", said Iñigo. After a while his voice no longer quavered.

A couple of urchins grinned at him. "L'Home del sach—el home del sach", they screeched.

The "man in the sack" went on begging.

After a while an old woman gave him a piece of bread and asked him to pray for her, which he promised.

He fulfilled that promise as soon as she had gone. Then he made the sign of the Cross over the bread and began to eat it.

# CHAPTER TWENTY-SIX

"IT'S TAKEN US A LONG TIME," said Uli, "but we're here. Feeling tired, Juan?"

The boy was gazing out the window. What a busy town Valencia was. Or was it that the streets were so narrow? They seemed to overflow with people, masses and masses of people, donkeys, mules, carts, *carretas*, and again people; it made one dizzy just to look at it.

"I asked you whether you're tired, Juan."

"N-no, not very. This must be about the thousandth *posada* I have seen."

"I suppose it is." He had some difficulty keeping compassion out of his voice. "Made you see something of the world, didn't it? Very good for a boy."

"I don't know whether I want to be a boy all my life", said Juan. He was still gazing out of the window.

"You certainly won't be." Uli began to unpack his bundle. There was a girl's dress in it, but he did not touch it. He took out a cake of soap and a brush instead. "In a month or two from today you should be back to a normal life again. I'll take you to Barcelona myself."

Juan said nothing.

"Aren't you glad?" asked Uli.

After a while Juan said, "I don't know. Maybe I've become accustomed to wandering about like this. Mother always used to say that I have something of the gypsy in me. Perhaps I have."

"You want to see her again, don't you?"

"Yes, I do."

"She must be worried about you."

"I don't think so."

"Why not?"

"I wrote to her from Segovia and from Ávila, as you know. And she never really worried much about me. She said I was my father's daughter and not at all like her family, and I'd always fall on my feet like a cat."

The boy turned away from the window. He looked at Uli with a half smile. "Sometimes I think we are just like little Teresa and her brother."

Uli grinned. "You'll make me feel like coughing again. She was a nice child. But I don't quite understand what you mean."

"Well, marching and marching in one direction and quite convinced that it's terribly important we get to some place. And the grownups smile and think it's all rather foolish."

He thought that over. "Who are the grownups, in our case?"

"Perhaps people never grow up", said Juan. "Or—most of them. All chasing something silly. All thinking they'll be so happy when they get there. And perhaps little Teresa was the least silly of them all."

"Going to the Holy Land to become a martyr?"

He rubbed his chin. "I need a shave", he said thoughtfully.

"Going to the Holy Land", said Juan. "She was thinking of the end of things, not just of the next bit, as we are all doing. Did you see her eyes?"

"Yes", he said. After a while he added, "I've met a few Turks, you know. Arabs, too. In Hungary. They're not bad, on the whole, and they take their faith very seriously. More so than most of us. And they believe that they must spread it. And when they fall in battle against us, they believe they will go straight to heaven. So we go to the Holy Land to become martyrs there, and they come to us to become martyrs here. It's a mad world."

"Perhaps the Holy Land is everywhere", said the boy Juan. "But there must be something about the land where Jesus died. I—I'd like to see it. It's funny. I never thought of that before that little girl said it. And I've been thinking of it ever since. I wonder what will become of her. I'm glad I met her."

"She'll marry", said Uli. "She is pretty already. And her husband won't have much say in that marriage, I think. Now get out, Juan. I must wash and then pay my respects to the person whom I have never mentioned to you."

Juan walked to the door.

"Don't forget to tell her about Don Iñigo", she said. "She'll like that."

"What makes you think so?" he asked, surprised.

"She's a woman", said Juan and walked out.

Grinning, Uli began to undress. They had put a large pitcher of water in his room, and he splashed it all over himself. The soap smelt faintly of some flower or other, but that could not be helped. He rubbed himself with a clean towel from his bundle and started shaving.

After a while there was a knock.

"You can't come in now, Juan", he growled.

But the door opened, and one of the innkeeper's girls walked in with his other shirt freshly washed and pressed. She said, "Ooooh", and pretended to be shocked.

"Told you to keep out", he growled, turned her round, gave her a resounding slap on the rear, and shoved her out.

"You didn't." She giggled. "My name's not Juan. You are very strong, aren't you?"

By then he had closed the door behind her.

She was quite a pretty girl. The shirt looked as good as new. She looked a bit like the girl in Stuhlweissenburg, fiery little cat.

He pulled a grimace at himself in the stained mirror on the wall.

"You've got to set a good example to your little brother, you pig", he said. It sounded just a trifle bitter.

He began to dress.

Not much of an ambassador in these clothes, but there was no time to get others, and anyway clothes would never make him look anything else but what he was. A soldier. One didn't get that kind of a scar over the eye in the diplomatic service. A wash and a clean shirt were good enough.

Pike and two-hander he had left in the *carreta*, under the straw. He considered for a moment leaving his dagger at home, too, but then frowned and put it in his belt.

"You never know whether you won't meet somebody who needs a shave, too", he murmured.

He put on his cap and walked out.

The sentinel at the palace called an officer.

The officer asked, "Does Her Highness know that you are coming?"

"I have no idea," said Uli truthfully, and the officer glared at him suspiciously.

"Who sent you here?"

"His Worship the mayor of Basel in Switzerland", said Uli gravely and this time the officer did not doubt his word.

"Do they worship their mayors there now?" he asked raising his eyebrows.

"They didn't when I left", replied Uli innocently.

"Anything's possible with those damned heretics." The officer grunted. "You're a heretic, too, perchance?"

"I never worshipped a mayor," said Uli, "and I do not worship you either. Do you mind announcing me now? I've come a long way.

"Her Highness is not so easily approachable to anybody who just—well, maybe you'd better come with me. We'll see what Don Antonio Carbajal has to say."

They crossed the spacious court and entered the palace. Uli began to feel better. Once a man was walking on a soft carpet he had a chance. A sergeant was almost always a more difficult obstacle than a captain.

But Don Antonio Carbajal was no captain. He was a tall, lean, cadaverous-looking man in black velvet with a collar of very fine white lace.

"Basel?" he asked. "What on earth does the mayor of Basel want of Her Highness?"

"That's not for me to say, sir", was Uli's polite answer.

"Indeed it isn't." Don Antonio began to caress his graying mustache. Suddenly he said in Swiss-German, "How do I know that you are an *Eidgenosse*?"

"There is no way of finding that out", said Uli in the same language. "For if it is possible for you, sir, to speak the language of my people so fluently and without an accent, how could I possibly prove that I am not really a Portuguese or a Turk in disguise?"

Don Antonio smiled. He was flattered.

"We'll see what can be done", he said. "I shall ask Her Highness. You may wait here."

He disappeared, and Uli remained stockstill where he was. It was only too probable that behind one of those curtains eyes were watching him. Her Highness was well guarded, and that was only natural. She was a Frenchwoman by birth, and there was a war on between Spain and France.

He had always suspected the real reason why the commander had sent him as his messenger rather than one of his more experienced agents. A Swiss was not likely to have sympathies for either side.

194

Don Antonio returned. "You are a very lucky young man", he said. "Follow me."

The way went through a long series of rooms and ended in the most luxurious one he had ever seen.

He knew little or nothing about such things, but it was not difficult to gather that the carpets, pictures, and statues were priceless.

But the most glittering thing in the room was a group of three ladies and the most glittering one of the three was the one in the middle, a small, round lady with a heart-shaped face smiling from under a sparkling tiara and a high collar of lace that made the one on Don Antonio's collar look like a kitchen towel. She had round eyes, and yet they managed to look haughty. She had a small, arrogant nose, and that smile meant nothing except that it showed two rows of pearly teeth; it belonged to her dress and her makeup.

If she weren't a Christian princess, thought Uli, she'd make a damned good heathen idol.

Her hair had the color of spun copper.

It was quite impossible to judge her age, she was so carefully made up. Perhaps she wasn't an idol after all, but a dish, very elaborate and very sweet, a dish fit for a king, if the king had good stomach nerves.

He bowed as best he could, and the lady giggled a little and asked, "Why did the good people of Basel bleed you before they sent you here?"

And she passed a very white finger across a very white forehead, imitating the line of his scar.

Uli grinned cheerfully. "They knew full well I was going to meet the most beautiful princess alive, and they thought it would be too dangerous if I had too much blood."

"Young man—" began Don Antonio sternly, but the lady beckoned him to be silent. Still laughing, she said, "As you are no longer dangerous, I think we can dispense with etiquette."

The two ladies-in-waiting left smiling, Don Antonio not without reluctance.

"You have our permission to sit down", said the lady in a loud voice. He knew instinctively that this was unusual, but he obeyed, and he heard her whisper, "They can see you too clearly when you stand. Are you really from Basel?"

"I'm a Swiss, Madam," said Uli, "but not from Basel."

"I thought so. Who sent you?"

"General André de Foix", whispered Uli. "I have a letter. . . ."

She was no longer smiling. "Give it to me, but don't raise your arm."

She took it quickly, opened it, and read.

"*C'est de la folie toute pure*", she murmured.

"Yes, I thought it was a little mad", murmured Uli.

She began to giggle again.

"One should never have cousins", she said. "They will always ask for the impossible. This letter is dated—let me see—ah, I thought so."

"Before Noain", said Uli. "And long before Fuentarrabia. I thought it was out of date, but my order was to deliver it."

"You know the contents of the letter?"

He shook his head. "All I can do is guess."

"Guessing", said Germaine de Foix, "is a dangerous game. I think it would be very much better not to guess."

"I am very bad at it anyway", he lied cheerfully.

"And I believe everything I am told." She smiled again. "But I cannot make you out. You are not a noble. . . ."

"I'm a Swiss," said Uli, "and we believe that we are all nobles there."

196

"Oh, oh!" The lady smiled. "And they say it's the Spaniards who are proud. I am not going to inquire about your status. I will not even guess. It does not matter." She let the letter disappear in her corsage. "Perhaps we have paid too little attention to Switzerland— and the Swiss."

"Is there anything Your Highness wishes me to tell the— mayor of Basel?" asked Uli and then remembered that it was a breach of etiquette to ask questions when talking to a person of royal rank. But then, everything so far had been against all etiquette.

Germaine de Foix stared at him as if he had two heads, but she recovered quickly. "I do not understand", she said. "We often receive visits of courtesy from faraway countries. We wish each other all manner of good things, and that is all. Except of course, if we receive a written message—a letter. But ..." she leaned forward a little, "but we have not received any letter in this case."

He looked straight into her eyes, now very hard and commanding. "I see", he said.

"There has been no letter of any kind", she repeated softly.

He began to have a better opinion of her. She was not only a dazzlingly beautiful woman whom it amused to receive a simple man whose manners were different from those of her courtiers. She had brains. And perhaps she was even trying to be loyal to her new country ... or else she did not want to jeopardize her position. Or both. In any case it looked very much as if the general had made a mistake, and perhaps a serious one. He was not much good as a general; he seemed even less effective as a politician.

"The mayor of Basel", said Germaine de Foix, "must content himself with my good wishes for his well-being. It is the best I can do for him."

"I understand, Your Highness."

"You have an intelligent face", said the astonishing woman. "It's an ugly face, but it has its points."

He chuckled. He could not help it. "I understand also, Your Highness, that any man who has ever been in your service will dream of you as long as he lives. It is inevitable, however high or low his position. I shall have to dream in the future, like Don Iñigo de Loyola."

"Loyola? Loyola—where have I heard that name?" She looked up to the ceiling. The line from neck to shoulder was perfect; the best poets at court had competed in raving about it.

"I believe he was one of Your Highness' pages."

"Oh, now I remember!" She broke into silvery laughter. *"Le petit* Loyola. Yes. He used to read poetry to me, some of Montesino's and some of his own. My Spanish was not too good in those days, and he had such a hard Basque accent. *Le petit* Loyola! How is he?"

"He was badly wounded in the war", said Uli. "I took him back to his castle, and in his fever he talked of Your Highness all the time."

*"Tiens, c'est émouvant.* But surely—he was fighting on the Spanish side, wasn't he?"

"Indeed he was, Your Highness. He was defending the citadel of Pamplona, when he was hit in the leg by a cannonball. I had the honor of transporting him back to Loyola, because . . ."

"Because?"

"Because it was—a compatriot of mine, a Swiss who had fired the shot that wounded him", said Uli.

She read him like a book.

"Poetic justice", she said.

"Those were the very words of my—of the commander-in-chief, Madam." Uli nodded.

Germaine de Foix shook her head. "Men are incalculable animals", she said pensively. "Did my poor page know who had shot him?"

"Yes, Madam."

"*Ce pauvre petit Loyola*. And he is still devoted to me after all these years? It is really most touching. I ought to be very angry with you, Master Swiss! But I forgot: it was not you who half murdered him; it was only a compatriot of yours." She smiled. "In any case I think you ought to make amends for the action of a fellow-Swiss, don't you?"

"It will be as Your Highness commands", said Uli.

"Indeed it will, and I command it. You may not know it, but there is no actual war going on now between Spain and France. There are no French troops left on Spanish soil, and there is hope that they will come to some understanding."

Uli grinned broadly. "That makes my—mission—rather a ludicrous affair, I'm afraid. Here I go wandering through half of Spain, and in the meantime . . ."

"These things happen", interposed the princess curtly. "In any case your 'mission', as you call it, has nothing to do with it. You are concerned only with the mayor of the good city of Basel, and it would be most regrettable if you forgot it."

He bowed silently.

"But things being what they are," pursued the lady, "there can be no reason for you to hurry back."

"I can see that." He nodded.

"And therefore I want you to go on—what did you call it?—a 'mission'—for me. Will you do that?"

"If Your Highness commands", said Uli. "I'll go anywhere, even to the Turks or the Arabs."

He was a little surprised at himself. Faith, he thought. I believe I really mean it. What is the matter with the woman? How does she do it?

Germaine de Foix was not surprised at all.

"Very well, then", she said. "I want you to go and visit my poor little page and give him this ..." She took a ring from her finger and gave it to him. "Tell him to wear it in memory of me and as a sign that I have not forgotten him."

It was a very beautiful ruby set in gold.

"As for you", she went on. "Is there anything I can do for you?"

"The sun warms the earth," said Uli, "and the earth is very grateful."

"The sun—" the princess laughed—"must go into an eclipse now. Maybe you ought to have been born a noble— you talk like a courtier. But I forgot that all Swiss are nobles. They tell me, however, that even nobles need money when they travel. Open the little cupboard on the left for me, please—yes, that one. There is a purse there, behind all the knickknacks. Have you found it? Good. Keep it."

She rose.

"Your Highness overwhelms me", said Uli, and once more he meant what he said.

"Do I?" she asked, suddenly all woman. "It is a very pleasant thing to do, just a little like playing God. But that is a sinful thought, I'm sure." The next moment she was again royalty.

She stretched out her hand, and he kissed it, kneeling on one knee as a soldier does when swearing the oath of fealty or before going into battle.

He walked out in a dream.

A lackey, walking before him, showed him the way to the door.

The officer on duty now gave him a respectful salute, and the sentry followed his example. The fellow did not look like much, but he had spent over an hour at the palace. There had to be something in him.

Uli did not even notice. Holy Frundsberg! he thought. Holy mayor of Basel! One need not have a fever to rave about that little lady. And a man can get drunk on other things beside wine. Better snap out of it, or you'll reel about like the village idiot on his birthday.

But he was still mildly drunk when he reached the *posada*.

He knocked at the boy's door. There was no answer. He opened the door cautiously. The room was empty.

He frowned a little. He did not like Juan to wander around alone. He went back to his own room, but as he entered he saw that he must have made a mistake: there was a young girl sitting in it.

"I'm sorry", he began. Then he said, "What the devil is the meaning of this?"

Juanita said defiantly, "I told you I didn't want to be a boy all my life."

"That's no reason to dress up like this, here in Valencia of all places. What do you think you are doing, you silly— fellow? Walking in as a boy and walking out as a girl. Do you want to have us both arrested?"

"Arrested? What for? It's no crime to be a girl, is it?"

"Listen, Juan . . ."

"My name is Juanita."

"Your name will be dragged in the mud, whatever it is, if you behave like this."

She lifted her chin. "I know only too well that my poor dress cannot compare with the wonderful elegance of the lady you went to see."

"What's that got to do with it?" By all the devils and all the saints, how could a man ever hope to understand what was going on in the head of a woman! "Juan! You have even powdered your face and put salve on your lips. What's come over you? You look like a dancing girl!"

The little chin went still higher. Her eyes flashed.

"I suppose you paid similar compliments to that lady in the palace, did you?"

He stared at her strangely.

She had grown. The very simplicity of her little dress showed off the natural beauty of her young freshness as stiff brocade and glittering collars of lace could never have done. Only a few months, he thought. She was no longer a child. However much he might try to persuade himself, he knew that he could never again think of her as a child.

"I will have no nonsense", he said gruffly. "You'll have plenty of time to be a girl when you are safely back in your mother's house."

She gazed at him intently. "Is she *very* beautiful?" she asked. "Are you going to dream about her—like Don Iñigo?"

He burst into laughter, and she turned pale with rage.

"You don't think I'd mind that, do you?" she cried. "Why should I?"

"Quite", he said, still laughing.

"You may dream as much as you like", she decided haughtily. "And I hope you'll get a fever like Don Iñigo, too. The vanity of a man! I really think you thought it mattered to me. Well, it doesn't. Not a bit."

"Of course not", he said.

"There's nothing to laugh about either", she snapped at him. "Oh, you're-you're horrible."

She burst into tears and ran toward the door.

"Good heavens, little one, what is the matter with you?" he said. With three long strides he was at the door before she could reach it. "Little one—"

When he touched her arm, she went limp, and he stretched out both hands to keep her from falling. For the length of one breath or two she was in his arms, and he saw her young mouth, soft and inviting. Then her head drooped, and suddenly she gave a low, moaning cry, her body stiffened, and she struggled free.

"The ring, she gave you a ring."

He looked at her in dismay.

"Well, yes, but . . ."

"She loves you. I knew it would happen. I knew it all the time."

He ruffled his hair. "You crazy little idiot. How can you believe such a silly thing? She is a great lady. You yourself told me what she was and is. She . . ."

"She loves you. She is a woman, isn't she? And you have accepted her ring."

"Will you see reason, you stupid little bumblehead? She's given me that ring for your Spaniard, for Don Iñigo de Loyola. I'm to take it to him."

"I don't believe it", she sobbed, and ran out of the room, stumbling over the skirts she was no longer accustomed to wearing.

He sat down heavily on his bed.

It was all so absurd, and yet he could not laugh.

He wanted to laugh, to laugh it off; after all, most girls went through a stage like that when they grew up, silly little creatures. Instead he grunted angrily.

Only an hour ago he had been sitting before one of the world's most bewitching women, the queen not only of Spain but of Elf Land, and though it had gone to his head like sweet old wine, like the sparkling wine they made in the Champagne, he had never felt uncertain of himself.

And now he did.

It was pity, of course. She was so genuinely unhappy, a wounded little fawn. It was pity. What else?

He gave a deep sigh.

203

It had not been pity. Not that moment at the door when her little body went limp and . . .

He wiped his forehead.

It was time this journey came to an end.

Glumly he stared out of the window.

After a while there was a soft, coughing noise from behind him, and he turned.

The boy Juan was standing in the door. Uli saw that he had scrubbed his face. He held a bundle under his arm, and Uli knew it contained the girl's outfit.

"What is it—Juan?" asked Uli.

"I—I just wanted to say—I'm ready, if you want to leave." He gazed at the boy, at the bundle under his arm, and again at the boy's bleak little face.

"All right, little brother", he said wearily.

He rose.

"There's something else", said the boy timidly. "I'm sorry I said I didn't believe you. You never lied to me."

"I may start lying any moment now."

"You never lied", insisted the boy. "So, if you say the ring is for Don Iñigo, it's for him. He will be so happy, too."

"So would anyone be", said Uli. "Let's go."


CHAPTER TWENTY-SEVEN


THE WOMEN, scrubbing away at their laundry in the shallow water of the river Cardoner, never lacked themes to discuss, but lately the tongues had wagged harder than ever.

The wintry air struck sharply at their lips and nostrils without discouraging them in the least.

"L'home del sach" had passed by a few minutes ago, a small, shadowy figure with an unkempt beard and unkempt hair, nails like claws, and with his eyes half closed as usual.

"When I think how many people wonder where he goes when he disappears", said Concepción Valdez contemptuously. "And it's so simple. The cave, up there, near the old bridge. That's where he sits for hours, doing nothing."

"How can you know he's doing nothing, Concepción? He's praying, maybe."

"Plenty of time for that on Sunday at Mass", said Concepción resolutely. "Me, I work—and so do you."

Pilar Gónzalez nodded in silent agreement, but Rosa Bigorra shook her head vigorously.

"There is all kinds of work", she said. "And there's all kinds of people."

*"He's* not doing any work", insisted Concepción. "He's begging. Getting other people's work for nothing, that's what it is."

"Go on, you don't really grudge him a piece of bread, do you now? It's all he eats in a whole day. . . ."

"It isn't", snapped Concepción. "I saw him sneak away with a whole armful of good things, cake and meat and wine, too. Saw it with my own eyes."

"Cat", said Rosa Bigorra.

"What?"

"Cat", repeated Rosa Bigorra. *"He* never ate the stuff. He took it to Saint Lucy's and fed it to those who can't move."

"And how do you know that?" Concepción Valdez sniffed. *"You* don't live at Saint Lucy's, do you?"

"No, but my aunt does", said Rosa curtly. "Got it from her. And you knew my aunt's living there. Cat."

"Shame", interposed another woman. "Picking on him like that, I mean. Everybody can see the poor man eats next to nothing. Only skin and bones, he is."

"He frightens me."

"He doesn't frighten the children, though. That's always a good sign, I think. He's been teaching my little Carlos the catechism, very nicely and with a lot of patience, and María and Dolores Passos and Miguel Torres and Francisco Bijar, too."

"And you know what Señora Pascual says?"

They all listened now. Inés Pascual was a well-to-do lady whose word counted in the little town.

Rosa Bigorra looked around with satisfaction. "She says he is a saint", she told them. "Nothing less than that. She says it's thanks to him that we haven't got a single case of plague in Manresa, when Barcelona is full of them, with people dying like flies, she says."

"The saints preserve us", said Concepción Valdez hastily. "I didn't mean what I said about the poor devil—about—him, I mean."

"Doing a lot of good he is. They love him at Saint Lucy's, and the Dominican fathers have a bed for him any time he goes there. They wouldn't do that for most other tramps."

"Señora Pascual says he's a man from a noble family", said Rosa Bigorra.

Again they all looked at her.

"She says she can see it from his face and hands even if he lets his beard and his nails go the way he does. 'You can't deceive *me* about such a thing', she says."

"Anyway, the children like him. That's a good sign, I always say."

"They call him *l'home del sach*, don't they?"

"Yes, and he smiles at them when they shout it after him. *L'home sant*, that's what he is if you ask me."

"They found him in a dead faint the other day before Our Lady of Villadordis."

"Not enough in the belly, that's what it is. But some people would grudge him a crust of bread."

"I never said nothing", said Concepción sullenly.

"Who's mentioned names? And I dunno whether it's just the food. They say he often goes off in a queer way, eyes wide open and seeing nobody. My brother Pedro found him kneeling with his arms crossed, and he didn't notice him at all, and Pedro looking him straight in the face and making a noise, too."

"If he can keep the plague off Manresa, he's all right with me", said Concepción. "It's an awful thing when they get giddy and drop like they have been poleaxed and break out in spots and vomit black bile. . . ."

"Mercy, Mary! Hush! I can't listen to such things."

*L'home del sach* was sitting in his usual place again, in front of the little cave.

The Cardoner was deep here, a broad, green flood with a thousand little white eyes of foam.

He sat motionless, and if he was praying it was mental prayer. He did not move his lips.

Sometimes he foreknew that he would be taken again, and sometimes it came suddenly, without the slightest warning. Like lightning coming from a blue sky.

He never tried to make it happen. He knew it would be quite futile, like trying to make the sun rise at midnight or the stars at noon.

He was back in the womb here in the cave, and it was meet and just for one to be newborn.

He was a newborn child elsewhere, and like a helpless babe they had to feed him.

Slowly, very slowly, he began to see the new world in which he was to grow up.

The time when all this had been almost intolerably hard was gone now.

Gone also was the time when the sins of his past crawled up in him again and again, and with them the terrible fear that he had forgotten some of them at his general confession at Montserrat, and that he was still held by the secret pincers of the enemy.

He had almost killed himself with mortification and with an ever increasing number of strokes with the iron chain to defeat the enemy in the body, the old animal.

It had been like wading through black water in a river under the earth, without light and almost without hope, and many a time he had been tempted to make an end to his life altogether.

That was when he saw the thing for the first time, most beautiful with its thousand luminous eyes, a wondrous thing, vibrant with life. He had felt a strange delight. And the thought welled up in him how much beauty he was missing, and the question dropped down to his soul, noisily like the splash of water on stone: "How can I live like this—when it may be for another forty years?"

At once he recognized the enemy and fired on him, "Miserable being, can you promise me one single hour of life?"

And the shimmery thing paled and vanished.

That was not the end of his troubles, however.

The time came when he found no taste either for prayer or for Mass, and it was not like a time but rather like a darkness that suddenly fell on him like a cloak.

The priests he went to see could not help him. Again he felt tempted to throw himself from the high window of his cell in the Dominican monastery. But he remembered in time

Christ's own temptation to throw himself from the roof of the temple, and he cried out, "Lord, I will do nothing to offend thee!" and it passed—but only to return.

That time had gone now, too—ever since he had seen with the eye that was open day and night. It was not the eye that saw things awake and not the eye that saw things in a dream. It was an altogether different way of seeing, and yet it was just that: seeing.

But just as it required a new eye, it also required a new language to describe it. There were no words for it.

He had seen how God made the world—but all he could put into words was that a white mass was formed from which rays emerged, and from that God drew the light, so the mass became dimmer, as if it cooled down, and became hard, as if it were liquid metal cooling.

He had seen how Christ was present in the Blessed Sacrament, and that was even more impossible to describe.

He had seen the humanity of Christ—the principle, and yet also the Body, though without a clear integration of the limbs.

After that there was no further temptation, although the luminous thing with its many eyes still turned up from time to time. But it was weaker now, and he could chase it away with a single, vigorous movement of his staff.

This time, however, it was all different.

There were no images.

Was the river talking?

But it was not a voice either; it was almost the reverse of a voice, and it made all noise slow down and become mute. The murmurings of the Cardoner and the humming of bees and the faraway voices of women ceased to be.

He had not *seen* the tremendous black wings of the archangel that day in Montserrat, not even with that new, that

209

third eye, but he had known in his innermost heart that he was there, hovering over the church and filling it at the same time.

And he was here now. He was more here than Iñigo and more than the river.

He really *was*—Iñigo and the river were shadows, slow-moving specters.

It was he who was thinking, and he was thinking in Iñigo, and there had never been such clarity of thought.

There was no arduous climbing along a logical line to a conclusion, no weariness and no smug pride when it was reached.

It was not like an internal flash of light either, the way an idea reaches a man as it were from nowhere. One moment he was without it, and now here it was, and it made a man's eyes gleam and made him snap his fingers, I've got it, that's it, and a little glow of pride as if it were all his own.

It was a steady light.

Everything was lit up at once in length and past and breadth and present and depth and future, and this was the key to the door and the door itself and the room, to which it led and the person who was in the room, and he himself was that person, though he was also the key.

That was how his mind worked, and this was how a woman's mind worked, and a child's was such at this age and such again at another.

What time did to man and what sin did to man, and the mother's presence and the father's; the generation of the body, oh, the miracubus sequence and the generation of thought and the infusion of the soul and the keys to human music and what they mean to music on a different plane.

The mind of man and the wondrous way it could be played upon and the extension it could take in this direction and that, if it were put into a certain mold and shaped in a certain way.

The way of leaders of men in war and in things of the state and where they succeeded or failed and why and how the threads of success and of failure in the actions of a king and a beggar and a halfwit were woven into the golden thread of God and straightened out to clear lines in the geometry of Love.

When the wings withdrew, there was no loneliness. He was no longer overshadowed, but the mind seed was left in him, and he knew that it would grow and that he would pass it on and that this was required of him, and he rose and limped to the cross at the wayside, and he fell on his knees and gave thanks.

They found him there, under the cross, a few hours later, first two old women on their way to the church, then a young man of the name of Ferrer who insisted that *l'home del sach* should be taken to his father's house in town, and from a nearby farm he got a little *carreta* drawn by a donkey and a man to go with it, and they lifted *l'home del sach* into it. On their way to town they passed the women still washing their laundry, and Pilar said it was not surprising when a man had nothing in his belly, and Rosa Bigorra said that one could never know with a man who was probably what Señora Pascual had said he was, and Concepción Valdez said she hoped he would recover because it would be too awful if the plague came to Manresa.

Ferrer, a careful man, had looked into the cave before they left. All he found he put into the *carreta*. It was very little: a staff; a book with the title *The Imitation of Christ*; a notebook, almost full of notes in a clear, precise handwriting; a pen and an inkpot; and a second notebook, a little over half filled with notes and titled *Spiritual Exercises*. That was all.

# CHAPTER TWENTY-EIGHT

When the Puerta Neuva of Barcelona opened at long last, the girl Juanita raced through it like a hare, and Uli, despite his long legs, had difficulty keeping up with her.

For seven maddening days they had been kept in quarantine in a camp full of emergency tents, right in sight of the gate.

The plague in the city had subsided, but the city fathers were being careful lest new arrivals should bring in fresh cases and start the terrible race with death all over again.

They had been visited and examined by physicians who wore white, monklike apparel, the hoods drawn tightly over their heads, with narrow slits for eyes and mouth, and sniffed at phials filled with vinegar and spices.

Most fortunately there had been no plague carrier among them, or they would have been kept in the camp indefinitely.

Naturally Juanita had become anxious. The nature of their journey had made it impossible for her mother to answer her letters, and rumors had it that thousands had died of the plague within the last two months alone.

He had done his best to divert her, but she had been in a difficult mood ever since Valencia, shy and yet tense; he could not make her out at all.

It was as if she wanted to withdraw into herself and found the entrance blocked.

Now at last action released her tension.

They had left the *carreta* and the mules at the gate and hurried through the Calle de Corders to the Plaza de Lana and down the Calle Febres.

Twice in that short distance Uli had seen houses with a large black cross painted at the door, and he knew that she must have seen them too.

Suddenly she stopped before a small house, and he saw her falter. Her hands went up to her mouth.

"Mother!" she cried in a strangled voice. "Mother ... Mother ..."

Uli came just in time to catch her. With the girl in his arms he stared at the black cross on the door.

The long scar on his forehead began to pucker, and his mouth was grim. Hear a prayer, God, he thought. If you can hear at all what we are saying down here, listen now. Mothers must die, sure enough. We all must die. You gave us that present as well as the gift of offending you, as the priests like to say. You made the plague, too, didn't you? Or if you didn't, who else did? And if someone else did, why didn't you stop him? What's *she* done that this should happen to her now? When I bring her back after all she has gone through. But you don't care. You don't care. Up there somewhere in your great and horrible majesty you are happy—and we rot.

A constable walked up, but stopped at a healthy distance.

"Is the girl ill?" he asked.

"No. Fainted. That's her mother who is in there."

"Was in there", corrected the constable wearily. "She died ten days ago."

"Where does she lie?"

The man shrugged his shoulders. "She had to be buried quickly, with the others. You know how it is. Sure the girl has not fallen ill?"

"Quite sure. Can I get her in there now?"

"Are you mad? The house is unclean. Must be left as it is for three months. Are you her husband?"

"No."

"Brother?"

"No", repeated Uli.

"Do you know whether she has any relations here, apart from her mother?" asked the constable.

"No. Do you? She is Juanita Pérez."

"This is a big town", said the constable.

"Do you know a *posada* around here?"

"There's one at the Plaza de Lana. The Catalan. I'll help you to carry her there."

"No", said Uli again. No one else was to touch her. He stalked away on his long legs, the girl in his arms.

The constable looked after him. He had seen that so often. Like a walking cross, he thought.

He went on, crossing himself.

CHAPTER TWENTY-NINE

THE CHURCH OF SANTA MARIA DEL MAR, not very far from the port of Barcelona, was almost empty.

Only around the altar steps and on them a flock of children was listening to the sermon of an old priest, and in their midst a man in a simple black habit was sitting who might have been their schoolteacher. He had a huge, domed forehead and a small, pointed beard.

Further back two well-dressed ladies were watching, whispering to each other.

"That's how I saw him first, two weeks ago", said Isabel Roser. "And I was all aglow. I knew I had to meet him—

something kept urging me to call him, but of course I couldn't do such a thing. When I came home I told my husband—I didn't think he was going to listen to me, but he did, and he even helped me to find him. My dear, how much I owe you, for bringing him to Barcelona! I have never heard a man talk as he does, and yet there he sits, listening to poor old Padre Boñaz as if he were a child. How I envy you for having him stay at your own house!"

Inés Pascual shook her head. "I see very little of him", she whispered back. "He's using a small room in my house as his cell, that is all. He refuses to have a meal there. Instead he goes out and begs for bread in the streets, just as he did in Manresa."

"He is overdoing it."

"He certainly used to overdo it. He spent several weeks in the house of my uncle, Carlos Ferrer in Manresa, flat on his back, with his life in the balance. We nursed him back to health, and I talked to Carlos, and he persuaded him to put on this habit we had made for him instead of that sacklike thing he was wearing, and *that* wasn't easy. And that's all he would accept. I hope he won't let his hair and beard grow again the way he used to."

"Without you he would never have got here", said Isabel Roser fervently. "My husband and I shall never be able to thank you enough. I know only too well how difficult it is to do anything for him. He was going to sail today, as you know, on that little brigantine, the *Feria*, and we had the greatest difficulty persuading him to wait for a better ship sailing next week. The *Feria*, my dear—I would not allow a little dog of mine to sail in her. She's not only a bad ship, but the captain and the crew are either criminals or the nearest thing to it."

"He says he is going to Rome", said Inés Pascual.

215

"Yes, can you understand that, my dear? Rome! I know, it will always remain a holy city, but one hears so many stories—Fray Damaro said only the other day it was just as well not to wander about in the kitchen of God. . . ."

They giggled a little at that, but just then the old priest ended his sermon, and the children got up.

The two ladies, too, rose and walked toward the door.

The little, dark figure of a girl in one of the last pews caught Isabel Roser's eye. She has been crying, she thought with casual compassion. But—I know that girl, don't I? She came a little closer. Of course she knew her. It was María Pérez' little daughter, whom she had sent to—was it Burgos or Pamplona? Anyway, one of the two, and her name was Joaquita or Juanita.

She stopped beside the pew and bent down to the girl.

"You are María Pérez' daughter, aren't you?"

"Doña Isabel . . ." The girl struggled to her feet.

"There, there, so you haven't forgotten me. What is the matter with you, child? Is there something wrong?"

The girl's lips trembled. "My mother, Doña Isabel . . ."

"Oh, my poor lamb, I am so sorry." A terrible idea came to Isabel Roser. "It wasn't—your poor mother didn't have the . . ."

"Yes, Doña Isabel. She died of the plague, two weeks ago."

I will not recoil, thought Isabel Roser bravely. I will not, if it kills me. Well, it's two weeks ago . . . If the girl were infected, it would have shown by now. I can stop playing the heroine. And she said, "Were you with her, when it happened?"

The girl shook her head despairingly. "No. No, Doña Isabel. That makes it so much worse. I was not with her. I only arrived here a few days ago."

"Now they won't let you into the house, of course." It was a cruel law, but necessary. "Where are you staying?"

"At a *posada* in the Plaza de Lana. The Catalan it's called."

"What? A girl alone? How utterly impossible. I was a friend of your mother's. I cannot tolerate such a thing a moment longer. You come straight with me."

"But, Doña Isabel . . ."

"Don't say another word, my poor dear child. Just come along. *Santísima Virgen*, a girl of a friend of mine alone in a *posada*, where men sit and drink."

Over the good lady's shoulder Juanita saw Uli, sitting quietly in the last pew. She had not even known that he was there, that he was in the church. He must have slipped in behind her. She saw him nodding vigorously and pointing to Doña Isabel; he seemed to have heard everything, and he wanted her to accept.

Of course he wanted her to accept. She could not very well go on roaming with him across the country like—like a gypsy girl. She was a burden to him.

Her eyes filled with tears. "You are very good, Doña Isabel", she murmured tonelessly.

"Nonsense, child, now come along."

Still she hesitated. But now the children were all around them, a whole swarm of little heads. Swirling arms and energetic little shoulders swept them away and out of the door.

A sudden gust of wind made the women clutch their hats. Their long dresses billowed.

"Just as well he didn't sail today." Inés Pascual had to shout to make herself heard. The wind was whistling stridently.

Isabel began to explain about little Juanita, but had to wait till the wind subsided.

Uli had not budged. He stared ahead without seeing anything.

It's better this way, he thought grimly. It had to come sometime, hadn't it? It's better like this.

Perhaps it was even the best thing not to look her up at all. In any case he wasn't going to leave here till they had gone. Or else they would start questions again, like that constable. "You her husband? Her brother?"

He groaned.

The thing to do was to go to that confounded old castle of Loyola, give the man his ring—if he was still alive—and then go and look for somebody, prince, duke, or bishop, who needed a pair of arms in some war against somebody else. It's the only decent thing to do, he thought, with clenched teeth. And I'm going to do it—not because of you, God—in spite of you.

Then he saw the man walking slowly toward the door. He was limping a little.

He saw his face, a pale, white face with a pointed beard. I don't believe it, he thought. It can't be. I don't believe it.

But he scrambled out of the pew.

The man did not see him, although he passed so near that Uli could have touched him, and he walked out.

Uli followed, his head whirling. He saw the man join the little group of women and withdrew into the shadow of the door, watching intently.

It was Iñigo de Loyola. Without the shadow of a doubt it was Iñigo de Loyola.

He had not seen him in the church before he came walking directly toward him, but then he had scarcely seen anybody or anything, except that poor drooping head of the girl in the row in front of him.

It was Iñigo de Loyola. There was no need for that limp of his to make him feel certain about it. Although he had changed, and not only in dress.

Juanita was bound to recognize him, but would he recognize her? He had never seen her as a girl before.

He watched the little group like a hawk.

He could not hear what they said to each other, because the wind was whistling so loudly. It was growing dark, too.

The lady who had addressed Juanita now seemed to introduce her to Iñigo, and she curtsied a little. He could see Iñigo's face, void of expression, staring at the girl. Then the lady turned to the other one, explaining something to her, and he saw Iñigo's finger go up to his lips. He did not wish to be recognized.

A scream came from somewhere, shrill and terrifying, and they all looked in the direction from which it had come. It was the scream of a woman, a disheveled old hag, running across the plaza with her mouth wide open. "Sunk!" she screamed. "Sunk with all hands."

"Who? What?" asked a bald-headed man.

They came running from all sides now. The Plaza de Lana was never empty, and the woman's scream had been loud enough to awaken the dead.

"What's happened, Rosina?"

"Sunk", repeated the woman, wild eyed. "The first squall took her—went down like a stone. We all saw it—I saw it—and Antonio is on her—let me go, I must tell his father...."

Even the wind seemed to hold its breath.

"But what ship?" shouted the bald-headed man. "Not the *Stella Maris*, is it?"

"No—the *Feria*—let me go ..."

She ran on, screaming again.

"Oh my God in heaven", cried Inés Pascual. "The *Feria*—and you might have been on her...."

"God did not want it so", said Iñigo, and he pressed Isabel Roser's hand.

"Isabel," sobbed Inés Pascual, "you saved his life; you and your dear husband have saved his life...."

Uli watched the scene with cold eyes. He had seen it so often before. One man was saved from death—and ten, twenty, fifty others were drowned. Or fifty were saved, and one was drowned. And they tried to make a kind of justice out of the terror and confusion that was life.

So this man of Loyola had been saved again. You could not kill him with a cannon shot, and you could not sink him either, it seemed. Maybe he had nine lives like a cat. Or— like an old soldier.

The wind had subsided, but now the first drops of rain began to fall and broke up the group of women.

"We'd better get home quickly", said Isabel Roser. "I have a nice room for you, Juanita. You will like it, and it's quite near, in the Calle de Cotoners. Let's go quickly, all of us."

Inés Pascual was willing, but Iñigo shook his head and murmured a few words of excuse.

Isabel Roser made a half-regretful gesture as if to indicate that she had not really expected anything else. As she and Inés Pascual led Juanita away, Iñigo gave a courteous little bow. When the women had disappeared, he remained for a while where he was, without heeding the rain that now fell steadily. Then he turned and came up the steps to the door of the church again.

"Don Iñigo de Loyola", said Uli.

Iñigo stopped as if he had received a blow.

For the first time Uli saw his face from very near.

It was so changed that he marveled at having recognized him at all. It seemed to be molded of white wax. The eyes under their heavy lids were enormous, the mouth a thin, bloodless line; the hair had begun to recede at the temples and was graying; the cheekbones were prominent. But it was the expression of the face that had changed most, and he could not make it out at all. For surely it was as strong, as indomitable as ever, despite the suffering it showed so clearly. What was the change? What did it consist of?

"Don't you recognize me, Don Iñigo?"

"Sergeant Ulric von der Flue", said Iñigo slowly.

"That's right. And the little lady they introduced to you, you recognized her, too, didn't you?"

The shadow of a smile went over the emaciated face.

"She is a good girl", said Iñigo. "I always knew that. But a man does not always talk of what he knows."

"I think I understand what you mean", said Uli.

"I am a pilgrim", said Iñigo. "What I was before that does not matter and concerns no one."

"I understand." Uli nodded.

"Beyond that," said Iñigo, "I am most grateful to you."

"Grateful? To me? What for?"

"Because you shot me", said Iñigo, and he moved to walk on.

"Don't go", said Uli quickly. It was not easy to keep his thoughts straight, but it had to be done. "I have a message to deliver to you. And if I hadn't run into you here, I would have had to go all the way to Loyola castle."

"A message?"

"Yes, from a very great lady, who was the queen of Spain not very long ago. Queen Germaine. I have come from Valencia."

Not so much as a flicker went over Iñigo's face.

"You have seen the lady?" he asked courteously. "Is she well?"

"Very well, I should say." Was the man no longer human? He had enquired about Germaine de Foix as if she were an elderly relative.

"The lady has charged me", he said, "to visit you and give you this ring"—he took it from his finger and handed it over—"and to tell you to wear it in memory of her and as a sign that she has not forgotten you."

Iñigo looked at the red eye of the ring. The rain had suddenly stopped, and the sun breaking through the clouds made the ruby sparkle like a star.

"The man to whom the lady sent this ring no longer exists", he said softly. "Please take it."

Uli stepped back, aghast.

"Someone will find it", said Iñigo casually and dropped it. Then he gave his courteous little nod and walked into the church.


## CHAPTER THIRTY


X̱ERES WINE was a good thing.

When the third pitcher tasted as good as the first, it was a sure sign that it was good wine.

Anyway, it was the best they had at The Catalan.

It did not make a man drunk either. Not much.

I'm not drunk yet, thought Uli, taking another sip. But I shall be. I shall be very drunk, and what else is there to be in a world that's gone mad. It's the world. Not I. There's nothing in the least mad about me. I can still think. Quite clearly. But people don't make sense any longer.

He began to play with the ruby.

"I did not drop you", he said. "I picked you up. Because I'm not mad. You're worth a hundred ducats if you're worth a piece of copper. You're not the kind of thing a sane man drops on the steps of a church. Faith, the streets of Barcelona are not plastered with things like that. 'Someone will find it', he said."

He took another sip.

He had not just picked the ring up and walked off with it. He had put it back on his finger and waited. Not at the church door, but in the street, on the plaza, behind the well. After about half an hour Don Iñigo had come out and walked away. Uli had followed. He had been very careful about it, but it was quite unnecessary. Don Iñigo did not once turn his head. He walked up the Calle de Corders, very slowly, his little black cap in his hand, and begged. Begged.

Somebody gave him a few copper pieces and was thanked politely in the name of God.

And why not? He had thanked the man who had shot him for having shot him, hadn't he?

A man with the mind of a general.

He thanks me because I shot him, thought Uli. He refuses to accept a ring worth a hundred ducats. And he begs for coppers. I may be a little drunk, just a little. But it isn't I who is mad. Holy Frundsberg!

The trouble was he knew perfectly well that the man was not mad either. He was changed. He was another man. And when he said something it had a meaning.

What was going on in the man?

The way those women had looked at him, as if he were a saint. Well, women were easily impressed.

A pilgrim, eh? Where to? Why?

Bah, why bother?

He emptied his goblet.

"Why?" he asked aloud. He unbuttoned his doublet. The wine made him feel hot. Or perhaps it was hot. To shoot a man was one thing. To put him on an entirely different road was another. Who did that? Who made use of one thing to bring about another?

And the way he reacted to the name of the lady who had meant so much to him only a few months ago. His queen, his great lady. Juan had been so sure that he loved her.

How was it done—to forget—to get over a—a thing like that? Perhaps one should ask him how it was done. Perhaps one should ask him a great many questions.

But he was leaving. Going on his pilgrimage.

The girl was safe anyway. That was something. He had inquired right and left about that woman Isabel Roser. There was only one opinion about her. The girl was in good hands.

And that was that.

The pitcher was empty. Empty, he thought. Empty. Empty.

Well, he was free now. No need to go to Loyola castle, no need to go anywhere. Not much sense in trying to find André de Foix just to tell him that his beautiful cousin couldn't do anything for him, was there?

Free. Whatever *that* meant.

He knew what it meant. It meant swearing another oath of fealty to some great lord, or even a small one, carrying his confounded livery and fighting his confounded wars for him. It meant seeing another country's misery, more houses burning, more men slain, more women raped, more children made orphans. To be free meant that he could not see Juanita any more, because of Margaret. And it meant that he could not go home because of Margaret and Kaspar Jost.

To be free meant to be a chained slave.

The funniest part of all was that he ought to be happy. He was strong and healthy, he still had a fair number of golden ducats in his pocket, and he had a ruby ring worth a nice little farm anywhere he chose to buy it.

He ought to be very happy.

224

Why, by the seven-horned devil, wasn't he happy?

Was *he* happy? That pale-faced man who despised rubies and begged for coppers?

If he was, it was not the right kind of happiness for Long Uli.

Men were different. Their happiness was different.

When he was a child, they had often told him the story of his great-uncle, Nikolaus von der Flue, who had been happily married with a whole crop of children and then left his family to settle down as a hermit in the *Ranft*.

There he spent years and years, and the rumor went that he neither ate nor drank, but lived on three things alone: his faith, his humility, and the grace of God.

So they tested him. The council had his hermitage surrounded by sentries, who watched him day and night for weeks, ready to pounce at the slightest suspicion. They had searched him first and his cell. And when he went to the village church on Sunday, they went with him, keeping him under surveillance all the time.

And they found that he really did neither eat nor drink. The only thing he ate was the Host in Holy Communion.

He was supposed to have had visions, too, and when he died, everybody agreed that he was a saint, although the Church had not said anything about that.

Brother Klaus, they called him, and Brother Klaus had been quoted to him in his parents' house as the example of Christian life, till he felt so rebellious that he always ate double portions.

Well, maybe Brother Klaus was the example of Christian life.

Maybe a man could be good only when he cut himself off from the outside world, though what kind of a world it would be if everybody followed his example was another question.

Uli began to chuckle. There was not much danger of that. The thing to do was to go down and get another pitcher of Xeres wine, better still, get three pitchers and get really drunk. He half rose, and sat down again. A fool's remedy, he thought. Eating double portions again.

Brother Klaus was well out of it all.

*Dinmut* was the Swiss word for humility. *Dinmut*—"the courage to serve". There was something in that. The courage of total service.

A soldier could understand that.

Maybe the pious old great-uncle had been a soldier of sorts, too, after all. Maybe he had chosen for himself a better master than the dukes and counts his great-nephew had served.

Certainly, even if God felt indifferent toward him, he had not felt indifferent toward God. Maybe he thought, the old fox, that by his total service he could force God not to be indifferent. He just threw himself in God's lap. He stormed heaven by force.

It was an idea. Could God afford to be outdone in generosity?

What was it he always used to pray?

Uli frowned. He had not thought of Brother Klaus for many years. God knows why he was thinking of him now. What was that prayer? They had quoted it so often at home as his favorite saying. "What did you say, Great-Uncle?"

They were sitting round the dinner table, tin plates, tin mugs, folded hands. It was snowing outside. And even before they said Grace, Father would say Great-Uncle's prayer: "My Lord and my God, take me away from myself and give me wholly to thyself."

That was it. Then it went on: "My Lord and my God, take away from me everything that hinders my way to thee."

And it ended: "My Lord and my God, give me everything that makes me come nearer to thee."

Maybe he really was what they called a saint.

Strange thing, to have a saint in the family. Not that it helped much. A cardinal, now, that might have been different. An uncle or great-uncle cardinal could do all kinds of things.

Uli frowned.

No uncle cardinal could make him understand why God was indifferent to his world. No uncle cardinal could do anything about Margaret and Kaspar Jost, or about the fact that he would not see little Juanita again, or about the terrible, idiotic senselessness of it all.

And Brother Klaus. They said miracles had happened to some people who invoked his aid. People said so many things when the day was long. And even if some of that was true, maybe Brother Klaus did not believe in nepotism. No reason why he should believe in it, especially when it was the case of a grand-nephew who had never bothered much about him and ate double portions.

Somebody knocked at the door.

"Stay out", he shouted angrily. "Whoever it is."

He turned round in a fury when the door opened—and saw the boy Juan.

The boy Juan, dressed in the suit Uli had bought for him in Segovia, came in and closed the door behind him.

Uli stared at him.

"Holy Great-Uncle", he said. "I take it all back. Holy Great-Uncle."

"I had to come to see you", said the boy Juan.

"Wait a minute", said Uli. He got up and walked to the corner of the room where the heavy water pitcher was. It was full to the brim. He lifted it high up and turned it over, and the water cascaded over his head and body. He put the pitcher down, shook himself like a dog, ruffled his wet hair with both hands, sneezed vehemently, and stared at the boy again.

"Sure you are yourself?" he asked suspiciously.

The boy Juan looked at the array of wine pitchers on the table. "I am", he said. "Are you?"

"No", said Uli. He grinned. Then he began to frown again.

"Does the lady you are staying with know that you are here?"

"No."

"She doesn't approve of a young girl staying at a *posada*, and she's right."

"I've stayed at more *posadas* than I can count."

"She's still right. And when you get back, she'll . . ."

"I'm not going back."

"Oh, oh", he said. "Mutiny, eh?" His eyes narrowed suddenly. "They've been nasty to you? Just tell me . . ."

"Not a bit. Doña Isabel is very sweet, and so is her friend. But I'm not going back. I wish you'd listen, instead of interrupting me all the time. Don Iñigo de Loyola is here, right here in Barcelona."

"You surprise me", he said.

"So you don't have to go to Loyola castle to give him that ring."

"I see."

"But you'll have to come straight away", said the boy Juan. "Because his ship is sailing in three hours. And don't tell him I told you."

"So that's why you've come", said Uli.

"That's part of it," said the boy Juan. "I also wanted to say goodbye to you."

"Nice of you", said Uli. "Where are *you* going?"

"I am sailing with him", said the boy Juan.

"You . . . *What?*"

"He doesn't know that yet", said Juan.

"Just a minute", said Uli. "You are sailing—where? Why? What is this all about?"

"He's a saint," said the boy Juan, "and he is going on pilgrimage. And I am going with him."

"So you told me." Uli nodded. "And he doesn't know. And how are you going to pay for your passage? And where are you going anyway? Rome, I suppose."

"Pilgrims need no money", explained Juan. *"He* hasn't got any money either. Besides, I still have the ducats you gave me, and if that isn't enough, I can work."

"Has it occurred to you at all", he asked, "that he may not want you to come with him?"

"He doesn't", said the boy Juan promptly. "I know he doesn't. But I won't disturb him. I'll just go where he's going. He won't so much as see me."

"Ah", said Uli.

"I've seen him praying", said Juan. "It was as if I'd never seen anybody pray before. I've seen him begging, too. And I've heard him talk."

"I suppose that was as if you had never heard anybody talk before", said Uli drily.

"That's right. Doña Isabel says, when he talks heaven opens. She's right, too. They always want him to stay, wherever he is, but he doesn't. I heard him say goodbye to her, and he said—he said—"

"Well?"

The boy Juan looked at him gravely.

"Can you keep a secret?" he asked.

"I shall put you over my knee any moment now", bellowed Uli. "Out with it."

"He isn't going only to Rome", said Juan, quite un-ruffled. "He is going to the Holy Land."

"Oh, is he?"

"Yes. And I'm going with him."

Uli jumped. "Holy ... never mind. Do you know how you're talking? Exactly like that little girl we met at Ávila—Teresa Some-thing-or-other."

"Teresa de Cepeda", said Juan simply. "Yes. She gave me the idea."

"Perhaps you want to be a martyr, too", shouted Uli.

"I don't think so", said Juan. "But I wouldn't mind. Any-way, I'm going there."

"You're *not* going ..."

"I am. And you can't stop me. You can try as much as you like. If you take me back to Doña Isabel, I'll slip out again and again and again. If I can't get this ship, I'll get the next."

"The trouble with you", said Uli, "is that you won't let me finish a sentence. It's a very bad habit. I shall have to cure you of it. After all, you're my young brother. What I was going to say is you are not going alone. I'm coming too."

Juan's eyebrows went up. Then she gave a loud cry of joy and rushed into Uli's arms. "Oh, oh, it's too wonderful ... it's too good ..."

"That will do", said Uli, and he disengaged himself a lit-tle hastily. He began to button his doublet.

"I'm so happy", said Juan, her eyes filling with tears. "I hope Mother won't mind. . . ."

"Nonsense", he growled. "She wants you to be happy. Whether she'd approve of such a hare-brained plan as this is quite another matter."

"It's not hare-brained at all", protested Juan. "Now that you're coming, she would feel that I'm quite safe, and that *he's* quite safe too. He's so good, he won't do anything for himself. Now you'll be his bodyguard."

He grinned. "That's a great idea", he said. "I've been a bodyguard of the Pope. I've served under the emperor, under a duke, a count, a robber with a crested shield, and a town. Now I'm the bodyguard of a holy beggar." He took up his coat and bundle. "Just as well I sold the *carreta* and the mules", he said. "And I left the pike and the two-hander where they're safe. Can't take arms on a pilgrimage. Well, what are we waiting for? Out with you."

As he followed Juan, he thought: Brother Klaus, just in case it was you ... no, damn it. It *was* you. He gulped. "Thanks", he said tersely. Then he walked out.

## CHAPTER THIRTY-ONE

THE *Ciudad Real* was a good ship—and it had to be.

There was a squall soon after they had set sail, and a storm the next day.

The boy Juan was seasick and hid himself below deck.

The man whom they called "the black pilgrim" was seasick too, but remained on deck, telling his beads. When he saw Uli and the boy Juan on board, just before the ship sailed, he had bowed his head politely, and that was all.

Neither of the two tried to speak to him.

On the third day—the storm was still blowing with full force—Uli met the captain, a stocky little man with a fierce russet mustache. However, the mustache was the only fierce thing about him. He was a morose, uneasy man. The storm worried him. He had a wife and four children, and he wanted to see them again, he said.

Clutching a rope, Uli grinned at him. "I've been in tighter spots that this one", he shouted.

"Soldier, eh?"

"Yes, though this is a new kind of war to me ... in a wooden fortress that rolls from one side to the other."

"It's good to see a passenger so cheerful in a storm", said the captain glumly. He spat.

"Mustn't do that", said Uli reproachfully. "You're reinforcing the enemy. There's enough wet cavalry around us as it is, and all with white plumes on their helmets."

The captain pointed to the solitary little black figure, huddled up in a corner.

"Know anything about him?" he asked.

"Yes."

"Is he crazy, or is he a saint?"

"He isn't crazy", said Uli.

"Glad to hear it. I gave him a free passage. Don't know why I did it. I was very angry about him."

"Why?"

"Because he had some money. My mate told me. He had a few gold pieces! Before he came on board. Gave them away to half a dozen beggars. Gold pieces! Then comes on board and begs for a free passage. And I gave it to him. And then the mate told me about the gold pieces. So I was angry and who wouldn't be? Wondered ever since whether he's crazy or a saint."

"He's not crazy", repeated Uli curtly.

"Well, maybe he's a saint. Be a good thing then, to have him on board. Saints never drown, they say."

Two days later they landed at Gaeta and took the road to Rome.

As if in a silent agreement, Uli and Juan let Iñigo go on ahead alone. They followed at a distance. When he rested, they rested a hundred paces behind him. When he resumed his walk, they did, too.

A few times they lost sight of him, usually at mealtime. He had finished his bread and fruit so quickly that he was on the road again before they had eaten their soup.

But they caught up with him quickly enough.

"It's astonishing how well he can walk, though", said Juan. "He's so frail, and he eats practically nothing, and his poor leg . . ."

"He's doing very well", assented Uli. His tone of voice was gruff. He did not want to talk about Iñigo's leg. He did not want to think of the shot at Pamplona and its strange, incomprehensible consequences. It led, in turn, to a whole sequence of incomprehensible things. To Juan telling him of a wounded Spaniard's love for Queen Germaine and a few days later André de Foix sending him to that lady; to a little girl of six who wanted to go to the Holy Land and was laughed at; and to a girl of sixteen who was going to the Holy Land now and a long Swiss soldier who ought know better than be going with her—*and* with the Spaniard he had shot. If this was supposed to be a pattern, it was as crazy as that of a court fool's dress. And yet . . .

They spent the night at a village inn. Iñigo would not sleep there. They found him in the morning in the innkeeper's stable. He greeted them politely and then resumed the journey on an empty stomach, as he had done the day before. One meal a day, thought Uli, and not much of a meal at that. He won't stick to that for long.

The next night they spent at a farmhouse; it was too late and too dark to go any further.

233

The owner of the farm was an old man, much intimidated by the presence of half a dozen soldiers who had killed an equal number of his chickens and forced his wife to roast them for them. They had got hold of a small barrel of wine too and were now sitting down to a solid meal.

It made them feel sociable, and they invited the three newcomers to have some wine with them.

Iñigo declined the invitation and went out to look for a place to sleep, but Uli and the boy Juan accepted rather than to offend the men.

The wine was light, but even a light wine intoxicates when it is taken in quantity. The soldiers became hilarious and began to sing, the kind of songs that soldiers sing when they are hilarious. They began to tease Juan for not enjoying the songs as a young man should.

"He doesn't speak Italian well enough", explained Uli drily. "And he's young. Leave him alone."

But they would not leave him alone. Perhaps it was just their drunken mood, or else the wine had made them more clear-sighted. In any case, they first started teasing Juan for behaving like a girl, and then one of them even suggested that he might really be a girl in disguise.

"Sure enough", said Uli quickly. "He's the favorite wife of the sultan. And as you are not the sultan, you better leave him alone. Go to bed, Juan, you're tired. I'll go on drinking for a bit with these cheerful boys."

But the suspicious soldier was obstinate. "Sultan or not," he said, "I want to know. Just you come here, my little one, and let me have a closer look. Come here, I say."

"I told you to leave him alone", said Uli, frowning.

"So you did, Colonel", jeered the soldier. "We have a right to know with whom we're drinking, haven't we? I say the boy is a girl, and if he is a girl we are going to have fun."

He rose and staggered over to Juan, who had turned very white.

Uli too rose and laid a heavy hand on the man's shoulder. "Keep off, friend", he said. "I'm warning you for the last time."

The man laughed at him, gave him a push, and seized Juan's arm. "A nice, close look", he drawled.

The push made Uli reel back a step. Two arms seized him from behind and held him.

"You shouldn't do that, you know", he said. "It makes me lose my temper." He bent over with a sudden jerk, and the man who held him flew over his head and cannoned into the soldier holding Juan. Down went the whole group.

Instinctively Uli stepped aside quickly, and the heavy pitcher hit him on the point of the shoulder. A wave of pain billowed down his left arm. The three remaining soldiers jumped at him, roaring. He knocked one down, tore the hands of the second from his throat, and then saw the floor come up to meet him.

He sank through the floor to enormous depths, full of stars. Then he realized that he was not sinking at all but rising, rising past stars and moons and all kinds of strange forms till he reached the Puerta Nueva of Barcelona. It was closed, of course, and Saint Peter pointed out sternly that it could not be opened for him just because he had a saint in the family. Saint Peter had a large forehead and a little pointed beard. All the same there was not a shred of doubt about his identity. Uli offered him a ring with a beautiful ruby if he would let him in, but Saint Peter declined it contemptuously. "Show what you can do", he said. "You are a gunner, aren't you? Try and shoot the devil with it."

It was a lovely cannon, large and shimmery, and Uli spat into his hands and began to load it, but the ruby had grown to such a size that it would not fit into the mouth of the cannon, and it was no longer a ruby. It was the devil himself, and Uli struggled to bend and twist him into shape so that he could push him into the cannon, and the devil began to laugh because he was ticklish and thrust out a long red tongue and licked Uli's face.

"Stop that, you pig", commanded Uli and sat up.

He stared into the face of the boy Juan, who held a towel, dipped in cold water, in his hands.

"So that's the tongue of the devil", said Uli, and he laughed a little.

"Are you all right?" asked Juan anxiously.

Uli touched his forehead and winced. There was a swelling there, as large as an egg.

"I'm fine", he said. "What the devil happened? Where are they?" He looked around wildly. He and Juan were alone in the room.

*"He* chased them away", said Juan. "He came in just when they had knocked you down. . . ."

"Knocked me down? Well, I suppose they must have. Stupid of me. I clean forgot that third man. He must have hit me with a pitcher. They make hard pitchers in this country. What the devil *has* happened?"

Juan poured fresh water on the towel and laid it again over Uli's forehead. "Can you hold it up there yourself?" she asked. "Right. Now be nice and quiet. I'll tell you everything."

Uli half closed his eyes. "Where are the soldiers?" he asked again.

"Just be quiet and listen. You were lying here on the floor, and that—that man was trying to tear my doublet off. And *he* came in— and he shouted at them."

"I know." Uli nodded. "Saint Peter."

236

Juan gave him an anxious look, but Uli grinned at her, and she went on. "I've never heard anybody shout like that. It was like—like a trumpet. And that from him—who never raises his voice at all! They all stopped and stared at him, and he went on, thundering at them in Spanish. I don't think they understood a word of what he said, but they did understand it all the same—I'm telling this very badly. . . ."

"Go on. I know what you mean."

"He was quite white in the face, and his eyes were burning. And he pointed with his finger to the door, out, out— and they sneaked away like whipped dogs. All six of them. Just like that."

Uli nodded. "Once a general, always a general", he said.

"What?"

"Never mind. They didn't come back, eh?"

"No. And he looked at me and laid his hand on my head and smiled. And then he bent down and looked at you and he said, 'Put a little water on his head', and he walked out."

Again Uli nodded. "I'm a fine bodyguard", he said. "No wonder Saint Peter wouldn't open the gate of Barcelona."

"What are you talking about?"

"Never mind. Are you all right? Good. Go and get some sleep now."

Four days later they reached Rome.

It was Palm Sunday.

They never found out how Iñigo managed to get an audience with the new Pope, but he did and was given formal permission for his pilgrimage and a blessing.

Uli would not go near Saint Peter's and the Vatican, despite Juan's pleading.

"Been there often enough and long enough."

"You're a bad Christian."

"I am", he said. "But at least I know I am, and I don't pretend to be a good one. That's nothing to do with it, though."

"Well, then, what is it?"

"You go alone, little brother. Say a prayer for me. If it doesn't help, at least it won't hurt."

Sighing, the boy Juan departed alone.

The city was teeming with pilgrims, deputations, and delegations to the new Pope. They said he was a good man. Well, it was about time that there was a good man again at the helm of Saint Peter's barque. But however good and wise he might be, what did it all matter, unless God cared?

There were moments—moments—when it almost looked as if he cared. Perhaps, perhaps someone like Brother Klaus could still do something about spinning a thin, thin thread between heaven and earth.

And perhaps even that was an illusion, even if the thought tugged at his mind again and again.

But all this had nothing to do with not going to Saint Peter's. The Swiss were there, the Swiss Guard to which he had once belonged, the Holy Father's bodyguards. Some of them at least were likely to know him, and a letter might go to a certain little place in the mountains saying that he had been seen—alive.

## CHAPTER THIRTY-TWO

IMMEDIATELY AFTER EASTER they set out for Venice.

It turned out to be a difficult journey. The plague was stalking through Italy now, and quarantines had been estab-

lished everywhere. They passed Tivoli, Orvieto, Spoleto, To-
lentino, Macerata, and Loretto—they marched up the long,
long coast of the Adriatic Sea, passing Ancona and Sini-
gaglia, Fano and Pesaro, Rimini, Ravenna, and Comacchio.
Almost nowhere could they enter the towns.

When they got to the canals of Venice itself, the police
entered their boat and examined all the passengers. Uli had
great difficulty in diverting their attention from the boy Juan
and succeeded only by pretending to fall into the canal
through sheer clumsiness so that they had to fish him out,
spluttering and swearing, much to their amusement.

Of Iñigo, on the other hand, they did not ask a single
question. They did not even seem to see him, and he certainly paid no attention to them either.

The Most Serene Republic was at the very height of its
power, comparable only to that of ancient Carthage.

It was the center of world trade. Its ships roamed the Med-
iterranean. Even the great sultan himself thought twice before attacking it and preferred to send his vast armies into
Hungary and to try his hand at sea against the knights of
Rhodes, very small fry in comparison to the forces of Saint
Mark. His emissaries bought much of the elegant goods in
Venetian shops and storehouses. The Venetians were not
bluffed. They knew that Suleiman would attack them at the
least sign of weakness, but they also knew that the sultan
could not or did not yet trust the strength of his fleet. It had
been sufficient for Rhodes. It was not sufficient for Venice.
And even Rhodes had proved a hard nut to crack. The knights
there had repulsed one attack after another, and more than
once the sultan was near to lifting the siege. Letter after letter, envoy after envoy the old grand master of the knights
sent off—to the Pope who had no soldiers, to the emperor
who had no interest, to the king of France who would not

dream of helping the knights against a power he might need any day now against the emperor.

Eighty-five thousand nine-inch cannon balls were hurled at the defenders; mines by the dozen were laid.

Rhodes fought back, using "Greek fire"—burning naphtha—fighting for every inch of its fortifications, making Suleiman's most trusted war dogs, Ayas Pasha and Ferhad Pasha, look like tyros. And still no help came.

After more than five months, when there was a powder supply for only twelve hours, when there were not enough combatants left to man the walls, the grand master accepted Suleiman's repeated demand of capitulation.

Suleiman spared the lives of the surviving defenders— most unusual behavior for the Turks, and for him.

His janizaries marched into the fortress without their usual shouts of joy, their howls of *"Allah akbar"*, silently, quietly, almost overwhelmed by the fact that the grim knights had surrendered after all.

And the old, white-bearded grand master, Philippe Villiers de L'Isle Adam, standing erect and gaunt before the young sultan, said with a grudging admiration, "You are worthy of praise because you vanquished Rhodes—and because you showed mercy."

Uli knew that story. It had happened only last year. In Rome he had also heard the emperor's reaction when the capitulation was reported to him: "Nothing in the world has been so well lost as Rhodes."

In Rome he had heard too that during the last months of the siege the Venetian battle fleet had been lying at anchor—at Crete, with strict orders not to interfere, unless the Turks should threaten Cyprus. Two thousand volunteers had gathered at Rome to relieve Rhodes, but there had been no shipping for them . . .

Two thousand Christians, he thought grimly. It was not much, but it was better than nothing, though it did not help. The Christian princes had much to account for.

Meanwhile the doge of Venice gave his booming city the greatest show of the year: the feast of the marriage of the doge with the sea, the symbol of the power and wealth of the Most Serene Republic.

In a golden robe, with a golden diadem, under a golden canopy the doge sailed out in his galley, richly bedecked with priceless carpets and golden hangings, and threw a golden ring into the sea.

"He's getting himself a notoriously unfaithful wife", said Uli. "No wonder their marriage contract must be renewed each year."

But the pilgrims were well received and looked after in a city that lived on foreigners and foreign trade. Room and bed and food was provided for them for nothing.

Iñigo took no part in this. He went on as before, begging for his daily bread and sleeping in porticoes, doorways, and under the planks of the booths in the marketplace. Once a Basque noble recognized him as a Basque and invited him to his house. Iñigo accepted. The next day the man took him to the doge.

An hour later Iñigo went to see Uli and told him that he had been given free passage on the *Negrona* to Cyprus.

"I thought he had forgotten how to speak", said Uli drily when he informed Juan.

Juan shook his head. "It is not he who has forgotten anything, but you. I remember very well how loudly he spoke—and how effectively—to the six soldiers in the farmhouse."

"I can't remember that because I never heard him", said Uli. He grinned apologetically. "You're right all the same.

But now let's see that we get a passage too. But it won't be for nothing, you can rely on that."

It was not. He had to sell the ruby ring, for which the much respected firm of Messer Bontempelli—jewelery and banking—paid him the substantial sum of 130 ducats, more than enough for the ship's fare both ways. In fact, they were charged twenty-six ducats each for the round trip, and Uli looked with satisfaction at the finest passenger ship he had seen in his life, armed with nineteen cannons, just in case the Algerian pirates with their notorious chief Khaireddin should be encountered.

The passengers were asked to provide themselves with all the necessities of the voyage. They assembled and formed a council who undertook to buy biscuits, ham, Plaisance cheese, crates of eggs, live poultry, onions, dried fruit, sugar, salt, and, of course, a few barrels of wine. They also urged everybody to buy glasses, plates, pillows, medicinal drugs, gunpowder and perfume.

They all knew that Iñigo had no money, but a man called Fuessli, a bellfounder from Zurich, asked him with a twinkle in his eye what he was going to add to the things they were taking on board.

"An inexhaustible provision of confidence in God," said Iñigo, quite unruffled, and Uli chuckled behind his hand. "Serves Fuessli quite right", he said to Juan afterward.

Then the plague broke out in Venice after all.

They kept off the streets and away from all places where people assembled, but when Iñigo went down with fever, they feared the worst. The physician they called in—in his now familiar uniform of white cloth with hood and gloves—stated to their great relief that it was not the plague and then burst into a torrent of polysyllabic words in Latin.

"Is it dangerous?" asked Juan anxiously.

The physician said it was.

"We are supposed to sail in four days", said Uli. "Can he do that?"

The physician said he doubted it very much.

On the very day of the departure he came in again to give some medicine to his patient, and Uli asked him again whether he thought that Iñigo could travel.

"No", said the physician firmly. "If he does, you will bury him at sea."

When he had left, Iñigo looked at Uli and Juan.

"My inexhaustible store of provisions is already on board", he said. "I shall go with it."

They both had to support him on their way to the ship, but he made it. For the next three days he was seasick. Then they saw him sitting up on deck, with his rosary in his hands, and from then on all was well.

A month after their departure they arrived in Famagusta, where they had to change ships, and Uli had to pay another twenty ducats each for Juan and himself—the round trip to Jaffa and back.

"He has managed again to get a free passage", said Uli when he came back from a visit to the new captain. "God knows how he does it."

"That's right", said Juan gravely.

Uli gave him a suspicious look. "That's right, eh? Meaning, God does know. Tell you something *I* know, little brother: you're acquiring the same kind of sense of humor that he's got, and I never thought anybody else could have it. He says something with a perfectly straight face, and you take it literally, but you can't quite understand it, and then what he really meant suddenly dawns on you—if it ever dawns on you at all."

243

Juan smiled. "There's nothing wrong about acquiring a sense of humor, is there? If you can do it? But you're quite right about him. That's how he is. And do you know what?"

"What?"

"I think Jesus had that kind of sense of humor."

"Don't be silly."

"I'm not being silly."

"I never heard of such a thing. What makes you think so, anyway?"

"Well, do you remember the story of Zacchaeus?"

"No. Who was he?"

"Oh, a moneylender or tax collector or something like that, and he had become very rich...."

"Times don't change much, do they?"

"And when he heard that Jesus was passing through his town he did want to see him, but he didn't want to be seen...."

"Good politics—if you can do it."

"Or perhaps it was only because he was a very small man—anyway he climbed a tree. But when Jesus passed by, he said, 'Come down, Zacchaeus', and I'm sure with a perfectly straight face, too."

"I think I remember now. Old Zacchaeus did climb down, and not only from the tree. He gave half of what he had to the poor. An expensive tree, I call it."

"Not as expensive as the one in paradise."

"Juan, Juan, if you're not careful, our pilgrim friend is going to make a nun out of you."

"He could do worse", said Juan. "But that's no way to talk."

"I think you are having long discussions with him behind my back."

"He doesn't mind talking," said Juan slowly, "if it is about God. I think he likes it almost as much as saying nothing, though not as much as talking *to* God."

"You always got along well together—" Uli grunted— "even when you nursed him on the way back to Loyola castle."

Juan remained silent a while. Then he said in a low voice, "I've never seen such a change in a man."

Uli chuckled. "It is strange, isn't it? And all because I hit him with a cannonball. He meant nothing to me, and I meant nothing to him. I just wanted to show those idiots of gunners how to shoot, and he got hit. What a coincidence! And don't tell me it's all ordered and prescribed by God or that God trained that cannon for me. I know he didn't. I know I did."

"God did not train the cannon, and God did not climb the tree", said Juan. "But he made something out of it. He fitted it into his own plans somehow. He writes straight with crooked letters, we say in Spain. It's not our actions; it's something behind our actions. It's—it's like the silkworm."

"The silkworm?"

"Yes. It spins its thread. . . ."

"That's funny. I once thought—never mind. Go on."

"It spins and spins, and a man comes and gathers in what it has spun and makes a beautiful silk kerchief out of it."

"That", said Uli drily, "won't do the silkworm much good. They don't wear kerchiefs, as far as I know."

"No, but don't you see, that's just where it is different when the silkworm is a man and the man is God. And what's more—oh, I wish I could express it, I've felt it for so long now—I mean, even if it doesn't do that particular silkworm any good, it will do good to others, and the silkworm being man will know that."

245

"Possibly", said Uli lightly. "And he may resent it, too."

"Yes. Yes. Or he may claim that it is all due to his own merit."

"Well, what do you expect from a silkworm?" said Uli.

"Silk", said Juan, smiling very much like a girl.

Uli stared at her, hard. "If you know so much," he said, and his voice sounded a little hoarse, "perhaps you can tell me also why I should have passed by when a little lady ran out of her house, crying for help in the name of the Blessed Virgin— why I passed by the next day and she came with me—why the convent of the Franciscan nuns did not open their door when I knocked at it to leave you in their care—why we have been traveling through half of Spain together and . . . and many other things." He caught himself. "I'm sorry", he said. "I shouldn't have said that at all. You look quite frightened. . . ."

"But I'm not", said Juan, looking more like a girl than ever.

This was in Cyprus. In pagan times they had believed that it was the seat of the goddess of love, born at the shores of the island from the foam of the sea. It was warm and sunny and glowing, and the wind seemed to kiss the trees named after the island of the goddess.

Uli looked down on Juanita's upturned little face. "Why," he said breathlessly, "why did we meet, and . . ."

"Oh, there you are", said the guttural voice of Master Fuessli, the bellfounder. "The captain just told me he wants us to come on board at once. The wind is favorable, and he wants to set sail."

Uli took a deep breath. "Very well", he said. "We're coming. Come along, Juan."

"Somehow we never had much opportunity to talk to each other", said Fuessli genially. "Yet I think we are compatriots—or am I mistaken? I'm from Zurich."

"I am not", said Uli.

Fuessli gave him a surprised look. "There are two other men from Switzerland with us", he said. "Let's have a few goblets of wine together when we come on board and chat over old times."

"This", said Uli, "is a pilgrimage, I believe."

The good bellfounder was hurt.

"That's no reason to be unfriendly", he said. "You haven't made a vow of silence anyway. I heard you talk to this boy."

"This young fellow", said Uli, "is under my protection."

Fuessli opened his mouth to give a sharp answer, but thought better of it and walked on quickly.

"Weren't you rather rude to the little man?" asked Juan innocently.

"Yes. I don't like snoopers."

"But he was only trying to be friendly . . ."

Uli laughed. It was not a merry sound. After a while he said, "We may be silkworms, but I don't want any threads spun between these men and myself."

"But what have you got against them? They're from your own country, aren't they?"

"They are, and that's why. No more questions, Juan, my boy."

"You are just like Don Iñigo", said Juan.

"What? I? Nonsense. Why?"

"Because he also always avoids getting in touch with anybody who might know who he is. Perhaps you are a nobleman in your country, or even a prince. . . ."

Still there was no mirth in his laughter.

"I told a great lady once that all Swiss are nobles, but we are simple people, Juan. Perhaps I have committed a crime and do not want it to be known."

"Never", said Juan firmly.

"I wouldn't be so sure if I were you. Anyway, it is just as well that Fuessli got those answers out of me."

"Why? He didn't enjoy them."

"Neither did I enjoy giving them. But they reminded me, just in time, of something I had forgotten. And I mustn't forget it."

Men, thought the boy Juan, are strange people.


## CHAPTER THIRTY-THREE


THE FIRST GREETING the Holy Land gave the pilgrims was a cannon shot from one of the two towers guarding the roads of Jaffa. At the same instant the red flag with the white crescent went up.

The master of the galley had to soothe worried passengers.

"They're not shooting at us. It's a kind of welcome. But they won't be very friendly. No one is allowed to leave the ship till I have secured a safe conduct and an escort."

"It's only fair." Uli grunted.

"What do you mean?" asked Juan.

"Well, it all started with a cannon shot, didn't it? But I wish we could get off this ship. It stinks to heaven."

"It does stink", admitted Juan. "But not to heaven."

Uli's wish was not fulfilled for several days. Captain Francisco had gone to Rama and Jerusalem alone, and they even began to suspect that he had been killed.

Once a Turkish officer with a detachment of soldiers, armed with bows and arquebuses, came on board to examine the passengers. He contented himself with bellowing at them in Turkish, which none of them understood, and spitting contemptuously at irregular intervals. What he and his men really examined were the belongings of the passengers, a good many of which disappeared into Turkish pockets. One of the pilgrims, a Dutchman, protested violently. When he recovered from the consequences of his protest, his left arm was in a sling, and he was told by one of his shipmates who knew something about the art of Hippocrates that he was lucky not to have had his skull fractured.

At long last the captain returned with two Franciscan friars, and one of them spoke to the passengers. In fact he gave them a little sermon in Italian, which he repeated in French and in German. At the end he reminded them that they would need some of the humility of the Lord to go through what was in store for them here.

But the sight of the two Franciscans revived the pilgrims' spirits. They had sung the *Te Deum* and the *Salve Regina* when the Holy Land was first sighted. But ever since the cannon shot thundered the Turkish answer to their prayer, at least some of them had become a little depressed.

Now once more they sang: the *Pange Lingua* of Saint Thomas Aquinas and the thousand-year-old hymns of Saint Ambrose.

And again the Turks answered. The pilgrims were herded together, shouted at, spat at, and pushed before a number of dignitaries, every one of whom was resting on a beautiful carpet and every one of whom had to be appeased with ducats.

Their names were noted and their fathers' names. They were warned not to wear anything white; only true believers were allowed to do so, not Christian mud. They were warned that any arms found in their possession meant death, that any attempt on the part of a Christian to strike a true believer meant death.

To this the Franciscans added a further warning: "Don't look at women at all. The men here are all insanely jealous."

Then they were passed on to the escort, Turkish soldiers looking down on them disdainfully from the backs of camels, as they struggled to mount their own beasts—small and quite incredibly dirty donkeys.

The drivers went on foot and started their own little game, consisting of making the beasts buck or jump by prodding them suddenly with the end of a sharpened stick. A pious unbeliever who fell from his donkey was a source of great merriment, and the game was played endlessly, unless a pilgrim had the good judgment to buy himself off with more coins.

Uli was slowly beginning to boil with rage, and Juan had great difficulty keeping him from doing something imprudent.

Iñigo seemed completely oblivious.

Uli had been curious to see how he would extricate himself from the various payments they all had to make. After all, the people who had taken him on board their ships had been Christians of sorts; they could be moved, if not by their faith, by some kind of superstitious fear. But what in him could move a Moslem?

Iñingo gazed quietly at the representative of the emir of Rama; he looked past the chief scribe, who in vain asked him for his name—and he was not even asked to pay anything. After a preliminary stare they let him pass as if they had reached the conclusion that he was an optical illusion.

He would not mount the donkey they offered him. He walked. And when one of the drivers deliberately pushed him, he did not even look up but went on walking, his eyes half closed, his hands folded in prayer.

The man is an impregnable fortress, thought Uli, and then shook his head. The truth was probably that he was far away in his thoughts.

He was right. Iñigo was far away in his thoughts, but in time, not in space. He was fifteen centuries away.

He receded still further in time when a caravan of Jews joined up with them. The Jews were on their way from Egypt.

They spent one night in Rama and another halfway between that ramshackle town and Jerusalem.

It was about ten o'clock in the morning when the Franciscans told them that they would see the city any moment now. Ragged singing broke from parched throats.

Suddenly Juan clutched Uli's arm.

From behind the hill a cross became visible. Slowly it grew higher and higher. Then the man appeared who carried it, a simple wooden cross, no more than six or seven feet high. He was a Franciscan, and behind him came more of his brothers to welcome the pilgrims to the Holy City.

Uli pressed Juan's hand and nodded. He too had been strangely touched by the sight of that cross suddenly appearing over the crest of the hill, and for the first time he too felt that he was on sacred soil.

He was not the only one. All the singing ceased.

In deep silence they walked the last two miles toward the Holy City. But all suffering, all hunger, thirst, and humiliation were forgotten. They were singing in their hearts.

At the Jaffa gate they were halted and their luggage rifled by Turkish officials.

Then they entered, two by two, into the city.

The procession halted in front of the Church of the Sepulcher, built by Saint Helen when she had found the True Cross where it lay hidden under the dust and rubble of three centuries. The Turks demanded an entrance fee of seven ducats.

But what was that? What were all these little miseries and needle pricks to them now?

Heavily armed Saracens jostled them right and left; children threw mud and filth and stones at them; abuse was heard at every street corner, in front of every house.

There was no law of hospitality for the infidel.

It did not matter.

They were allowed to visit the Cenacle, where Christ partook of the Last Supper with the apostles, the very room that had seen the first Mass.

The Franciscans knelt before them, washing their feet in memory of the immortal scene one and a half thousand years ago.

They walked to the house of Caiaphas; they saw the place where Mary stood waiting the trial of her Son.

They stood at the place where Mary Magdalen first saw the resurrected Christ.

They walked, praying, up the Via Dolorosa to Calvary. They stood; they knelt on Calvary. It was there; it was here; it was a real place, stone and earth, the real place where he had died for them; they could touch it with their hands, with their lips.

## CHAPTER THIRTY-FOUR

FRA ANGELO DE FERRARA listened to the report of Fra Onufrio. It was the usual thing. Three pilgrims had fallen ill with fever; one might be dead by now. Two had been stoned by

Saracens and were now being attended to. Two others had died the day before; here were their names and belongings and the addresses of their families in Lisbon and in Utrecht. The worst bit came at the end: five hundred janizaries had arrived in the city, and the rumor had it that a mufti would arrive shortly, an envoy of the sheik ul Islam himself.

Fra Angelo sighed deeply. He could see the connection between the two things. The mufti would bring the order of eviction or at least of further curtailing of Franciscan activities. The new sultan was an even more zealous Moslem than the old one. Any day now he could take away the privilege Saladin had granted to Saint Francis himself, and then there would be no one to watch over the holy places.

"Anything else, Fra Onufrio?"

"The little Spanish pilgrim is here again—the one who limps. I told him you are busy, but he said he would wait. He has been here three hours."

"I suppose it is a courtesy visit. You should have told me earlier. Show him in."

The Spanish pilgrim who limped came in. His was not a courtesy visit. He came to ask to be allowed to join the community.

Fra Angelo liked him for it, but he had to refuse. The Order could not afford it.

The pilgrim pleaded with him. All he wanted were a cell and a confessor.

Fra Angelo pointed out that he could not increase the number of his monks beyond twenty-four. Other pilgrims had tried to stay on in some way or other, only to be killed by the Saracens or to be sold as slaves.

The pilgrim answered that it did not matter what happened to him as long as he could serve God in the country where Christ died.

"I know how you feel", said Fra Angelo gently. "Believe me, I do. Do you think I like saying no to you? Go back with the others."

The pilgrim said quietly that he had made up his mind to stay and that he would stay.

Very gently Fra Angelo said, "I must forbid that. The Holy Father has given me the power to excommunicate those who will not obey my authority. I shall show you his letters."

The little pilgrim's face became a tragic mask.

"The word of a religious is enough for me", he said in a low voice. "I will obey."

Looking up, he saw in the sad old Franciscan's face the perpetuation of the suffering and humiliation of Christ.

He knelt before him, kissed his hand, and left.

He left in a dream. Today, this very day he would have to leave Jerusalem behind him, perhaps never to see it again.

Every single day, every single sight within these days must be anchored in his heart, never to be forgotten, never lost.

The caravan of the pilgrims was to set out in two hours. They had to make preparations, pack their belongings, pay their bills. Not he. He had two hours to be as near to his Lord as he could be.

He felt an intense longing to go once more, just once more to the Mount of Olives, to kiss the rock from which Christ had ascended to heaven.

What could happen to him if he did? They might arrest him. They had arrested Christ. They might whip him. They had whipped Christ. They might kill him—they had killed Christ. He would go.

The guards stopped him. He gave them his penknife, which he used to sharpen his quills. They let him through, and he mounted the hill.

From here, from this rock the Lord had left the earth. Here was the point where an invisible thread led from the earth to heaven, just as an invisible thread led from heaven to earth into the cave at Bethlehem.

Here he prayed, and praying lost all sense of time.

The pilgrims assembled for their departure, and the Franciscans counted them carefully. The Turks were just waiting for a slipup to pounce on the last vestiges of Christian rights in the birthland of Christ. One pilgrim was missing.

"I'll go and look for him", said Uli, who had been worrying about Iñigo's absence even before the Franciscans discovered it. "You stay here, Juan. Don't budge from here under any circumstances till I come back."

He joined the Franciscans swarming all over the place.

"It is so foolish", wailed one of the brothers. "What difference can it make to him, a few minutes more? It endangers him—it may endanger us all."

He was not in the Church of the Sepulcher or at Calvary? Mount of Olives? It was a possibility.

They ran.

There was a wild debate between a Franciscan and a Turkish guard. "He has been here and back and gone again", explained the Franciscan hastily. Uli shook his head. But the next moment he saw Iñigo coming down the mountain, closely followed by a lay servant of the monastery, a big fellow, brandishing a heavy stick. Uli ran up to them, tore the stick out of the man's hand, broke it in two, and said with a dangerous gentleness, "I had to promise not to use violence against any Moslem. You are not a Moslem, are you, friend?"

The Turkish guard grinned. It was clear enough that all Christians were the most utter fools. The little fool had given him his penknife to be allowed to go up a small mountain. Then he had come back. Then he wanted to go up the mountain again, to have another look. For that he had given him his scissors. Now he was having trouble with his own people. Allah had darkened their minds so that they were like little children playing games and running up and down for no purpose at all.

Iñigo said nothing. The little incident with the stick he had not even seen.

## CHAPTER THIRTY-FIVE

"There", said Isabel Roser with an appreciative nod. "Now you look like what you really are—a very pretty girl, a young señorita with good manners—and not like a half-savage youth, traveling all over the world like a gypsy."

Juanita fiddled nervously with the folds of her wide, honey-colored skirt. "I don't feel right, Doña Isabel", she said in a quavering voice. "I feel like—like a fraud."

Isabel Roser laughed. "A fraud is what you were till now, little one. And believe me, it could not have lasted much longer. That little bodice of yours is well rounded. There's no need to blush, child; that's as it should be, and it will be pleasing enough to the man you marry one fine day."

She smiled at the girl's confusion.

"I think I even have a fair idea who he might be", she went on.

"Please, Doña Isabel . . ."

The older woman took the girl's hands into her own. "Do you love him, child?" she asked kindly. "That's what really matters, you know. That's what your poor mother would ask you if she were still alive. Do you love him?"

"Yes, Doña Isabel, I love him. But . . ."

"Well?"

"But—I'm not sure—whether he loves me."

Doña Isabel snorted. "He'd be a greater fool than I think he is if he didn't. I've seen him look at you, too. He loves you all right; don't you worry. We shall have to do something about your dowry, though. I've taken good care of your mother's little house. It was just as well that no one dared to enter it, not with that cross on the door. And when the time of quarantine had elapsed, I made sure that it was guarded by the authorities."

"Oh, Madam, you are too good to me, to everybody."

"Nonsense. I only wish there had been more valuables in it than there were. And the man you love is not exactly wealthy either, I believe. Poverty is not a bad thing, and it may well be indispensable for holiness. But a young couple should have enough money to manage on. Well, we'll see what can be done about it. There are many letters and documents, too, which I packed away. Study them whenever you want to. I've put them all into a little red leather case; it's in your room. Now will you do me a favor, child? You've been back four days now, the three of you, and I've seen *him* only twice for a few minutes. You know how he is—he insists on going on begging for his food, he has the prayer life of a monk, and now he is studying Latin . . ."

"I didn't know that. I thought he knew everything."

"Yes, it is strange. And yet it isn't. It is as if he had been born again when he came to Manresa, where he could do nothing for himself. They had to feed him, nurse him, look after him in every way. That was his infancy. Then that pilgrimage of his—the child began to walk alone, gather its experiences in a hostile world full of Saracens and Turks. And now he is going to school. No, don't laugh, child. It is a strange thing to see a giant grow up to full stature. And a giant he will be, believe me. Have you ever seen a sculptor at work? When he tears big chunks off a formless heap of clay and molds them in his hands till they seem to come alive under his touch? That is how men like that treat history. They form it in their likeness as God has formed man in his likeness. And I think that and the forming of human life itself are the two greatest miracles in the world."

"He has so many names now." Juanita smiled. "You call him a giant. Uli—that's . . ."

"I know who he is."

"Uli calls him the general. And I call him my saint."

"He is all these things, I believe. And all of them make a man very lonely and give him little time for those who want to be his friends. He did not tell me anything about your journey. I should be very angry with you, my child, for running away from me the way you did and roaming the world, dressed in a very unbecoming manner. But you were in *his* company, and so I can say nothing. For nothing wrong can happen when he is there."

"That is true," said Juanita eagerly. "It has proved true again and again."

"Tell me about the journey then. Everything, everything that you can remember—even if it takes hours and hours."

It did take hours.

Isabel Roser listened, her eyes closed, her slim white hands, sparkling with rings, resting in her lap. Twice Juanita thought that she had fallen asleep, but each time when she paused, she was told, "Go on. I want to know everything."

Juanita told about the dreary way back to Jaffa, where many of the pilgrims died of illness, exhaustion, and the filthy food.

How the voyage to Cyprus took twelve days instead of five because the ship sprang a leak and because there was not a breath of wind for days.

Of their horror when they found out that the captain of the *Negrona* had not waited for them, although he had sworn he would, but had sailed back to Venice and left them stranded.

How they tried and tried to get passage on board another ship with what little money they had left.

There was one large, well-built Venetian ship that belonged to the brothers Contarini. They could have sailed on it, but the greedy owners insisted on being paid every penny left in their pockets, and even then they would not take Iñigo.

In vain did the other pilgrims tell the Contarinis that he was refusing passage to a saint, and one of the brothers, Girolamo, answered tartly, "If he is a saint, let him walk over the water like Saint James of Compostela." And the other brother laughed.

So the large, safe Venetian ship went without them, and a little later they found passage on a tiny boat, belonging to its captain, Ser Bigarelli. He took Iñigo for nothing. But for several days they could not leave. When at last they sailed and reached the first port, Limissa, they heard that the large Venetian ship had broken up in the storm and had gone down.

Isabel Roser crossed herself. "The *Feria*", she murmured. "It's the *Feria* all over again."

"That's what Uli said", Juanita nodded. "When the Contarinis refused to take my saint, Uli said, 'Now that's the first time that somebody has been able to resist him. It's just as well. I almost thought he could do anything with people.' But he was furious about it all the same. Then, when the news came that the *Leone* had gone down, he said, 'It's safer to be with him in a nutshell than without him in Noah's

Ark. Do you know what? The man is lucky, that's what he is.' But he didn't mean that either. I know him—I think."

"Go on."

How they came to Rhodes and ran into a storm again and could not get away from Crete for weeks. How cold it was at Christmas in Cephalonia and how they had to change over to a ridiculously small boat at Parenzo. How they came to Venice and then marched cross-country to Genoa. How on the way Iñigo was taken prisoner twice, once by the Spaniards and once by the French—they had not even known there was a war again—and how Iñigo escaped because he was so completely indifferent to the threats of the Spanish captain that they thought he was weak minded. . . .

And the last passage from Genoa to Barcelona, and Uli saying to the captain, "Lucky for you that you have taken that friend of ours for nothing. I'll lay twenty to one that we'll arrive safely."

Isabel Roser laughed and cried. "It is a beautiful story", she said, wiping her eyes. "And I will write it down. People will want to know it when all of us have gone. But what a terrible thing it is that a Christian cannot visit the holy places without being robbed and insulted and humiliated all the way."

"I don't know", said Juanita slowly. "Perhaps that is what ought to happen to us when we follow in his footsteps."

Isabel Roser looked at her sharply. "Did *he* say that?"

"Yes. When he was talking about the Crown of Thorns one day."

"I wonder", said the older woman pensively. "I wonder whether anybody can go on such a pilgrimage and come back just as he left. I know *he* hasn't. But you too seem to have changed, and even your Swiss friend—talk of the devil!" She laughed, interrupting herself. "Here he comes. I can see him entering the door from the street, and he's carrying a pike and a bundle and a terribly long sword. Does he think my house is a fortress?"

She gave a nod to the servant announcing Uli and went up to him graciously when he came in.

"Welcome, warrior," she said, with a friendly smile, "but I'm glad you left your horrible weapons outside. I hope you will not mind, but I must look after a few things around the house. In the meantime, the señorita will keep you company. I ought not leave you alone with her without a duenna present, of course. But I am told such is not the custom of your country, and I will make an exception—just this once."

Another gracious nod, and she was gone.

A smile on the lips of the girl fluttered and died. She had smiled because it seemed so incongruous that she should need a duenna's presence when talking to Uli, when she had traveled alone with him countless hundreds of miles over many, many months; and her smile had died because she suddenly felt that miles and months had faded into nothingness and that she was alone with him for the first time.

It was quite absurd, of course.

She could not look into his eyes, and her heart beat so hard that she thought he was bound to hear it.

He said very softly, "Little one, I hate this hour."

Now her eyes opened wide. Blank surprise changed to quick, piercing anxiety. He was ghastly pale, and his mouth and hands were unsteady.

"You are ill", she said breathlessly. "You are . . ."

He shook his head.

"I hate this hour", he repeated. "It's one of the two worst ones I ever had. What's more, they're related."

All the blood drained from her face.

"What do you mean?" she whispered. "Why do you look at me like that? What have I done?"

261

"You? God bless your heart, nothing. It's me. I always thought I was a good soldier. But I'm not. A good soldier has courage. And I am the world's worst coward."

She cried out, "Don't talk like that!"

But he went on, relentlessly. "I am such a coward that I wanted to sneak away without so much as a word. I had packed my things. Then I couldn't bear to leave without passing by the house where you were. And then I couldn't bear that either. I had to come in."

"You were—leaving?"

He nodded.

"But . . . why? Where to?"

"Where to, I didn't know myself. It doesn't matter either. Why? Because I love you, of course."

Her little face lit up. "But you dear fool, don't you know that I . . ."

"Don't say it", he interrupted her hoarsely. "Don't say it. You mustn't."

"But why, why . . . what is wrong?"

"Everything. I must tell you now. God, how I wish I didn't have to. But you have a right to know."

She sat down. Looking up at him, round eyed, she was a child once more, a frightened child.

"I served in the papal guard as a youth", he said. "I told you that, I think. But I did not serve in it for long. I couldn't keep my mouth shut. Had been brought up by good Christians. The Holy Father was the successor of Saint Peter. But what I saw was not—holy. I said so. My captain laughed at me first; then he became angry. I was told to get out. I went back home. There I met a girl—Margaret. She was pretty enough, and I fell in love with her. I was nineteen; she was seventeen. I told her I wanted to marry her. She laughed and said, 'You haven't got a house for us to live in.' So I built the house. And we married."

Juanita said nothing. Her hands were like ice.

"War broke out", went on Uli. "With the French. I had to go. It was only a few months after our marriage. Margaret cried, but so did many wives that day. I didn't feel like leaving her, but there was nothing else to do. And I didn't have a bad foot like Kaspar Jost. Kaspar Jost was a boy who had wanted to marry Margaret. Not a bad boy. And he was in love with her. Well, she married me." He took a deep breath. "The war went badly", he said. "We lost one skirmish, then another. In the second one I got this . . ." He pointed to the long scar running up his forehead. Pale as he was at this moment, the scar looked a deep red, as if the wound were fresh. "It put me out for some time, and the French packed me on a cart and took me away with them. I was a prisoner. At first they thought I would die. I wish I had died then."

"No", she whispered. "No. No."

"It would have saved me a good deal of trouble", he said with a dark smile. "To say nothing of—others. I pulled through after four months. But I was still a prisoner. All might have been well if I hadn't tried to escape. I wanted to go home. They caught me, and I was put in prison. There they forgot me. Happens sometimes, you know. The war was over; the Swiss army had been back a long time. I was still in that damned prison. There seems to have been some mixup. They thought I was somebody else. I spent two years in that French hole. Chained, too. Then, quite suddenly, I was told it was all a mistake, and I was free. I had no money, no clothes, nothing. I begged my way through, but believe me, I didn't feel holy for doing it. I came home. On the way there I met a few people I knew, but they didn't recognize me. I was as thin as a skeleton, and there was this scar. Then I reached my village. It was evening. And the first man I saw was Kaspar Jost. I called him by name, and he stared at me. He didn't recognize me either at first. But then he did, and he crossed himself and babbled a prayer. He thought I was a ghost."

Uli gave a harsh laugh. "I had to shake him to convince him that I wasn't. And then he broke down. He cried and cursed and howled; I couldn't make it out at all. In the end he told me. I had been given up as dead long ago. Two men said they had seen me fall. Most likely it was quite true. They said I had my head split by a French two-hander, and that was true, too. Anyway, I was declared dead. And Margaret waited a year like a good widow and then married Kaspar Jost."

"Oh, God . . ."

"I wanted to kill the man, but I couldn't. Wasn't his fault, was it? Wasn't Margaret's fault either. It was no one's fault. It just happened that way. And there was poor Kaspar, howling, 'What am I to do—what am I to do—what's to become of all of us—what's to become of my son . . . ?' That settled it. He had a son by her. Three months old. It was his son. And Margaret's. I was out. I was dead. So I said to Kaspar, 'Go home to your wife.' He looked at me like a lunatic. He asked, 'What about you?' And I said, 'Forget about me. I'm dead.' And I told him to go away quickly before I changed my mind. He ran. There I was, alone on the road. I could see the roof of my house—of what had been my house. I turned away and walked into the woods and waited. When it was dark I sneaked up to the village and to my—to the house. And looked through the window. I saw them all. Margaret was suckling the baby. She looked happy enough. Kaspar was sitting in a corner, staring at her. I didn't stay long at the window. Someone might pass by and see me. I went back to the woods and slept there. Or tried to. In the morning I went away. Begged my way again till I was far enough to be fairly sure I wouldn't run into people who knew me. A farmer gave me some work, light work at first, till I had become stronger. After six months I had my strength back. I went on working for him. Then I left him and joined up with the Bavarians. They're rough people, but at least I was out of Switzerland. I served the duke of Landshut. I served the emperor. I fought under old Frundsberg, and I got as far as Hungary when we went out against the Turk. But after that day, when Kaspar Jost told me that I was dead, I couldn't believe that God looked after his world. Margaret, Kaspar, I—none of us had done any wrong. There was no guilt. Yet—it happened. I decided I'd fight decently and live decently—not because I wanted to please God—I knew he wouldn't care either way—but because I wanted it so. Then one day I took service under his lordship Charles of Gramont, bishop of Couserans. He and his troops joined up with General André de Foix, to reconquer Navarre. You know the rest."

She said nothing. Her tear-stained face was as white as his.

"Or perhaps you don't", he said hoarsely. "I picked up a young boy in Pamplona. He was a bit of a nuisance. Not much, though. But there were moments when he looked like a girl, and then he was a nuisance. Somehow I couldn't get rid of him. Then I found I didn't want to get rid of him. Then I found that I couldn't imagine what life would be without him. In Barcelona—here—when Doña Isabel first took care of you—I thought it was all over, and I wanted to get drunk and forget it. But I couldn't forget it. I couldn't even get drunk. Instead I thought of somebody—my grandfather's brother. I've told you about him a few times— Brother Klaus, the hermit. I thought of him because I had thought of Don Iñigo and the change that had come over him. He seemed to have become happy—as Brother Klaus

265

was happy, living for God alone. And I remembered a prayer we used to say as children; it was Brother Klaus' prayer: 'My Lord and my God—take me away from myself and give me wholly to thyself.' And: 'My Lord and my God, take away from me everything that hinders my way to thee.' And: 'My Lord and my God, give me everything that makes me come nearer to thee.' And then *you* walked in, and you said you were going on pilgrimage with Don Iñigo. And I felt— Brother Klaus had heard what I said and allowed me to be with you a little longer. Maybe he did, and maybe he didn't. Anyway, I was happy."

"And so was I", said Juanita tonelessly.

"I loved you, then," said Uli, "but like a fool I wouldn't admit it to myself. And yet I knew it all the time. I knew it couldn't last. Sooner or later I would have to tear myself away. I thought: let it be tomorrow. Not today. But now . . ." He breathed heavily. "We've been at the holy places", he said. "And they are holy. All the Moslems and all the dirt and the vermin and the rest of the damned nonsense can't change that. We've been to the holy places, and we had a guide. I was supposed to be his bodyguard—but it was he who protected us. One of the Franciscans told me he wanted to stay. It was his dearest wish. The brother guardian did not permit it. So he left. He's still a soldier. A holy soldier. And a soldier, holy or not, must know how to obey. So here I am. You're safe now. Doña Isabel is going to take care of you."

He stopped for a moment as if to brace himself for a tremendous effort.

"I wanted you to know that I love you", he said in a strangely clear voice. "I've never loved anyone as I love you, and I never shall. Please, don't say anything. God bless you, Juan, my little brother, my girl, my love, I . . ."

He turned abruptly and was gone from the room before she could speak.

She wanted to rise, to run after him. She could not. Her limbs were leaden.

She wanted to cry out. Her voice would not come.

She sat, immobile, mute, a forlorn little figure with her hands folded in her lap.

She could not cry. She could not even pray.

# BOOK THREE

# CHAPTER THIRTY-SIX

BACHELOR FRIAS, member of the ecclesiastical tribunal of the Inquisition, shook hands with Padre Francisco de Mendoza and Padre Pablo Hernández.

"The case you are interested in", he said, "will be heard any moment now. They're fetching the prisoner from the palace."

"From the palace?" asked Padre Hernández, wide eyed. "Since when are the prisoners of the Holy Office kept in the palace? Have you no jails left in Salamanca?"

"No safe ones anyway." Bachelor Frias laughed. "Explain it to the good father, Mendoza, will you? I must go."

He fluttered off, a large black raven, in the direction of the courtroom.

"Everything is slightly unusual about this case." Mendoza smiled. "Frankly, I wonder what they are going to do about it."

"What's so unusual?" asked Hernández gruffly. "Just another wild preacher without any learning or office going about and stirring up the people. If it's the first time, admonish him and let him go. If it's a relapse, let him stay in jail for a while. And if his so-called teaching is grossly heretical and has caused people to stray from the true faith . . ."

"Easy now, firebrand," warned Mendoza, "lest it be said that the egg wanted to be wiser than the hen. But it's a relapse all right. The man's been arrested before, in Alcalá, for very much the same thing. Went about preaching and catechizing, with a few others—four in all—dressed the same way. The Gray Robes, they used to call them."

"There you are", said Hernández. "These people are a plague."

"That's what some of the secular clergy used to say about the Dominicans, when they had just been founded."

Hernández became red in the face. "You're not thinking of making that comparison, are you?" he spluttered. "Why, Saint Dominic was a saint, and the clergy at that time . . ."

". . . was frequently dissolute and needed reforming badly. True. And how are things today? Do you think that fellow Luther could be so successful if it hadn't been for so many of us having gone too sour or too sweet?"

"That's no reason for allowing heresy to be preached in the streets of a Christian city", said Hernández.

"Certainly not. But does this Iñigo preach heresy? He didn't in Alcalá, you know. They examined him. . . ."

"Who presided?"

"Figueroa."

"Well, he's sharp enough."

"Quite. And all he could say was that it was unbecoming for those four to go about dressed uniformly as if they belonged to an order. They were sentenced to dye their garments in different colors, as they were too poor to buy secular clothing."

"Figueroa contented himself with that?"

"Yes. But the prisoner didn't. He demanded to know whether the court had found anything about his teaching to be heretical. Figueroa didn't like that, but he had to answer it. So he snapped at him, 'If the court had found that, you'd burn.' And the prisoner answered as cool as ice, 'So would you, if you spread heresy.' "

"Cheek."

"Yes. But the truth. And that is just the trouble with the man. It's going to be the trouble at this session too, you'll see. Anyway, he insisted on a testimony that there had not been anything wrong with what he taught. And Archbishop Fonseca received him after the trial and was very nice to him, they say. Made him a present, too."

"Is that why he is staying at the palace here now?" asked Hernández ironically.

"Not exactly, no. He was in the ordinary jail. But there was a jailbreak—some of our worst criminals escaped. They opened all the cells, broke the prisoners' chains. Iñigo stayed where he was."

"Like Saint Paul in the Acts, eh?"

"Yes", said Mendoza quietly. "Like Saint Paul. I visited him, before the jailbreak, and asked him whether he found his chains very hard. He said, 'There are not so many posts and chains in Salamanca, but I should desire more of them for the love of God.' And strangely enough, I had a letter from a learned physician in Alcalá, Jorge de Naveros. He had visited Iñigo in the Alcalá jail. D'you know what he wrote? 'I have seen Paul in prison.'"

"Extraordinary fellow." Hernández fidgeted. He hated to show that he was moved. "Why can't he be an ordinary decent Christian like everybody else? Why must he go and set himself up as a preacher when he's a layman?"

Mendoza smiled. "Maybe we could do with a few extraordinary men", he said. "And as for everybody else being decent Christians ..."

"All right, all right, I concede that point. They're not. We're not. But where would we be, if we let all those wild men go about and do what they like? There was that girl from Piedrahita who called herself the 'bride of Christ', prophesied all kinds of nonsense right and left, and told everybody that the Virgin Mary always walked beside her, so she always bowed politely to let the Virgin go through first before she entered a room; there is that horrible fellow Medrano with his shameless practices and his 'cult of light', making people meet naked at midnight and dance and utter blasphemies. And the *illuminati* with their crazy ideas ..."

"I never said", interrupted Mendoza quietly, "that the Holy Office has no legitimate business. It must deal with such people, and it does. But every case must be decided on its merits, and I very much wonder whether they will find anything against this particular man. When they found him praying as usual in his cell, with the door wide open after the jailbreak, they decided to put him up at the palace. And there's Doctor Santisidro now. They're starting the case."

The four judges, Doctor Santisidro, Doctor Paravinhas, Doctor Frias, and the bachelor of the same name opened the session. They had read the book of the accused, *Spiritual Exercises*, but whether or not they had drawn any profit from it was impossible to tell.

Bachelor Frias opened the questioning, asking the prisoner for his opinion on a case of canon law.

The prisoner replied that he had not studied canon law, but would answer the question, as he was under obligation to do so.

Doctor Paravinhas then asked him to explain how he understood the mysteries of the Trinity and of the Eucharist.

The prisoner's answers were faultless.

Doctor Santisidro felt that the time had come to take a hand. His learned colleagues made it too easy for the accused.

"You tell us that you are not a learned man. Yet you go about teaching. Can you give us a full explanation of the meaning of the First Commandment?"

The frail figure seemed to grow. The pointed beard lifted challengingly. His eyes half closed, Iñigo began to speak.

274

He spoke of the tremendous revelation of the first words, "I am the Lord thy God"—disclosing in its "I" that this God was a personal God, disclosing in its "I am" that God was Being and the Principle of Existence and making "Him Who Is" the very name of God—giving clarity to the word of Christ when he said to the Jews, "Verily long before Abraham was I AM." Disclosing further that God demanded acknowledgment of his supreme rule over mankind, as well as the divine courtesy—for in these words God deigned to introduce himself to his creature, man—"I am the Lord thy God, who brought thee out of the land of Egypt and out of the house of bondage."

He gave a shattering sermon on the theme that God had commanded: "Thou shalt have no strange gods before me."

He spoke about the meaning of the words "Thou shalt not make to thyself any graven thing, nor the likeness of anything that is in heaven above, or in the earth beneath, nor of those things that are in the waters under the earth", and their close and direct link with the grave admonition, "Thou shalt not adore them nor serve them."

Here was the commandment to worship the one true God by faith, hope, and charity and by religion, the commandment to avoid false religions, willful doubt, disbelief, or denial of any article of faith, the stern warning against culpable ignorance of the doctrines of the Church. Here was the warning not to expose oneself to danger by listening to unbelievers or infidels, by reading books on false teachings, by sinning through despair and presumption. Here above all was the warning not to give any creature whatsoever the honor which belonged to God alone, to deal with Satan and his demons, to believe in anything superstitious.

Two or three times Doctor Santisidro tried to interrupt, and once even the presiding judge, Vicar General Frias, made such an attempt, but the attempts were rather feeble, and in any case of no avail whatsoever.

They had unchained the eloquence of the accused as they had unchained his legs and wrists, and now he would not be stopped.

They had demanded a *full* explanation of the First Commandment, and he was giving them a full explanation.

Iñigo spoke about the sins of sacrilege and of simony, about the sin of giving angels or saints, relics, crucifixes or holy pictures divine honor or worship.

He spoke of the necessity to accept everything revealed by God, the duty of knowledge, the sin of neglect.

The man who had needed three days to explore his conscience before making his general confession at Montserrat now spoke for two solid hours on the First Commandment of God alone.

Doctor Paravinhas looked appealingly at the presiding judge. It was after the time for the midday meal, yet the accused was still in full swing.

Vicar General Frias looked pointedly at Doctor Santisidro and gave a very slight shrug. He felt sorry for poor Paravinhas, but Santisidro had insisted on a full explanation, and now he was getting it.

Meanwhile Iñigo started the third hour of his speech.

Not only the heretics in the north, but the Catholics everywhere, even here in Spain, even in Salamanca frequently sinned against the First Commandment. He quoted what he had heard; he described what he had seen.

Vicar General Frias made a real effort now. He raised both his hands and succeeded in making Iñigo pause for a moment.

"That", said the vicar general quickly, "will do."

Doctor Paravinhas blew up his cheeks and released his breath noisily. "I should think so", he murmured.

"Just a few more questions", said Frias. "You have determined the difference between mortal and venial sin in your *Spiritual Exercises*. Surely only a theologian should be allowed to determine such difference."

Iñigo gazed at him steadily. "Determine yourselves whether what I say is true or not; if it is not true, condemn it."

The vicar general passed the back of his hand over his perspiring forehead. "The court is adjourned", he said resignedly.

A few days later it reassembled, and sentence was pronounced. No error had been found either in the life or the teaching of the accused, and therefore he was allowed to continue to teach the catechism and to speak of the things of God. He must not, however, determine what is venial and what is mortal sin until he had studied for four years more.

The prisoner was set free forthwith.

The judges came up to him, one by one, to congratulate him.

"It is my duty to obey", said Iñigo calmly. "But I do not approve of your judgment. You have not condemned me, yet you have shut my mouth and prevented me from helping my neighbors according to my ability."

They reasoned with him, and he listened courteously and with bowed head. Then he said slowly, "While I remain in the jurisdiction of Salamanca, I shall do as you have commanded me."

Padre Francisco de Mendoza heard him say it and understood at once. He tried to make him stay, as did a good many others. The story of his trial was all over Salamanca.

But a scant two weeks after his acquittal Iñigo set out for Barcelona and Paris, on foot, leading a small donkey laden with his books.

"It is a pity", said Mendoza to Hernández.

"It probably is", agreed Hernández grudgingly. "But there are others, you know."

"There are many other donkeys laden with books." Mendoza nodded. "But not so many men who can preach a sermon to the Inquisition. Faith, do you know what I think?"

"You are overrating my abilities", said Hernández.

"I think he has the quality poor Savonarola lacked so completely: a sense of humor."

"Well, what if he has?"

"My dear Hernández, the man's a saint. And that's the greatest thing that can be said about mere man. But a saint with a sense of humor to me is the crowning glory and goes right to my heart."

"I don't know what you mean." Hernández grunted.

"You don't know what you miss." Mendoza smiled.


## CHAPTER THIRTY-SEVEN


"I'VE HELD COMMAND in fourteen wars", said George Frundsberg. "Or is it fifteen? Never have I seen such a pigsty."

"It is indeed most regrettable", murmured the duke of Bourbon, looking at his slim white hands. "But what can you do, my dear General? They have not been paid for a long time. It's like refusing a tiger his ration of meat and then being surprised when he snarls. I did my level best for you, General, even to melting down gold plate and other things rather dear to me. Even so I cannot pay twenty thousand men from my own poor pocket."

"Pigsty", said Frundsberg. "Gold plate! I've staked every penny I have on this expedition. Look at me! I am a beggar without a penny to his name for the sake of His Imperial Majesty. Look at me!"

The duke looked at the fierce, ranting German with ill-concealed distaste. The bullet head with its stiff whitish hair like a brush; the enormous, thick neck; the wide shoulders; the squat, graceless figure; the short, thick fingers; the wine stains on doublet and sleeves.

Nevertheless, this uncouth bull was a past master of war, the best soldier of his time, and his fame reached across all Europe. There was no need to embellish the stories that were told about him. The facts were fantastic enough.

"The trouble with this war", said Frundsberg, "is that everybody is cheating everybody else. The trouble with our time is that everybody cheats everybody else. My gracious emperor tells me, 'Frundsberg, go and march into Italy, and if I ask you to take Rome, take Rome. I rely on you.' Right. I go. But he sends me no money. Instead he makes all sorts of little deals with the Pope, with the Colonnes, with Ugo Moncada, with God knows whom. And my men don't like it. Naturally. If I can't pay them, they must get loot. The loot is just in front of them, and I can't tell them go and take it. Not as long as I haven't got clearer intelligence reports. So they're grousing. My gracious emperor is my gracious emperor, but he shouldn't cheat me."

He caught the duke looking at the two guards at the entrance of the tent.

"You needn't worry about *them*", he said. "I know how to pick my men." He rose, and it seemed to make him smaller. He had short, stumpy legs. He crossed over to the entrance of the tent. "That's Ilsank", he said. "A Bavarian. Served under me before, against the French. And this is Uli von der

Flue. Swiss. With these two I'll take on any half dozen men you can pick, Duke. What? Am I right? And they know that listening is a fool's game. Hey, you, Ilsank, what's a mouth for?"

"Eating and drinking, General", said the Bavarian, grinning.

"That's right. Not for gabbing. And you, Long Uli: What are ears for?"

"I don't know, General", said Uli stolidly. "I haven't got any."

Frundsberg roared with laughter. "See what I mean, Duke? I know my children. And they know that I don't cheat them even if my gracious emperor cheats me."

How childish they are, thought the duke. But they were strong, these childish men. The Venetians and the Milanese had found that out at their cost. . . . Twenty thousand men—and no enemy to use them against. If this went on a few more weeks there would be mass desertions. Even now there was fighting among the men every day, the Spaniards and Italians against the Germans. Almost all of Frundsberg's Germans were Lutherans. To take Rome had a very special meaning for them . . . or for some of them. He wondered where Frundsberg stood as far as that issue was concerned.

He said softly, "Perhaps you have doubts whether a Christian should go to war against the Holy Father? Perhaps you have qualms?"

Frundsberg stared at him. "Qualms? I? The Pope is my emperor's enemy. His worst enemy. He's allied himself with Francis the First, with the Venetians, with Milan—the Holy League. My holy father is the emperor. And I'll see the Pope hanged before I die—if I have to hang him myself!"

Once more the duke glanced at the two guards. They were standing like statues. Their faces told nothing.

"My family", said he softly, "holds no brief for the Medici, even if one of them does sit on the chair of Peter."

Frundsberg grinned. It was always a family matter with these Italians: somebody had poisoned somebody else or had him done away with nicely by some hired ruffian with a mask on his face. But in the case of the duke of Bourbon there was something more to it than that. He had deserted his own master, King Francis the First, had gone over to the emperor, and was partly responsible for old Francis' defeat at Pavia. And Francis had refused to hand him his sword; he had given it to Lannoy instead and altogether had treated the duke with the utmost contempt.

Frundsberg poured himself another goblet of wine. A man hates a traitor, he thought. But it is nothing compared to the hatred of the traitor for the man he has betrayed. Nothing would incense the king of France more than the fall of Rome. Therefore the duke wanted Rome to fall. It was as clear as the next move on the chessboard.

Now if it was true that the holy man in Rome still thought the matter could be settled peaceably, and if it was true that he had dismissed the major part of the mercenaries for that reason . . .

His thoughts were interrupted. Outside the tent a nervous voice asked to be let in at once.

"It's Captain Hauser", said Frundsberg. "Let him in, children."

The officer came in, pale and distraught. His report was breathless.

"Nonsense", said Frundsberg genially. "My men never mutiny. Pull yourself together, Hauser. You look like an old woman who's burned the roast. Excuse me, Duke. I must go and spank my boys. Tomorrow I'll have the final reports, I think. We'll march on Florence and get cash there, and then we'll go and hang the Pope."

He stomped out of the tent.

The duke followed slowly. He could hear the muffled noise from afar, the noise of thousands of men shouting at each other, herding together at a dozen and more places in the huge camp. His sensitive face twitched. He called for his aides and his horse, mounted, and rode off to his own tent.

Ilsank grinned. "His Grace has no taste for that sort of thing. Lets the old man do the job alone."

Uli said nothing.

"What's the matter?" asked the Bavarian. "Got a bellyache?"

"I don't like it", said Uli.

"Who does? But the old man will come out on top; he always does."

"I didn't mean that."

"Then what the devil do you mean?"

"The only apostle ever hanged", said Uli grimly, "was Judas Iscariot—and he hanged himself."

Ilsank was a little slow, but he got it after a while.

"There are lots of people who talk about the Pope like that now, you know."

"Yes. But it's wrong."

"Well, I don't know." The Bavarian shifted his helmet a little and scratched his head. "There are popes and popes, aren't there? And we've had a few that didn't do us much good. Maybe God wants them to pay for it. Maybe God wants the old man to hang this one—what's his name?"

"Clement", said Uli. "And God doesn't want him to hang."

"How the devil do you know?" asked the Bavarian, surprised. "You get visions or something?"

"No. But I'm using my head. Peter was the first Pope, wasn't he?"

"Yes, but he was a saint."

"He became one", corrected Uli. "But there was a very black deed in his life before that: when he committed high treason three times in one night. Denied he had ever known Christ."

"I think I remember something of the kind", admitted Ilsank. "But what's that to do . . .?"

"Think, dunderhead. It wasn't the cardinals who picked Peter; it was Christ himself. And even so he wasn't perfect. So why expect every pope to be perfect? And what did Christ do when Peter had committed high treason? Did he have him hanged? Or did he leave him in office?"

"Maybe there's something in that." Ilsank grunted.

"I joined up with the old man because he's a great general and I served under him before", said Uli. "But I didn't know what he was up to. Tickle the Venetians and clip the Milanese; that's all right with me. But you don't hang the Pope. You just don't."

"Maybe it isn't healthy", agreed the Bavarian. "But the old man always comes out on top."

"If he does," said Uli, "I want no part in it. But I don't think he will, and I don't like it."

"Holy Frundsberg," snapped the Bavarian, "how's a man to know what he is to believe, with the Pope shouting this and Luther the other, and the princes all split up, and the learned men all split up, and everybody telling us he's the fellow who knows? The Lutherans tell me I mustn't trust the Pope because he's breaking his word and thinks only of his own luxury and I must trust Luther because he's honest and speaks German. But I've seen the peasants who believed in what Luther had promised them. I've seen them when one of their own chiefs read out to them what Luther had written, and what he had written was against the peasants and for the princes. First he called them up; then he dropped them. And it was written in German, too. Maybe they all get like that when they get to the top. Me, I just do what I'm told, as long as I'm paid. And that's the end of it."

"I thought like that myself once", said Uli, with a bitter smile. "But it doesn't work out."

"No? Why not?"

"Because sometimes you do something, and it leads to quite a different thing, a thing you never wanted to do, you didn't even dream of doing. But it's there, and you caused it."

Ilsank shook his massive head. "I don't get that at all", he said. "Things like what?"

"You shoot a man," said Uli, "and you wound him, and he changes and becomes a saint. You hear a little girl of six babble about going to the Holy Land, and you laugh at it, and a few months later you're on your way there yourself. You get a girl away from a ruffian—not because of her at all, just because you're angry—and you find out that life without her is—no fun at all."

"Was she very pretty?" asked the Bavarian eagerly. Then he shook his head again. "What's the matter with you now?"

"Something's wrong", said Uli. "There's no more noise at all."

"He's got the better of them", said Ilsank. "I knew he would. He always comes out on top. I told you that before."

Uli strained his eyes. "There's a group of men coming up here", he said. "But I can't see the general. I know one of them, though. It's Doctor Becker."

"They're carrying somebody", said Ilsank. "Holy Frundsberg, it's the general. They've murdered him, the damned swine!"

"It's him all right", said Uli, and his voice shook. "But he's not dead. I saw him move his left arm."

A few minutes later six men carried Frundsberg past them into the tent. He was breathing stertorously.

From the corner of his eye Uli saw that his face was ashen; the mouth drooped queerly on one side, and his right arm hung down lifelessly. Doctor Becker shouted instructions.

The two guards remained where they were. Neither of them said a word. Tears were running down Ilsank's stout cheeks. Uli looked frightened.

After a while a number of high-ranking officers came and with them a whole pack of physicians. They did not stay long. A large cart was brought up, and the body of the general lifted into it. He was still alive, but he did not seem to recognize anyone. The tent was closed, the guards ordered back to their units.

There they found out what had happened.

There had been a mutiny all right. Frundsberg had sailed into it, first jovial, then angry, finally so furious that the nearest men recoiled from him. But those behind them pushed forward, and Frundsberg saw pikes lowered at him—the pikes of his own men, his boys, his children. It was too much for him. He tried to roar at them once more, could not get a word out, and fell headlong. It was a stroke.

What he could not achieve with all the strength of his personality, with all his bellowings and ranting, he achieved by his fall. The men, thoroughly frightened, dispersed and went back to their tents in glum silence.

"Think he'll recover?" asked Ilsank.

Uli shook his head. "He'll never again be the man he used to be. And—he won't hang the Pope."

A few hours later the duke of Bourbon ordered a general alarm and march formations. Soon enough the news went through that they were going to Florence.

The Lutherans—the majority of Frundsberg's mercenaries—were furious. They wanted to go to Rome. They were told that the Florentines had more money than they needed, and it cheered them up for a while.

"I'm going to get out of this army as soon as I can", said Uli to Ilsank.

"Don't know that I blame you." The Bavarian grunted. "Frundsberg was Frundsberg. I didn't sign on to fight under that pale-faced fop, duke or no duke. But at least we are going to get some Florentine money soon."

They did not. The duke received the news that Florence had been reinforced by the duke of Urbino and Venetian troops and would not even negotiate with him. He could not afford to lay siege to the town. He knew only too well that his troops marched only because they wanted to loot. They had not been paid, their boots were going to pieces, they looked like scarecrows, and they were in an ugly mood. Something had to be done and done quickly to appease them. Reports came from Rome. Pope Clement had said only a few days ago that peace was as good as certain and that there was no need to worry. He had dismissed practically all his auxiliary troops. He had only six thousand soldiers left and his Swiss guards, who numbered 189 officers and men.

Rome was presented to an invader on a silver platter.

Maybe the king of France would get a stroke like old Frundsberg when he heard that it was taken.

## CHAPTER THIRTY-EIGHT

"IT'S ROME AFTER ALL", said Ilsank.

Uli nodded. "I heard the Germans cheer."

"The duke's a Catholic, isn't he?" asked the Bavarian. "I don't get it. Do you?"

"No. But I wouldn't like to be in his shoes. And I wish I could get out of it."

"Fifteen deserters drawn and quartered yesterday", murmured Ilsank.

"I know. But it isn't that. To get a pike into the belly is no fun either. And before they can draw and quarter me they must catch me. They caught those fifteen because they were all together. It was worth their while to pursue them. If I slip away alone and at night and go into hiding in one of those farms on the hills . . ."

"You've thought it all out, haven't you?" Ilsank looked at him anxiously.

"Yes. But I'm not going to do it. I've never been much of anything in my life, but I've been a good soldier, and a good soldier keeps his word. I signed on, and here I am. But I won't kill. I'll defend myself, but I won't kill."

"I dunno what's come over you", said Ilsank.

"Maybe it's because I was in the Holy Land once", said Uli slowly. "I learned something there. I learned that there can be something holy about a place. Take Jerusalem now. It's filthy dirty, full of Moslems, who spit at you and jeer at you, and you can't make the sign of the Cross in the street without getting a stone thrown at you. But it's a holy place all the same. I know all about those Roman stories. I was in the Pope's guard myself when I was half a boy. It's a city full of courtesans and intrigues, and there are a lot of bad priests there, though no worse than at some other places. But it's still a holy city. It is where Saint Peter died and Saint Paul and the martyrs who died in the Circus. Ever thought of that, Ilsank? They died in the Circus. But Rome isn't only a circus! See what I mean?"

287

The Bavarian looked at him, open mouthed. "Holy Frunds-berg, the way you talk! You'll end up as a monk."

Uli gave a harsh laugh. "That'll be the day", he said.

They camped early that night. They had marched so quickly that only those among the inevitable camp followers who had provided themselves with mule carts had been able to follow them.

Usually these people were made to stay at a distance, not in the regular camp, and trips there to buy extra food or wine or to visit "a friend" had to be announced to the troop leader, a sergeant or even a captain who could give or refuse permission. But discipline had ceased to exist. This march had not been the progress of regular troops, but the forward sweep of eager marauders.

The officers looked at each other, but did not interfere.

What little wine and spirits there still were in the carts would soon be consumed, and it was better to let the men have their fling than to antagonize them.

Uli could hear the crude voices of the drunks and the rough laughter of the women. They weren't all "bad" women. He remembered some who had looked after the wounded better and with greater knowledge than the leeches, others who had fought like tigers when the enemy had broken through into the camp, like Mother Walburga of Landshut and Iron Clare. But there were old harridans, too, who let young soldiers write their mark on pieces of paper when they could not pay for their drinks and then altered the figures and claimed half of the youngsters' money on payday; and there were younger women, no longer good enough for the pleasure of townspeople and always ready to barter fresh loot for other values. And all of them had a vocabulary of vituperation no mere man could compete with.

One of the women called to Uli as he passed by on his way to his tent, and he said, "Thanks, but I'm not thirsty", and then turned and looked at her and stopped.

He began to move toward her, very slowly and a little unsteadily, as if he were drunk.

Perhaps the woman thought that he was drunk, for she laughed and opened her red-painted mouth to joke about it. But the joke did not come, and her eyes became wide and glassy.

She put down the goblet that one of her customers had given her to refill. There were three soldiers lingering around the small table with the tin pitchers—Spaniards, all of them.

The woman was trembling now.

Uli said to the Spaniards, "*Por favor, compañeros*—go. Go, quickly."

They turned. They saw the stony face with the long scar; they saw the two-hander, as tall as they themselves. They slipped away quietly.

Uli needed a long time before he could speak again.

"You are not surprised, Margaret."

"No."

"You knew I was alive."

"Yes. Kaspar told me."

Uli nodded. "I thought he wouldn't be able to keep it to himself. Where is he?"

"He's dead."

"But the child—your son?"

"Dead", repeated the woman dully. "They were both buried by an avalanche, two years ago. I sold the house. It was a good house ... No, don't! Don't touch me. I'm—ill."

He had seen the red splotches of the French disease under the makeup before he had spoken his first word.

"Margaret", he said. "Margaret."

"No use crying", said the woman. "Things are as they are. A body can't do anything about it. But it was a good house. Kaspar was good to me, too. I don't know what happened to the money. It just went. It doesn't matter. We'll all be rich a week from now."

"Margaret, I . . ."

"You mustn't touch me. Not you."

He took a deep breath. "Listen, Margaret. I thought I'd done the right thing that day—the good thing—the only thing I could do. There was the boy, and . . ."

"Don't. That's all done and finished. It is as it is. Who knows what's right or wrong? Not even the big ones, the princes and the cardinals. No one knows."

"But you can't go on like this. I'll . . ."

"It's all right", she said. "I can manage. And in a week we'll all be rich."

"Don't talk like that, Margaret. Here, take this. It's all I have at the moment, but I'll get you more. But go home. I'll get you everything you need, but go home. At once."

She weighed the little purse and let it drop on the table. It tinkled. She gave a little laugh. "You were never mean, I'll say that for you. But what is that when I can get everything they'll give me in Rome." She put the purse into a large leather bag.

"Margaret, I beg of you, don't say that. It's foolish talk. War is an ugly thing, but war against Rome is worse. No one will be happy from anything won in this war."

"Happy . . ." said the woman.

He was cut to the heart.

"Go home, Margaret", he whispered. "I'll get everything for you, I promise. Just go home. What I've given you will keep you going till I come back with more. I'll look after you. I'll do everything. Trust me, please, Margaret. I built you a house—I can build you another one. . . ."

For a moment or two there was a dreamy look in her eyes.

"We'll go to Brother Klaus' tomb", he said hoarsely. "Maybe he'll help you to get rid of . . . to get well again."

"Think he could?" Her voice sounded high, childlike.

"I don't know. We'll try. Pull yourself together, Margaret. Pack your things, right away. And go home."

"I'll think it over", she said.

"There's the trumpet", said Uli. "I must go. Don't think it over, Margaret. Do as I tell you. Now."

"I'll think it over", she said. "Have you married again, too?"

He gulped. "Of course not. How could I?"

She gazed at him thoughtfully. "Must have been kind of hard on you. Where did you get that scar? Never mind. You'd better go now; there's the watch coming any moment."

"You'll go home, won't you?" he pleaded once more.

"Maybe I will. Goodnight—soldier."

He stared at her, hard. "God bless and keep you, Margaret", he said hoarsely.

When he had gone she cried a little.

Uli lay wide awake, his thoughts biting each other like dogs.


CHAPTER THIRTY-NINE


HE SAW HER AGAIN twice during the march and each time succeeded in talking to her for a while.

There was still time for her to go home. She had money enough for that, and he would send her more, come back, build her a house.

Sometimes she seemed to listen to him; sometimes she merely laughed. She had become accustomed to the kind of life she was leading, and she did not complain about it. Only once she seemed a little worried, when Uli told her about Frundsberg's words, just before his death: that he was going to hang the Pope. She had heard German mercenaries say similar things, and it frightened her. "It's unlucky", she said.

"It's unlucky to be in this war", said Uli.

"You're in it yourself, aren't you?"

"And I wish to God I weren't. If I desert, they'll draw and quarter me, but nothing is going to happen to you. Go while you can, Margaret. Get out of it, I implore you."

"I don't want to see the Pope hanged", said she. "I've seen a picture of him, and he looks nice—a nice old man." She talked some more about the picture, and Uli realized that it had been of Pope Adrian VI, and not the present Pope at all. He did not say anything. Clement VII was a nice enough old man, too, though a failure as a statesman and much too optimistic.

She did not want the nice old man hanged, but she was convinced that they would all get rich in Rome, and she was not going to miss her chance. "Even the pillars of the houses there are made of precious stones."

She had always had a hankering for possessions, but now it seemed almost to have passed the bounds of reason.

His eyes were anxious. "Margaret, listen to me. . . ."

"Now you go along, Uli. There are customers coming. I must look after my business."

A dozen thirsty Italians began to crowd the little table, and Uli slunk away.

292

A few hours later they were again on the march.

By now the Romans knew, of course, that the imperial army was approaching. The imperial army, consisting of almost twenty thousand soldiers and driven forward by the idea that they were about to grasp the richest prize of all.

The Romans knew. But up to practically the last moment Clement VII believed that peace was secure. He had accepted the imperial conditions a long time ago; he had paid out the huge sums the Imperial envoy demanded; he had dismissed the greater part of his soldiers. When the news came that the imperial army was approaching in spite of all his efforts, last minute preparations were made in feverish haste.

The gates were closed, the citizens asked to join the colors, the walls reinforced.

But the citizens reacted very slowly and sporadically, and work was handicapped by lack of money, for all available money had gone to the envoys of the same emperor whose army now approached the city.

One of the richest Romans, Domenico Massimo, offered the Pope one hundred ducats, at heavy interest.

The only thing that made the few defenders feel somewhat better was that the assailants had little or no artillery.

But on the morning of May the sixth a sinister ally came to the help of the imperial army: fog. It rose from the pestilential depths of the Pontine marshes and rendered everything invisible up to the very walls of the city, and in it.

Rome was not large. It could not compare with London or Paris. Its circumference was no more than sixteen thousand paces.

The attack started at the Ponte Molle, at the Trastevere, at Porta Torrione, Porta delle Fornaci, and Porta Santo Spirito.

The first two attacks were repulsed.

The duke of Bourbon saw both Germans and Spaniards recoil, although the guns of the defenders fired into the dense fog without much idea of what they were hitting or even whether they were hitting anything at all.

Uli saw the duke raise himself in the saddle, shriek a command, and gallop forward. It rallied some of his men.

We are all ghosts, thought Uli, looking at the shadowy figures around him, ghosts, ghostly vermin, nibbling away at a fallen man. He shook himself. Rome had not fallen, but he knew it would; he did not know why.

The duke had jumped from his horse and was now ascending a ladder—no, he was lifting a ladder up to the wall.

The next instant he fell backward, shot through the heart.

Uli saw Ilsank's face, the Bavarian's mouth was wide open, and he shouted something, but it was inaudible in the din of the battle.

They were next to each other at the ladder a moment later, and Ilsank was still shouting, "It's got him, too, it's got him too." But instead of running he tried to ascend the ladder and fell, shot through the chest like his commander.

Somehow the duke's death was known to the soldiers in less than a quarter of an hour.

They were terrified. But they knew there was no way back for them. Their commanders had told them that hostile troops were in their rear, and even without that danger there was no way back through a countryside they themselves had laid waste. They could only flee forward, and that was what they did.

They fled up the ladders, killing everybody in their path, and suddenly found the ramparts empty and the city theirs.

It shocked them into a state of blind, stark, overwhelming fury.

Uli found himself pushed up the wall; he dodged the sword of a defender and ran on blindly.

Around him rose the first wild shrieks of women.

He knew Rome. Here, where men were butchering that fat man who was bellowing for mercy, he and his fellow guards had sat, drinking a goblet of Saint John's wine before returning to the Vatican. Over there, where they had killed two women who had dared to defend themselves, was the way to the little church where he had been to Mass many a Sunday. It isn't right, he thought dully. O God, it isn't right.

He had seen this sort of thing before, more than once. He never liked it. It was the disgusting part of a soldier's business. But something must have happened to him; he just could not stand the sight at all.

He tried to stop a Spaniard from killing an old woman who wore a golden brooch and found the Spaniard lunging out at him. He jumped back and raised the two-hander.

The Spaniard rushed him, and he clubbed him down with the broad side of the blade.

A couple of German mercenaries, taking him for one of the defenders, came up, swords drawn, and though he tried to explain to them what happened, they were too far gone in blood lust to pay any attention. He had to defend himself in earnest, and he slew one of them just as a whole troop approached from the direction of the gate of Santo Spirito.

He fled into the maze of pillars of a *palazzo*, where he saw four Germans driving an old cardinal before them with the points of their pikes. The old man stumbled and fell, and they began to tear his robes off him.

It isn't right, thought Uli again, and he sailed into them, swinging the two-hander. "It isn't right." He found himself roaring the words at the top of his voice.

The men gave up after a few strokes of the two-hander; they wanted to have their fun and to loot, not to fight; they had done their fighting and there was no need to risk one's life senselessly against some madman. But the old cardinal was dead by then.

Bleary eyed, Uli looked about. "It isn't right", he repeated. Over there was the Vatican, was Saint Peter's. . . . They were fighting on the steps of the church. He could see the uniforms of the papal guards, the yellow, red, and blue of the Medici, for the fog had lifted by now.

They don't have a chance, thought Uli, not a dog's chance. One hundred and eighty-nine men and officers.

He began to make his way forward, flanked by wild-eyed Germans, yelling obscenities and screaming their hatred.

"We'll make Luther Pope today!" roared a deep voice.

Uli pushed his way through, sweating and trembling with a fury whose cause he did not discern clearly at all.

Moslems, he thought, they're all Moslems.

Perhaps it was a vague memory of the address the duke of Bourbon had given his troops the day before when he told them the city was theirs for the taking and that there would be "Mohammed's law"—free looting and killing for everybody. Or perhaps it was a memory reaching further back into time when certain pilgrims went to the Holy Land. But that was so far away; it was in another life . . .

His doublet was torn in half a dozen places, and there was blood running from his shoulder. Where had he got that wound? He did not remember.

He reached the steps, where three guards were fighting off half a dozen attackers with their pikes.

"Moslems!" he shouted. "Down with the Moslems!"

He swung the two-hander, jumped up three steps, turned, and fought the attackers, side by side with the guards, who were too busy fighting to be baffled by this sudden aid from a half-naked madman with a sword the length of a man.

He was back in the guards, back with his old friends. He shouted at them in Swiss German, and one of them gave him a strained smile, as they retreated up the steps, fighting for all they were worth to join up with the last thin line of the company, slowly retiring into the main gate of Saint Peter's.

It's the end, thought Uli with a strange kind of joy. It's the end, but a decent end.

He split a German helmet, dodged the pike of an Italian soldier and saw him fall, pierced by the pike of the Swiss next to him. "Lovely work", he said appreciatively.

All the fog was gone out of him, and he saw everything with an almost unendurable clarity. Perhaps that happened when one was dying. They were slipping backward through the gate now and into the long, dim church itself, and here too there was fighting.

He slipped on a pool of blood and saw the man who had made it, a Swiss guard vomiting more blood.

Uli did not fall. He caught himself just in time to ward off the blow of a sword not much shorter than his own, and he hit out with the two-hander and saw the man drop, a huge German with a flowing mustache and a cavernous mouth screaming underneath it. There were little groups fighting everywhere within the largest church of Christendom, but it could not last long; they were streaming in now through all the gates.

A deep-voiced bell was ringing somewhere, and there were trumpet calls. Perhaps it was the day of judgment after all, the day when all hell was loose for the last time in one final, horrible paroxysm of evil.

Uli felt a searing pain in his shoulder; his left arm was dead—what did it matter?—the rest would follow soon enough. He saw old Sturzenegger fall, he had known him well, and with him three others, flax headed, clean boys the age he himself had been when he was one of them.

Back, back to the proud edifice in the middle of the church, the tomb of the Prince of Apostles, of the first Pope, of Saint Peter himself. Right over his head the battle went on, but it was not a battle any longer; it was butchery, with sixty or seventy guards fighting ten, twelve, twenty times their numbers. No better place to fall, unless it was on Calvary itself. But the two-hander was too heavy for one arm; he threw it in the face of a howling Spaniard and took the man's sword as he fell.

Somebody pushed him away from the milling mass round the Tomb. He was caught in a stream of men, carried away into a corner of the nave and out through a small door. The sun was shining suddenly, and he heard that deep-voiced bell again, ringing and ringing, or was it in his ears?

So compact was the mass of men around him that he could not see anything; he was swept forward, down steps, across cobblestones. A bridge loomed up, pikes and swords gleamed, but the fear of the fleeing was stronger than the fury of the attackers, and here were the moat and the drawbridge still down and behind it the massive strength of the Castel Sant'Angelo, and they streamed across into the dark, cold belly of the fortress, and behind them rose a baffled roar of fury, fear, triumph, and panic all mingled together. The last thing Uli felt was an enormous weight pressing behind him, as if he were pushed forward by the hand of a giant as large as a house. The last thing he heard was the shout of a man, "They're raising the bridge!" and the screams of those who were too late. Then all went black.

He did not fall. He could not fall. He was kept upright unconscious as he was by the mass of men who had poured in with him. It took a long time before that mass could be sorted out and the wounded carried away, still deeper in the belly of the fortress, to be looked after by the physicians, of whom there were five.

He was treated by one of them, but he did not know that.

He became half-conscious a few times and sank into oblivion again.

On the sixth day he awoke and was given some thin soup to swallow. The man who fed him was a Swiss guard, with his arm in a sling, Walter Erb he said was his name, and he was from Solothurn.

He talked a good deal, but Uli was not able to understand.

He could not move his left arm. It was bandaged, and so were his shoulder and his neck.

The next day he felt a little better.

If this was the beginning of purgatory, it was good to have a man from Solothurn with him, he thought.

Then he found that he must have said something of the kind, for Erb laughed and told him that this was the Castel Sant'Angelo and that they were all right, except that there was very little to eat.

Later Uli found the strength to ask him a few questions, and Erb proved to be a fountain of knowledge.

The Castel Sant'Angelo was the only place in Rome that was still holding out and had a chance of holding out for some time to come. Rome was a shambles.

Of the 189 Swiss guards, only forty-two had escaped, under Lieutenant Hercules Goeldli. All others had been cut down, most of them in Saint Peter's.

"The Holy Father?" asked Uli.

He was here, safe enough. He had been praying in his chapel, and they had thrown a purple cloak over his white vestments and hustled him to Sant'Angelo through a covered passage, only just in time, as the Germans stormed into the Vatican.

"We have quite an assembly here", said Erb. "Eleven cardinals, the French ambassador, the English ambassador, all eating thin soup like you and me." He was talking almost gaily, but Uli saw the furrows of grief around the young mouth and the redness of his eyelids.

"And—outside?" he asked.

"Hell", said Erb laconically.

Uli nodded. He closed his eyes.

After another week of fitful sleep, thin soup, and occasional visits from one of the physicians, he found himself capable of getting up for a few minutes.

A few more days, and he could stroll about a little in the dank, musty corridors of the fortress.

Once he saw the Pope, a broken old man with a long, gray beard, praying before a crucifix.

He made the sign of the Cross and slunk away.

He heard some of what was going on outside. He did not want to hear it, but it was thrust on him from all sides.

The prince of Oranien, serving with the imperial army, was afraid that his own horses might be stolen by the mercenaries. He was keeping them in the Sistine Chapel.

Nuns as well as the wives and daughters of nobles had been auctioned off and sold to the highest bidder.

Every church in the city had been desecrated, profaned, and robbed.

The ninety-year-old bishop of Terracina was asked to pay thirty thousand ducats for his life and freedom. He had no possessions at all, so he was placed publicly on sale.

The streets were full of corpses, and no one bothered to take them away. Plague would break out any moment. The orgy of extortion, rape, plunder, murder, and profanation continued day and night.

The very tombs of the popes in Saint Peter's had been opened and robbed, the relics of saints trampled underfoot.

Uli staggered over to the group of Swiss guards, huddled together in sullen silence.

Many of them were wounded.

But sentinels were posted at the lookouts, and pikes, swords, and arquebuses were held in readiness.

He was told about the death of the captain of the guard, Kaspar Roeist, who had been wounded in the head during the attack on the Porta delle Fornaci and carried to his home. There the Spaniards found him and murdered him, although his wife threw herself over his body to protect him with her own. The stroke of one of the murderers cut off three of her fingers.

"I'm one of you", Uli said hoarsely.

He felt as if he were talking to the last decent body of soldiers left on the earth and was proud that they welcomed him.

"I wish they'd take that poor woman down", said one of them.

"What woman?"

"She came up two days ago with a basket of fresh vegetables and shouted she wanted to give them to the poor Pope, who did not get enough to eat. She was sorry for him, she shouted, because he had such a nice face. She was probably a little weak in the head, poor creature."

Uli's eyes narrowed. "Say that again", he gulped. "What did she say about the Pope?"

The guard repeated the story. "They hanged her", he added. "The Spaniards did. Just in front of the lookout over there."

In three strides Uli was at the lookout.

"Margaret . . ."

Then he fainted.

## CHAPTER FORTY

PAUL III, Pope, Vicar of Christ on earth, Servant of the servants of God, was busy reading an extraordinary dossier.

From time to time he looked out of the window and down to a peaceful Rome, pulsating with life.

Nothing there to remind one of those terrible days, actually not very long ago, when his unfortunate predecessor was besieged in the Castel Sant'Angelo, when, as in the days of Alaric and Genseric, Rome was in the hands of barbarians and its population sank to less than thirty thousand souls. When many—of little faith—had believed that it was the end of Christendom, the end of the Church.

The gates of hell had been open wide enough—but they had not prevailed.

The emperor, frightened, and rightly so, at what had been done in his name, had negotiated, and Clement VII had been set free. And slowly life flooded back into the Eternal City; the churches were consecrated again. The barque of Peter had weathered that storm as so many before.

But what a legacy they had left to him . . .

He smiled thinly, caressing his beard. They did not think he would be Pope for long when he was elected, aged sixty-seven, and just after a severe illness. He had every intention of proving them wrong. There was too much work to be done. He could not afford to die, not for a long time yet. He did not have an ounce of superfluous flesh; the dark, penetrating eyes were deeply set; the nose with the flaring nostrils was strong and a little curved above the patriarchal white beard. It was a face that strangely combined the majestic and the shrewd, the spiritual and the worldly. He had been Cardinal Alessandro Farnese under Alexander VI, Julius II, Leo X, Adrian VI, and Clement VII. He had seen the times of corruption and of degeneration; the feuds of the Borgia, the Colonna, and Orsini; the rise of Luther, Calvin, and Zwingli.

Old as he was, he was determined to create a new age.

He had to bring about the reconciliation of the two most powerful Christian monarchs, Emperor Charles V and King Francis I of France, and he had succeeded, although both these crowned gentlemen had behaved extremely badly and at one time even seriously considered fighting each other in single combat.

He had recognized the Turkish danger for what it was and rallied a new Holy League against it, including the emperor, the king of France, and the Venetians.

Only a few weeks ago he had inspected the new fortifications of Civita Vecchia. After all, the Turks were near enough—in Dalmatia.

And there was Doctor Ortiz, ambassador extraordinary of Charles the Fifth in the matter of the divorce of Henry the Eighth of England from his queen, Catherine of Aragon, Henry who had said when informed of the death of Clement VII, "I care not who is elected Pope. I will take no more notice of him than of any priest in my realm."

Paul had retaliated by making the imprisoned bishop John Fisher a cardinal while he was in the Tower.

And Henry VIII had threatened to send the bishop's head to Rome, "so that the cardinal's hat could be fitted to it".

And now, into this maze of political upheavals, of warring ideologies, of crowned heads fighting each other, seceding from the Church, and blustering with arrogance, of threatening Turks and pleasure-loving, greedy priests, came this dossier, the dossier of a man in whom he sensed an entirely new force.

A Basque gentleman by the name of Iñigo de Loyola had renounced a successful military career to become a hermit and a pilgrim to the Holy Land. Returning, he had started preaching the gospel and teaching the catechism, had been arrested by the Inquisition in Alcalá and Salamanca and in both cases freed without a stain on his character or teaching.

He had gone to Paris, where he studied at Sainte Barbe, a man among youths, acquiring his livelihood by begging.

He made friends with a number of students, all considerably younger than he and of various nationalities: the Navarrese Don Francis Xavier, the Savoyard Pierre Favre, the Spaniard Salmerón and Lainez and Bobadilla, the Portuguese Rodriguez. And these friendships were all based on one and the same central experience, although these young men seemed to be very different from each other in character as well as in social standing. The layman Iñigo de Loyola had written a little book, a kind of manual, called *Spiritual Exercises*. And somehow he managed to make his friends go through these exercises with him, each of them separately. The retreat took thirty days.

And the men emerging from that retreat were transformed.

There seemed to be something well nigh magical about that slender book—or was it the comment given by the teacher rather than the book? Or was it both and behind it—grace?

It welded them together in a common ideal. It made them forget whatever ambitions, ideas, hopes, and wishes they had previouly lived for. One by one they succumbed to the transformation, and from then on all of them lived in the same way as their teacher: for the greater glory of God alone.

They studied for the priesthood, the teacher as well as his pupils, and actually one of the pupils became a priest before the teacher, who had started his studies so late in life.

Then on the Feast of the Assumption of Our Lady into Heaven, all seven went at dawn to an unused little chapel halfway up the slopes of Montmartre, the chapel of the martyrdom of Saint Denis.

Favre, then the only priest among them, celebrated Mass. All of them received Holy Communion. And one after the other each took the vow that made the seven like one man, because henceforth they would have one single will: the vow to renounce "on a specified day" all their possessions except their clothing and subsistence money; to go to Rome and ask the Pope's permission to make the pilgrimage to Jerusalem; to remain in Jerusalem, serving God there for their own sake and that of their fellowmen. Should it be impossible to make the voyage within the space of a year, or should it be impossible for them to remain in Jerusalem, they would be obliged to place themselves at the Pope's disposal and do what he commanded them, to hasten wherever he might send them.

Such was their vow.

Seven masters of arts of the University of Paris, seven glowing idealists. To many a man it might sound like a nice story of small importance.

But there was something about these seven young masters that rang a bell in the ears of an old man who had had ample opportunity to study men and to appraise their qualities.

Above all there was the personality of the master planner and what he had done next. He traveled to Spain to settle the affairs of the Spanish members of that curious little congregation. He settled his own affairs, too, going to Azpeitia, where he refused to stay in the house of his ancestors; he stayed in the poorhouse instead.

After a most arduous journey he met his disciples again in Venice, and they too had journeyed dangerously across the many zones of danger. Their numbers had grown: three Frenchmen, Le Jay, Codure, and Broet, had joined their ranks, and their entire luggage consisted of a Bible, a breviary, and their private papers. When they were stopped by French soldiers, the Spaniards became deaf mutes and the French did all the talking; when they met Spanish troops it was the other way round.

There was no pilgrim ship in Venice that year, so they had contented themselves with looking after the victims of leprosy and the French pox in the Hospital of the Incurables.

A little over six months later Iñigo de Loyola was ordained a priest.

The next part of the dossier was remarkable.

Father Iñigo—or Father Ignatius as he was called now, perhaps because he had a particularly strong feeling for Saint Ignatius of Antioch—did not celebrate Mass right away when he was ordained. Not for a long time. Not for over a year. He had said that he needed time for preparation.

The Pope thought of his own ordination, now so very long ago. He thought of the countless men whom he himself had ordained. Celebrating one's first Mass, living through that tremendous experience—neither he nor any man he knew could have waited a single week. He knew of only one who had gone still further—Saint Francis of Assisi, who had never been ordained at all, because he felt himself unworthy of so high an office.

He made a mental note of the willpower of that man Ignatius.

There were many more items in the dossier.

But from here on the Pope himself remembered what happened. Some of Ignatius' disciples arrived in Rome, and he had received them. He had them invited for dinner, where they were to give a little theological debate, right at the dinner table. He wanted to see their minds at work, and he did.

He remembered that dinner with real pleasure.

The debate was brilliant. The enthusiasm and zeal of those young men were backed not only by extremely sound knowledge, but also by a dialectical skill and a fighting spirit the like of which he had not seen in years, if ever before. Some of the older theologians present—learned and erudite men—had tried to break in, only to find themselves put out of action in the most courteous manner. A defeat seemed possible only between the young men themselves, and the coup de grâce was dealt as gracefully as it was received. Only a diamond could cut a diamond. They were all strong, individual personalities: Father Favre was a saintly man with the eyes of a mystic; young Xavier was like a fiery steed; Bobadilla bubbled over with a cheerful sense of humor, a most endearing fellow; and Lainez was possibly the most brilliant of them all, with a mind like a sharp dagger. Yet they all seemed to be wearing an invisible uniform, officers of the same regiment, trained by the same commander, trained in the commander's own image.

He had invited them again and again, at least once every two weeks. His first impression had not changed; it had deepened.

He had told them, mildly, that they had his permission to go to the Holy Land, but that he was doubtful whether they would get there. When they returned to the theme, he asked them a rhetorical question: "Why is it you so greatly desire to go to Jerusalem? If you wish to have fruit in the Church of God, then Italy is a good and true Jerusalem."

There was no chance whatsoever for them even to set out to the holy places, not with the Turkish war looming up more and more ominously, and he knew they would understand at once.

One did not have to tell them things twice; they were not only extremely quick of mind, but extremely eager to fall in with what was wanted of them.

He had proof of that. The first time they came for dinner their debate had been such a success that he had given them a purse of gold, and the prelates present had followed his example. They asked to have the money sent to a bank, to serve as fare for the sea voyage. When they dropped the plan, they paid the money back. The Pope knew the exact amount: 210 ducats, paid back in full, by people who were begging for their livelihood.

That too was worth a mental note.

So was the report about their activities in Rome itself.

The winter had been bad. People had perished by the hundred of cold and starvation. Many were found frozen to death in the open streets.

These pilgrims without pilgrimage, these energetic new men had gone to work on that problem. Their ramshackle old house near the Torre Melangolo became a hospital and hostel for the poorest of the poor. They gave them their own beds; they begged for them and gave them comfort. Sometimes they had three hundred, four hundred wretches under their roof, and each was treated with such love and respect as would be accorded the Lord himself. Apart from that they cared for the needs and came to the rescue of another two thousand starving people. And all that was the work of ten men.

So that commander of theirs must be an organizer as well.

They were living pure lives. But when they were attacked slanderously from the pulpit by a cranky monk, not without influence, Father Ignatius did not rest till his "case" was brought before the authorities, and the very men who had tried him earlier in Alcalá and other places now testified for him. The outcome of the case was symptomatic: they were acquitted most honorably of the charges they had dragged into the open, and their accuser, the monk Agostino, left Italy and turned Lutheran.

It was a clear enough picture.

But now these men had come forward with the idea of forming a new Order. As if there were not Orders enough already.

What was more, they had made a suggestion along most unusual, unheard-of lines. An Order without a choir! An Order that insisted not only on the three usual vows of poverty, chastity, and obedience, but also on a fourth, that of absolute and complete readiness to be at the disposal of the Pope.

But the most upsetting thing of all was the name they had decided to give their Order—if there was to be an Order. They had called themselves the Iñiguists at first, from the name of their commander when still a layman. But somehow they had come to answer, when they were asked who they were, that they were "the Company of Jesus". And now they seriously suggested that this should be the name of their new order. The Company of Jesus—the Society of Jesus.

At the mere mention of the most sacred name of the Savior, every priest up to and including the Pope must bare his head. It was a fine thing, if the Pope could not mention the name of one of his Orders without having to take off his cap!

The Company of Jesus indeed.

The Pope closed the dossier with a flick of his fingers. But his long, thin hands went on playing with it. If this man, this commander whom the Pope saw, as through a glass darkly, in his disciples, had the secret of transforming men into expert, indomitable, supremely skillful fighters for the Church Militant, what a field of activity would open for them! They could reform the monasteries; they could restore the faith everywhere and build walls and ramparts against the flood of heresy; they could carry the torch to the New World. There was no end to it.

The Pope rang the bell. He took off his ermine-trimmed cap and laid it beside the dossier on his desk.

To the entering secretary he said casually, "I want you to summon Father Ignatius of the Company of Jesus."

Mechanically the secretary took off his cap and placed it back on his head. He looked a little flustered.

"Your Holiness said Father Ignatius of . . . I'm afraid I did not quite understand Your Holiness' words?"

"Father Ignatius of the Company of Jesus", repeated the Pope, and the secretary took off his cap again and put it back.

"We may have to get accustomed to that name", added the Pope drily. "You'll find him at the house near the Torre Melangolo."

The secretary, still flustered, bowed himself out.

The Pope put his own cap back on his head. Under the grim, white beard lingered a smile that no one saw.

# CHAPTER FORTY-ONE

THE LONG, THIN SERGEANT of the papal guards saluted stiffly as Father Ignatius walked past him, led by a maestro di camera. He did not bat an eyelid, but his thoughts were in a turmoil.

It's he, he thought. Great Mother of God, it's he. He didn't look up. He didn't see me. Though you never know with him. Hopes, dashed so often that they were scarcely alive, flickered up wildly, and were held down with an effort of supreme pain.

Three quarters of an hour later Father Ignatius came back from his audience. Again he walked past the sergeant without looking up. He had changed, but not a great deal, except that his hair now receded so much that he seemed almost bald. His limp was scarcely noticeable.

For two maddening hours more Sergeant Ulric von der Flue had to remain at his post. Then he was relieved. Ten minutes later he found out that Don Iñigo de Loyola was now called Father Ignatius and was living in a large, old house near the Torre Melangolo. Another ten minutes and he had obtained permission to go to visit a priest and made off.

He found the house in a cheerful uproar.

One of the fathers was ladling out soup to a dozen rather dirty children; another wriggled his way through with a heavy load of firewood; a third and fourth came clattering down the stairs with large sacks on their backs and almost ran over him.

The apparent disorder did not deceive an old soldier.

Everybody here knew exactly what he was doing and why, although their cheerfulness made it all look like playing games.

Perhaps they were not always so cheerful. Perhaps the audience of Father Ignatius with the Pope had been a special success.

A fifth father enquired politely what he wanted, asked for his name, and disappeared round a corner. He came back almost at once. "Will you come with me, please?"

Father Ignatius was in a room on the street level. He rose behind his little desk as Uli came in.

"Sergeant or pilgrim," he said affably, "you are very welcome."

The door closed softly behind Uli. He stood there, trembling.

"Don Iñigo—Father Ignatius—I . . ."

"Sit down, please", said Father Ignatius gently. "What can I do for you? I am very grateful to you. I told you so once before. In Barcelona."

"Barcelona", repeated Uli. "That's where it started. That's where I left the girl—Juanita. I had to."

Ingatius nodded. His face was inscrutable.

"I had to because I was married", blurted out Uli. He began to tell his story, at first haltingly, then faster and faster.

Father Ignatius did not interrupt.

Frundsberg's death. The march on Rome. The way he found Margaret again and did not at first realize that her mind was a little disordered. The storm on Rome and how he joined up with the guards again. Margaret's death . . .

"She died with her will set toward an act of charity", said Father Ignatius.

Uli stared at him. "I never thought of it in that way", he said in a choked voice.

Father Ignatius smiled. "Go on", he said. "There is more, isn't there?"

312

"Yes, Father. When there was peace I went to Barcelona as soon as I could, to look for Juanita. But Doña Isabel Roser had given up her house, and no one knew where she was. No one knew anything of Juanita either."

Uli took a deep breath.

"I used to think that God was indifferent to us", he said hesitantly. "That he didn't care. Then things happened that showed me it was not so. There was something, something like a thread, a pattern behind it all. There was a moment—in Barcelona, just before we went on pilgrimage—when I thought I could see it. I had—help. Then later I doubted again. . . ."

"The pattern of God", said Father Ignatius gently, "is not always clearly visible to man. We must pray as if everything depended upon God alone. We must work as if everything depended upon our efforts alone. Now in regard to your present problem . . ."

In the hall Father Lainez asked Father Xavier whether he could go in now.

"Not yet. There's somebody with him. A sergeant in the Swiss guards. He's been in there for quite a while."

"Well, if he's a bothersome fellow, Father knows how to get rid of him", said Father Lainez.

"I wonder. He's too courteous to cut anybody short."

"Who said anything about cutting people short?" asked Lainez. "Don't you know how he got rid of that tiresome old Count Fuggio the other day? He just began to talk to him about the pains of hell. The poor man tried to switch the theme to something more pleasant, but Father always came back to the pains of hell, and after ten minutes of it Count Fuggio fled. What is the matter with you? You look as if you hadn't slept at all."

"I wish I hadn't", said Francis Xavier. "I feel crushed. I dreamed I was carrying an Indian on my back, and he was so heavy I could not lift him."

"Now what on earth makes you dream of an Indian?" said Lainez, shaking his head.

The door opened, and a tall sergeant came out. Beaming all over his face, he ran past the two fathers and disappeared at the end of the corridor.

"It doesn't look as if Father has been talking about hell to him", said Francis Xavier gravely.

By then Uli was racing through the streets. A few times he had to pause to catch his breath.

He reached the house at the Piazza Fosca.

A servant, badly frightened by the sight of the wildly excited guard, led him into the garden, where two ladies could be seen.

They looked up.

"Santísima", exclaimed Doña Isabel. "Didn't I always tell you? I knew one day he would . . ." She broke off.

Juanita was no longer at her side.


Father Ignatius had listened to Father Lainez' problem about the staffing of boys' schools and advised Father Salmerón about a number of letters to be written.

He did not share the midday meal of the fathers because of a violent attack of pain in his side. There was no need to call in a physician. He knew that pain. It was an old friend. Drawn and exhausted, he rested for a while. When Father Favre asked him anxiously how he was, he answered in a low voice, "I am as God wants me to be."

He recovered a little later and sat down at his desk.

There was still a great deal of strategy necessary to get the Order as such established. The audience had gone well, but he did not deceive himself about the finality of its outcome.

He knew he could count on Cardinal Gaspar Contarini and on Thomas Badía, master of the Sacred Palace, but difficulties could arise from other quarters, possibly Cardinal Ghinucci.

The Pope had been gracious, but things in Rome could be regarded as accomplished only when they were signed and sealed.

It had not been his original idea to have his headquarters in Rome.

But Christ had changed that on the way to Rome, at La Storta, when it happened again to him, just as he entered the little shrine with his companions. And he was filled with a great and lucid certainty that he would be favored in Rome.

One day history would know the meaning of this moment of utter and serene clarity.

He had thought at first that it meant he would be crucified in Rome. Even now he was not sure whether that was not true—in some way.

But what mattered far more than even a martyr's death was the work itself.

He saw, still dimly, the grand strategy of years to come, with castles, fortresses of the Lord built in all the countries of the world, small, highly trained communities, spreading the gospel, teaching at schools and universities, instructing, advising—and all fortified and supervised from headquarters.

First things first. The charter of the Order had to be drawn up.

The Holy Land?

The Holy Land was everywhere where work was done for the greater Glory of God.

He began to work.